GUARDIAN DEVILS

GUARDIAN DEVILS

Nick Englebrecht #4

K.H. KOEHLER

The Monster Factory

GUARDIAN DEVILS

A NICK ENGLEBRECHT MYSTERY

K.H. KOEHLER

Copyright © 2021 by K.H. Koehler

All rights reserved. No part of this publication may be reproduced, stored or transmitted in any form or by any means, electronic, mechanical, photocopying, recording, scanning, or otherwise without written permission from the publisher. It is illegal to copy this book, post it to a website, or distribute it by any other means without permission.

This novel is entirely a work of fiction. The names, characters and incidents portrayed in it are the work of the author's imagination. Any resemblance to actual persons, living or dead, events or localities is entirely coincidental.

Paperback ISBN: 979-8-8692-4112-2
Ebook ISBN: 979-8-8692-4113-9

Cover art and interior design by KH Koehler Design
https://khkoehler.net

No part of this book was created using artificial intelligence.

CONTENTS

1	The Birthday Massacre	1
2	Frenemies	13
3	One Hot Mess	23
4	How to Save the World (In Ten Steps or Less)	33
5	Royal Rumble	46
6	Grampa Monster	58
7	Coitus Interruptus	67
8	Hybrids	80
9	Going Down	92

10	Black Buddha	106
11	All in the Family	115
12	Cluster**ck	127
13	The Angry Red Planet	141
14	The Greater Arcana	147
15	Revelations	155
16	A Discovery of Witches	168
17	The Cabin in the Woods	179
18	Yahtzee	192
19	Cowboys in Hell	200
20	The Revenge of the Angry Red Planet	209
21	Beyond Escape	221

| 22 | Sweet Home Pennsylvania | 233 |

ABOUT THE AUTHOR

| 1 |

The Birthday Massacre

I WOKE UP and immediately remembered that today was my birthday, but I didn't expect anyone else to remember that. Old Scratch is one of those peculiar celebrities who get blamed for a lot of shit—most they are not even responsible for—but almost no one ever thinks to throw him a surprise birthday bash.

I wasn't disappointed. By the time I had stumbled through my shower, wrapped a towel around my waist, and returned to the bedroom suite in the old Victorian the nice Satanists had given me, I noticed my bed partners from last night were up and gone already. Probably off to do their early-morning Satan-y duties.

Amber and Henry. Over the past year, they had become something of a fixture in my life. I wouldn't call it love, exactly, but I cared an awful lot for them. They were fun and didn't make demands on my loyalty, and that worked in our relationship.

I glanced at the empty bed, mourned the loss of an early morning romp, and then returned to the bathroom to fetch a second towel to finish drying my hair. Over the course of the night, it had grown around six inches and now hung mid-back on me. By tonight it would be somewhere near my hips. That was the sad (and stupid, if you asked me) blowback from a spell gone terribly right last year. I'd opened a cosmic highway to a distant world, but because I was pretty much a shit witch barely in control of the craft, I was being "punished" with a quickly and continuously growing head of hair.

I don't make the rules. I don't follow them well, either (obviously).

I picked up the pair of scissors on the vanity and thought about cutting it yet again. Then I glanced down at the bathroom garbage can, at all the blond hair stuffed into it, and decided against the move. Cutting it just made it grow faster as if it was mocking me. Instead, I tied it up as best I could in a messy sort of man bun, threw on yesterday's clothes, and went down to scrounge up some morning tea. Morgana needed me at the shop early today to take her shift so she could attend a Wiccan convention in Scranton.

As I descended the stairs, I fully expected to see the nice Satanists as they went about their early-morning routines, which consisted of all the normal things one comes to expect of a working commune. There was early morning worship, cooking, laundry, and attending to the grounds. The greenhouse alone required constant attention. But the house was eerily silent as I moved through the collection of neat, dim rooms—and that struck me as odd.

The Victorian here on Lake Ariel was the summer residence for the Children of Endor. Normally, they stayed in the big manse in Philadelphia, owned by the Alexander twins, Juliette and Justin. Justin was the money man who kept their corporation and the coven going while the magus, Juliette, moved seamlessly between her place and this one, usually accompanied by a small retinue of her followers, including her daughter, the powerful Sun Witch—and my unofficial bodyguard—Sada.

As a result, members of the coven were known to come and go in various numbers. Amber and Henry, fraternal twins (but no relation of Juliette's that I knew of) were the only permanent fixtures here, and they stayed because Juliette was convinced the reigning Lucifer on Earth could develop more control over his powers if he had plenty of outlets for his baser desires. In other words, the more sex I had, the more powerful I could potentially become. All that sounded ideal, I know—a real Hugh Hefner-style life with magical Playboy bunnies—but what she was secretly telling me was that I needed to get better at my craft and stop screwing shit up before I did real damage to myself or this world. It was a sobering reminder.

As I passed the common room where we usually had game night or otherwise did important rituals—depending on the time of the year—I felt a subtle electrical current pass across my skin. The house was too dim, too quiet. The hair on my arms stood at attention, and I stopped dead about ten feet from the door that led to the large, industrially-outfitted kitchen.

Maybe I was being paranoid. A year earlier, I'd had a nasty run-in with some Arcana, angel-eaters with a particular taste for Nick flesh. They believed I was the key to helping them ascend to the level of God. Not a god; the Big Kahuna. I was just smart enough to know it had left me with a touch of PTSD. I felt hyper-vigil and hunted almost all of the time, and I slept with one eye open these days. All of my dreams were of me trying to escape from one situation or another.

Something was out there, I knew. *I knew.* It was lying in wait for me—relaxed and unhurried, waiting for the best time to strike. To take me out. Or perhaps to cage me and do unspeakably what the Arcana have always done to angels. I could feel it as if someone was slowly dragging a pin down my back.

That feeling of being watched and wanted in the worst possible way intensified as I reached the kitchen door.

Reaching for the belt of my jeans, I freed the athame I kept with me at all times now. It was bathed in the battle blood of angels and would kill damned near anything, whether it was Otherkin or human. Securing my grip on the ornate hilt, I turned sideways to minimalize myself as a target and moved to stand just outside the door. I put my hand on the knob and turned it slowly, making no sound.

Stopping, I took a deep breath and held it deep in my chest. I wasn't afraid, exactly. I'd been through too much shit to be afraid of much of anything. But I was concerned enough to be extremely cautious. If whatever was on the opposite side of this door wanted a piece of me, and God Himself knew those kinds of creatures existed, they were in for a rude awakening. I'd spent the last year practicing relentlessly with the athame and with the craft. I know self-defense from the force, and I knew magickal defense from my classes with Juliette. I knew how to hold my own.

That didn't mean I would most assuredly win in a battle, fair or not, but I knew if I lost, I would be taking it down with me.

I kicked open the door so hard it bounced off the wall and swung back around, but not before I glanced into the absolute darkness of the kitchen. It didn't matter if it was dark, though, I knew someone —possibly many someones—were in there. But before I could even react, the light went on and about two dozen familiar, glowing faces shouted a traditional birthday "Surprise!" at me.

I stood stock-still, utterly floored. A demon rage-lunging at me would have been easy; I had no coping mechanism for dealing with *this*.

The whole coven was assembled in the kitchen. Amber was holding aloft a ginormous two-tiered white and blue sheet cake lighted with a lot of candles, Juliette and Justin were here, blowing party poppers, and Sada, Antonia, and Henry were clustered around them all, holding flowers or balloons with my name on them.

It was…it was really surprising. Embarrassing, even.

And then it got worse. All of them begin singing to me. I saw the room was decorated with black and white paper streamers and balloons. A full breakfast with all the fixings had been cooked. At the end of the long, communal kitchen trestle was a small pile of birthday gifts in colorful wrapping paper. They even hung a large banner from the ceiling that read WITCHY BIRTHDAY!

But I just stood there like an animal caught in the headlights of an oncoming car. Any one of them could have slaughtered me in that moment.

It took me a long moment to step inside the kitchen. *Just a surprise birthday party—that's all it is, Nick.* As the adrenaline wore off, I discreetly slid the athame into the back pocket of my jeans and then smiled. Internally, I breathed a sigh of relief that it wasn't some crazy cult member who wanted to eat me, a forest monster who wanted to fuck me, or a god who wanted to destroy me.

When your job is to fill the role of Lord Lucifer, king of the fallen angels, you meet some whack people in your life.

* * *

Antonia sat on the bench beside me and set a large block of marbled birthday cake down in front of me. A plastic fork was sticking out of the white and blue icing. "Sorry we scared you, Nick," she told me apologetically, looking remorseful. "I explained to the others that you don't celebrate and it might upset you, but they wanted to do something nice for you. I think this is more for them than you."

"It's not that I don't celebrate," I told her. Well, she was right, actually, but I didn't want the nice Satanists to feel bad about all the thought and planning that so obviously went into this.

I picked up the fork and licked the tines of sweet icing just so no one thought I was a snob. "Why would you say that?"

Antonia watched me carefully, and not for the first time. She was dressed neatly in a black pantsuit and white shirt. The outfit screamed "uniform" in that men-in-black kind of way. Her long russet-black hair was tied up in a tight bun, though a tendril had fallen to surround her cheek. Recently, she had put some red Manic Panic streaks into it. I wondered how her boss felt about that.

Sheriff Ben's daughter had just completed her training at Quantico and was working her way through the Special Agent Selection System—an arduous, year-long work program where she'd be expected to do a series of grunt jobs where she'd be running glorified errands and assisting on different investigations. It was meant to pinpoint her strengths and weaknesses and was required to join the team. By this time next year, she would be a full-fledged FBI agent, solving crimes and saving the day. Special Agent Antonia Oswald. It had a nice ring, but I sometimes wondered how she balanced being a cynical and pragmatic investigator with also being a natural-born witch.

She shrugged at my question, then smiled all close-lipped. "I'm a good investigator."

"You saw I don't list my B-day on Facebook."

Her smile grew into a grin, and I knew I was right. "You know, one day, I'm going to be better than you at solving mysteries."

"Is that so?"

"Absolutely."

I watched her watch me lick the fork. I knew she was flirting. She was being pretty obvious about it too, which concerned me.

About a year ago, just as she was graduating from state college, Antonia came into the shop and expressed an interest in learning the craft. That didn't bother me. I was happy to tutor her. But then she mentioned joining the Children of Endor as a full member, and that...yeah, that bothered me a little. No, a lot.

She was a grown woman, sure. And her wanting to be a Luciferian witch was her own god-given decision. But I think the reason it bothered me was that it had to do with...well, me. I was a bit of a lightning rod for pretty terrible supernatural stuff. That, combined with the fact that Antonia had chosen to go into an especially dangerous field, didn't sit well with me.

For a while, I'd tried to dissuade her, but Antonia was as stubborn as her dad. And now that she had made friends here at the coven house—even if she wasn't an "official" member yet—I felt she was sealing her own fate. I couldn't seem to shake her.

I pushed the cake aside. "Aren't you going to be late for work?" I knew she had returned to the field office in Allentown for reassignment, a good hour's drive from Blackwater.

She checked her old-fashioned Mickey Mouse wristwatch. Antonia liked old tech; she seemed drawn to it. "Yeah, I need to get going. But I wanted to be here. I wanted to wish you a good one."

Getting up, she came around me and gave me a hug that lasted a tad longer than was absolutely appropriate. "Happy birthday, Nick."

While she was hugging me, she pressed a tiny present into my hand, which made my heart knock uncomfortably in my chest because it looked like a jewelry box. Then she stepped back and nodded at the gift in crinkly silver paper. "Open it."

"An engagement ring? You shouldn't have."

She laughed. "Just open it!"

Inside was a car key. I held it up.

"I won't be needing the Monaco. I'll be riding with my new senior partner soon," she explained. And then, sensing I was going to rebel, she quickly added, "She doesn't pass regulations anyway. Too old. So I want you to have her."

The other members of our coven had given me very small gifts as if they knew I had an aversion to them—which I do, by the way; getting gifts has always felt awkward to me, maybe because it's such an unfamiliar situation. I got a few silly joke cards, Henry gave me tickets to a big, dumb action movie playing in the Mahoning Drive-in, Amber gave me Halloween-themed undershorts, and Sada gave me a beaded feng shui bracelet that she said was blessed by a Buddhist monk and would enhance my power. This, though, was too much.

I tried to give it back to her, but Antonia held up her hand. "I won't take it, Nick, and if you force me to, I'll just sell her. She's practically a classic now!"

"She's no classic," I laughed. The beat-up, dirty white Monaco that Antonia had found online was worth maybe $400 in a good economy. She had rusty panels and a questionable transmission. But then, after a few awkward seconds, I clenched the key. "Compromise. I'll just keep her for you until you want her back."

"Fair enough." She stared at me long and hard. I could feel the question coming on. She wanted me to make her one of my many brides. So far, I had turned her down every time. I don't know. She seemed so young to me, so full of promise. I couldn't understand why she would want to attach herself to my fucked-up world.

"Toni!"

After another awkward second, she looked around and spotted the guy in the coven she said she was dating but was most assuredly not sleeping with. I knew because he was calling her "Toni" and Antonia despised anyone calling her that.

She partly grimaced at him before turning back to address me. "I'll see ya later, Nick." She gave me a little finger wave before going off with him.

I watched her, my heart aching a little inside of me. She's been through a lot with that nasty Simulacrum business last year, then had been through more when we both took shelter in hell. All of that had changed her. It changed us both.

Maybe I really should talk to her, I thought. It was her decision to be part of our little coven, not mine. But before I could make any decision regarding Antonia, someone grabbed my hand.

David Beyer, who had arrived late to the party. He looked tired and smelled like iodine. I suspected he'd just gotten off his night shift at Blue Ridge Medical.

Last year, we'd had a pretty big breakup. It was bad and we both walked away angry at each other. I couldn't blame David, though. He'd had more reason to be angry than I. Admittedly, I'd been an asshole to him; I put him in a very awkward position as the "other woman (or man, in this case)" in my then relationship with Morgana. So when he showed up on my doorstep six months ago, telling me we had to talk, I decided it was time to stop running and start taking responsibility for my very long string of relationships that had crashed and burned.

Reluctant but determined, I sat him down and told him everything about me. *Everything.* Even the crazy stuff.

He looked at me strangely for a full minute before uttering, "Well…shit, Nick."

I couldn't believe he actually believed me, David being a surgeon, a creature of science and reason, and not usually inclined to such things. Once, long ago, he'd wound up at odds with his Hasidic Jewish family.

It took him a day to process, but then he came back and told me he was cool with everything, and if I couldn't commit to just one partner due to my unusual circumstances, he could live with that. He could live with just being one of my many brides.

But I didn't take him up on his offer. We needed to establish a foundation of trust and friendship before we moved to any higher ground. A lot had been wrecked last year. So friendship it was.

Problem was, I didn't think that was what David wanted. Or it wasn't all he wanted.

Three months later, David committed to going full Satanist. It was a huge move on his part, one I questioned, but he said he was ready, and that he knew his place was with me, so we initiated him into our little collective. He said he had no regrets about his decision.

"Nick, I really need to talk to you," he said now. His voice was pained and urgent. His hand tightened just slightly around my wrist. "This really can't wait."

"Oh? What's happened?" Suddenly, my heart was in my throat again. "Is something wrong?"

"Nothing you can't fix. I think." David glanced around at the others talking, eating, and communing. "Can we go somewhere private to talk? It won't take long, I promise."

"Sure. I guess."

We retreated to the large walk-in pantry at the back of the kitchen, a private room stocked to the rafters with foodstuffs for our decently-sized commune. Once we were alone, David kicked the door shut, pulled the chain for the overhead light, and reached for a nearby stool. "Have a seat."

I looked at him nervously, not liking this much, but took the stool. I was super tall and David was maybe an inch below average. That put us at almost eye level when I sat down. "Okay. So, what's this about?"

David leaned forward, wrapped an arm around my neck, and kissed me. It was a slow, sensual, and somewhat apologetic kiss. "Sorry, I was late for your big day, man. A patient kept me."

"It's ok—"

David kissed me again, this time longer, fiercer. He ran his hands through my hair, undoing the still-damp strands so they fell all around us, tenting us in. I'd been hating on my long hair since last year when the blowback happened, but then, one night, Amber and Henry informed me that they liked it when I tickled them with it. After that, it didn't bother me so much.

When he finally let me breathe, I said, "You said there was a problem..."

"Yep," David agreed with a mischievous half-grin. "You haven't been in my pants since forever, you slacker. I'm starting to think you don't like me."

I chuckled at that. "I promise you that's not it."

David, still wearing that sexy grin, got down on his knees in front of the stool, his hands resting atop my jean-clad thighs. He gave me the most desperate come-hither look ever.

"David," I laughed. "What's all this about, man?"

He grinned up at me as he worked at opening my jeans. "I'm giving you your birthday present, you big dumb lug."

"Ah," I said, big, dumb lug that I was.

"I know you don't like gifts. But you like this, right?" And he started doing things to me that are best left to *Penthouse* forum letters.

Best. Birthday. Ever.

David was talented in so many ways. I was thinking seriously about pinning him to the wall between the canned goods shelves when my cell went off. I ignored it so I could concentrate on coaxing David up so I could kiss him again, but after a half minute of us fumbling around and driving each other crazy, I realized whoever was calling was desperate and not about to give up.

"Answer it," David said. I thought about telling him not to talk with his mouth full, but he let me go so he could look up. "Then tell them to fuck off while I suck off Satan's cock."

I laughed and looked at the caller ID. I didn't recognize the number. I was about to slide the icon to the red when that bad feeling I'd had earlier returned in spades. The sense of foreboding ticked away at the base of my skull and stiffened my spine—and that had nothing to do with David or his talents. I slid it to green.

"Eng…Englebrecht!" I said, jumping at little under David's wicked ministrations.

"Nick."

It took me a moment to place the voice. It had been some years since I'd heard that gravelly tone.

"Malach?"

David stopped when he heard the dire tone of my voice and stood up, his brows knitted with concern. That was disappointing…

Of all the people to phone me up, Malach (aka God's Hitman, aka the angel that hated me and once punched me in the face hard enough to crack a tooth) was the very last one I expected to hear on my special day. I didn't even know Malach owned a damned phone.

"Nick," he repeated, sounding more concerned than threatening now. "I need to see you. We need to speak. It's important." A beat. "A matter of life and…existence, actually."

That bad feeling filled me in all kinds of ways, and I felt my stomach sink to my shoes.

"What's all this about? Don't be cryptic or I swear to God I will hang up on your angelic ass," I growled into the phone. "If this is a joke—"

But Malach wasn't here to play. "This isn't a joke, Nick. I want to hire you as a private investigator. The…the whole world hangs in the balance. How quickly can you meet me?"

| 2 |

Frenemies

THERE IS NOTHING like a cryptic "you need to come and save the world, kthxbai" phone call to get the blood pumping in the morning.

A thousand scenarios went through my head as I piloted Antonia's Monaco down the back roads on the way to the address Malach had given me. The car, as big as a boat, bounced along on the barely-paved roads. Winter and rock salt had stripped all semblance of civilization away and turned the road into barely better than a glorified goat path. Still, it was nice to feel those roads rumbling away under the ponderous, slightly fishtailing car. In the months since I'd wrecked my own Monaco (rather, had it totaled on me), I'd been using any of the coven's many vehicles for any excursions outside the town limits, but they were all modern hybrids or electric cars courtesy of the Alexanders' green-energy corporation, Synergy. They were fine cars, modern and silent. But nothing was quite as fun to drive as a vintage 1970's cop car.

The ride out to New Hope was longer than I expected, but not unpleasant. The drive into the wilds was even longer, though not unwelcomed. It gave me time to contemplate what I was about to step into. Unfortunately, it also allowed my darker and more morbid thoughts to run wild.

I had to stop twice and look at the sheets I had printed off Google Maps based on Malach's address. Seriously, my old frenemy's safe house was really deep in the woods. Eventually, I hit the gate that marked the end of the last gravel road to nowhere. I had to leave the Monaco behind, sling a backpack on, and hike the last two miles in.

It was a frosty morning on this first of November. The trees were mostly bare, their blackish limbs clattering together like goblins rubbing their hands together over a nefarious plot. It tasted of snow—tonight or maybe tomorrow early. I was happy I'd opted for a warm pullover and my puffy jacket in case I was stuck here overnight—which I dearly hoped I would not be. Seriously, the Pennsylvania woods are scary as fuck after dark, and I was even one of the things that went bump in the night.

It was rough going with a lot of switchbacks to scale and long drop-offs, but I had brought my hiking gear and good Skecher boots, which I owned but rarely used because I was so not a hiker. Walking around in the mountains and possibly stepping into a gopher hole is not my idea of a good time. But sometimes, if you wanna help the police find someone, you gotta go off-grid.

I topped what felt like the hundredth hill, found a deadfall to climb for a good vantage point, and scanned the woods with my field glasses. I finally spotted the tiny hunting cabin Malach told me would be there. It was pretty rustic looking, and the area looked wild and uninhabited, which made sense, seeing how he was guarding the anointed future God of Planet Earth.

He must have spotted or otherwise sensed me coming because halfway down the footpath to the cabin, Malach threw open the door and walked toward me over the rickety front porch. The bad feeling I'd been having for hours intensified when I reached him.

"Thank you for coming, Nick. You may enter this dwelling," he announced, which removed any wards that might have kept someone of my kind from invading the place.

I glanced around as I shrugged off my heavy pack. It was a one-room, Amish-built cabin with no running water or electricity. Hand-carved living room furniture, a table with two chairs by the window, and a loft. Hunting trophies were scattered across the walls, along with some old photographs and other things like a bow and arrow set and hand-sewn snowshoes. I spotted a mattress and some blankets in the loft—probably where Malach slept. Or at least rested. I had no idea if angels slept.

The big man himself moved like a small, leather-clad mountain through the tiny space, making it feel smaller still. I told you I'm tall. Well, Malach towers over even me at a little over seven feet—probably more. He was dressed in his long hitman's coat and lace-up, shit-kicking boots. He looked as if he'd just sprung from a WWE match, except I spotted the pancake holster where he kept that gigantic golden gun with all its fancy angelic glyphs. He was scowling as he moved to stand behind little Cassandra Berger, who was seated in her wheelchair and paging through a book I had given her years earlier. *The Velveteen Rabbit.* He put his hand on her shoulder, absolutely dwarfing the little girl, who finally glanced up.

Cassie was five years old when Malach and I liberated her from her angel-eating, psychotic mother. She was nine or ten now, but she still looked small and frail from the Tay Sach's disease that kept her chair-bound, her little head supported by a brace. Still, her eyes lit up at the sight of me, and she dropped the book and made grabby hands toward me. She seemed to be trying to say my name, but it came out as soft, kitten-like mews.

"Hello, honeybee," I said, immediately going to one knee before her chair so she could put her hands all over my face.

She looked me over rather solemnly before nodding her approval. Then she grabbed my hand in both of hers. I wasn't sure what that meant, if she wanted to tell me something or not, but Malach said, "She understands much more than she says."

"I'm sure she does," I said, unable to look away from the little girl whose hand was wrapped around several of my fingers. As always, I experienced a profound sense of peace around little Cassie. She was a Nephilim. In essence, half-angel like me, but unlike me, her angel side lived in a state of grace and that made her surprisingly powerful. For some reason, little Cassie liked me. Maybe because I had taken a real beating to protect her. And yes, I would do it again.

"Cassandra wants you to know that she trusts you. That she knows you will take her to the throne someday. She has faith in you," Malach explained.

"I'm honored," I told her honestly.

Over the years, I had learned a great deal about myself and my family. One of the more surprising things was that those born into the Lucifer line were god-makers by design. I mean that we literally put God on the throne once, and we would need to do so again since there was a vacancy at present. As the reigning Lucifer, it was a job I'd been told would soon fall to me. My task was to see to it that little Cassie got to the throne as the Anointed One with no misadventure.

Malach indicated that I should follow him. "I need to talk to you. In private." He started toward a door that presumably led to the back of the property. Cassie tugged on a few long strands of my hair, so I gave her the candy corn in my pocket. I had bought it just for her on my way up. Then I retrieved her book and kissed her little hands. "I'll be back soon, honeybee," I told her before standing up and following Malach out back.

There was a small porch jutting off the back of the cabin—rickety and missing a few boards. But more surprising was the fact we weren't alone on it. I damned near had a heart attack when I stepped out and spotted the figure sitting in what looked like a hand-carved wooden rocking chair.

He turned his head, then immediately sprang to his feet. He was tall and excruciatingly thin like a willow tree without branches or leaves. Unlike Malach, he looked young—painfully so. He resembled a teenage boy with short hair and big ears. His mop of brown hair fell into his huge blue eyes—too large for anything human—and stuck there. Mostly because a long, never-ending stream of tears was running from them and down his cheeks, forming pools on the worn boards of the porch.

Before I could react, the young man was on his feet—it took microseconds, if that—and two large, owl-brown wings suddenly manifested themselves, though I didn't need to see them to realize what he was. The stink of Heavenly Host clung to him like the sickly-sweet aroma of cherry Twizzlers left in the sun to melt. The stench of magick surrounded him...

Malach held up his hand to stop the angel from charging me. "No, Cassiel."

"But, Malach," said the outraged angel, "it's Lu—!"

"I said *no*," Malach boomed, and the angel stopped mid-dive and reversed his trajectory so he was hanging in midair like he was being suspended on wires. He twisted his face into a silent snarl and showed his pointy little angel teeth like some feral Chihuahua.

It irritated me, so I leaned forward and made a half-hearted little snarl myself, showing off my own teeth.

Malach had to turn to me next and told me the same thing. I realized after a second or two I was standing primed, my athame in hand, ready to cut a bitch. That bitch being Cassiel. I didn't even remember pulling it from my belt.

Tears ran in rivers down the angel's angry face. Cassiel. The Angel of Tears. See, I remember my catechism.

"What's he doing here?" I demanded to know, gesturing with the knife. I was getting angry now and this was starting to feel like a setup. "I thought Cassiel and the other angels were loyal to Gabe and Mike."

Malach raised both of his hands. "Cassiel is with me now, Nick. And with Cassandra." But his explanation didn't explain anything.

Cassiel, in his reedy, annoying little boy voice said, "What is this, Malach? I will not work with Lord Lucifer!"

"Yeah, well, the feeling is mutual, you weepy, feathered twerp—" I told him.

Cassiel started retorting with something, but a loud gunshot cracked the quiet of the woods, and both of us switched our attention back to Malach. He had his big-ass golden gun pointing toward the sky, and the near-sonic boom he'd shot off was making some of the remaining leaves fall off the trees around us.

"Malach—" I said, and he said, "No!"

"Malach!"

He turned back to Cassiel. "I said no!" After a second or two, he finally lowered the gun and said in a more reasonable voice, "That's enough, boys. I need both of your help, so you'll need to set your difference aside for a time."

* * *

Malach put us both into time-out.

Cassiel went back to sulking in the rocking chair and Malach told me to sit at the bottom of the stairs that led off the back porch. He wedged himself between us so we wouldn't do anything stupid. Who, me? Do something stupid?

I didn't know much about Cassiel except he was a minor angel, a middle-ranking soldier in God's army. Sort of like a Sergeant First Class in the American army. He worked as an advisor and assistant to a platoon leader, but he had never done anything very exciting that I knew of and was utterly forgettable.

Malach cleared his throat. "I asked you here because I need your help."

It took me a moment to realize Malach was talking to me. He didn't normally use so many words, so I knew this was important. I turned on the stairs, leaned against the banister, and crossed my legs. "You, I'll help. Cassie, I will always help. That guy"—I pointed to Cassiel, still weeping his useless tears in that rocking chair of his—"can fuck the fuck off."

Malach raised his hand in an "easy" gesture. "Cassiel doesn't work for the boys any longer. He's aligned himself with me and with Cassandra."

"My ass!"

"Nick..." Malach began, but Cassiel stood up, interrupting us.

"Malach, I think it is unwise to involve Lord Lucifer in this matter."

Malach turned to him next. "I disagree, Cassiel. Nick is exactly the kind of ally we need right now."

"He is the prince of lies!"

"Nick isn't his father!" Malach insisted, which bolstered my mood just a little. "I want to take him into our confidence."

"For the record, I think this is a bad idea." Even so, Cassiel started explaining the whys and wherefores of their issue. He said in that reedy, annoying voice that he'd arrived only the day before. A few days ago, the Host had held a parliament and made some decisions about the currently empty throne.

I didn't like the sound of that. "What decisions?"

"They voted to put one of their own on the throne of the world." Cassiel was pacing, and he sounded ticked about that. "They decided to ignore the Anointed One"—Cassiel turned his head to acknowledge Cassie, still inside. She had discovered a moth that had found its way inside her book and been squashed by the pages. I watched in wonder as she cupped her hands around it and, one quick spark later, the white moth suddenly took wing and flew away, much to her delight—"and place Archangel Michael on the seat instead, seeing how he has always been the closest to Ha-Shem."

Ha-Shem. That's the big guy, for those not in the know.

I held up a hand. "Excuse me, but he would be wrong. That would be my granddad, Ha-Shaitan—God's red right hand, if you will." My grandfather had put God on the throne after an extended battle with the Old Ones, ancient gods and goddesses who had wanted complete control of Earth back in the day. Not long after, God gave Grampa a quick kick in the pants for trying to convince him to rule fairly. That's what you get when you work for a lousy boss.

Cassiel eyed me keenly as if I was lying. "After Ha-Shaitan was cast down, Michael took his place at our Lord's right hand. He has helped to rule fairly ever since."

"Sure, he's doing an awesome job, considering the state of the world," I quipped, folding my arms. "Maybe you should have left Grampa in charge."

Cassiel frowned, insulted. "You know as well as I that the Lucifers are a line of god-makers. You create the light that leads the young God to the throne. You cannot *be* God."

I rolled my eyes. Of course, His Holiness had completely missed my sarcasm.

Already tired of this, I stood up to leave, but Malach moved between us like a referee, which was totally unnecessary. I'd cooled off and didn't want to fight with Cassiel. I just wanted to go back to the coven house in Blackwater and be the nice, easygoing Lord of Hell I was.

"Nick, please...hear him out," Malach pleaded.

With a sigh, I stomped forward a few steps and pointed my finger at Cassiel's face. "I don't give a shit about the throne or ruling or any of your angel business. In fact, I have no idea what I'm even doing here—"

"About a week ago, Michael threatened Cassandra's life," Malach blurted out.

Not much could have kept me there but that did it. I stopped scowling at Cassiel and looked at Malach. "Threatened a disabled little girl? What the actual fuck?"

"Yes," Cassiel confirmed. "And that is the reason I will no longer work for Michael's court."

"And the reason I am helping Cassiel," Malach confirmed.

"Why did he threaten Cassie?"

My voice must have sounded really growly because it took Malach a moment to respond. "After God's Nephilim abandoned the throne, the Host abandoned all hope of placing someone with human blood on it again. They do not trust the humans to make a good God."

That made sense, I guess, but...hell. Hurting a little girl was pretty much the antithesis of what angels were supposed to be all about.

"I'll gut the bastard if he hurts Cassie!" I said, meaning it. I probably couldn't do it. I wasn't a full angel, sure, and I'd fail horribly, but I'd sure as hell try. And it wasn't like I didn't have mad skillz. Under Juliette's tutelage, I was growing to be a pretty good witch with a side of chaos demon.

Malach nodded slowly. "I knew I could count on you, Nick." He glanced over at Cassiel, who nodded for Malach to continue.

Malach turned back to me. "All of this is devolving into a pretty dire squabble…"

"I'd say!"

"And that's the reason I need to speak to Michael. I need to see if I can talk him down from his plans to hurt Cassandra."

"So talk to him! I'll even go with you if you want." And I meant that. I even took out my angel-eating athame and tossed it in my hand. Cassiel watched the blade keenly. "Be your heavy if he gets fresh with you."

Malach nodded once. "Yes. I believe you would. And Cassiel and I do want to speak to Michael, but he's disappeared."

Before I could ask about that, Cassiel took a bold step forward, the tears still running down his cheeks—which, by the way, were really off-putting. "Completely vanished. Malach and I can no longer feel his presence…anywhere. We have searched individually and as a team, to no effect. We have spoken to our brothers, and they too cannot find Michael. It's as if he's gone from this universe."

I gave the angel some serious side-eye then. "So what exactly do you want from me?"

Malach filled in. "You are a private investigator and you have good instincts and a keen intellect." I think that was the first compliment I had ever heard from Malach's lips. Aww, I thought, he must really love me! "We want you to find where Michael has gone. We cannot offer you anything in return, but you would be saving Cassandra from Michael's wrath."

| 3 |

One Hot Mess

I DROVE BACK to Blackwater with one of those thin, flimsy Trapper folders on the seat beside me. A pair of rainbow-colored frolicking unicorns by Lisa Frank graced the front of it. The folder was so old, it was faded and the edges were torn. Inside the "dossier" (as Cassiel called it) were a few sheets of paper—all the info that Malach and Cassiel could give me regarding Archangel Michael's whereabouts. They consisted of a few smudgy pictures of a man in profile that was supposed to be Michael, but they looked like they were taken from a CCTV in the dead of night, some notes that Cassiel had written up on Michael's last movements, and newspaper clippings about a variety of crimes scattered across NYC. The two angels thought they were all leads on Michael, but most of it looked like random crap to me.

Halfway home, I pulled into a rest stop, opened the folder, and threw out all the stuff I knew wasn't of any help, which was almost all of it. The one thing I kept was a grainy pic of a group of men playing poker inside a warehouse of some kind. The pic was taken from an awkward angle far up. I didn't recognize the middle-aged, balding black man in the center-right of the picture, but the man beside him resembled the Archangel Michael.

I knew this unfortunately because one day long ago, while I was working Vice down in New York, I responded to a distress call in lower Brooklyn, and when I got to the ramshackle, coldwater flat, someone was waiting for me. He surprised me and threw me against the wall.

The dude was so strong that I broke through the plaster and wound up entangled in the studs in the wall. But before I could react, call for backup, or even get my piece out, he pulled me out, dislocating my shoulder in the process, and threw me to the floor. The entire building shook and I thought for a second I was going to go right through the floorboards. Then he planted a booted foot on my chest and glared down at me.

"Rude," I grunted.

He had a sword that was, literally, on fire. I didn't need a name to know who I was dealing with. My dad had warned me this could happen, though I'd shrugged it off. I figured he was just overreacting and I wasn't important enough for Michael to turn a rheumy eye on. Obviously, I was wrong.

The creature pointed its sword at me, singeing the little hairs on my face, and said, "You are he? Ha-Shaitan's whelp?"

I pushed against his leg, but it was like trying to move an iron statue. My panic made me a dumbass, no surprise there. "No, I'm a Jonas Brother."

Not one of my finer moments. Archangel Michael seemed to glow and I got a glance at the fucking scary way he looked when he wasn't disguising himself as a human, all giant, prince-like, armored, and with grotesque scars running all over his face from his many battles. Milky wings, tattered and torn were covered in bronze and gold armor. Not a pretty angel, and grinning at me like a hungry lion. He drove his burning sword into the floor beside my head and said, "Beware, Satan's son." Then he vanished like he was never there.

To tell you the truth, I'd never figured out if he meant beware *him* or someone else. I also never discovered why he didn't just kill me when he had the chance. As a Daemon, I wasn't protected from being hunted by Otherkin. Maybe he felt sorry for me or figured I wasn't much of a threat?

It was a mystery I'd never solved.

I wasn't hot for Malach's mission. Michael could have killed me and he hadn't. He still could. I had no fantasy about overcoming a full-blooded archangel who had it out for me. He'd skewer me like a shish kabob long before I got a single tine of the bident into him.

"So what the fuck's wrong with you?" I asked myself as I looked at the grainy pic of the mobsters playing poker. Michael's attention was squarely on the black man beside him, and they were smiling like they were old pals. But I already knew the answer to my question: As the god-maker, I had to protect Cassie. If something happened to her, especially when I could have prevented it, I would never be able to live with myself.

I had screwed up a lot of stuff in my life—careers, relationships, just being human—but I couldn't fail in this task.

I snapped a pic of the photograph with my phone, then used Google's reverse image search to discover the identities of the men in the picture. Michael didn't return anything, but I matched the black man to a name: Papa Lacroix, a Haitian drug lord who ran a lucrative business out of downtown Brooklyn—my old stomping grounds. He specialized in the trans-shipment of cocaine and marijuana. According to my Google-fu, Lacroix once worked under the Colombian drug lord Griselda Blanco, a pioneer in cocaine trafficking. Lacroix was one of his top bosses and was responsible for more than 200 murders over the years. Then, a few years ago, Lacroix and a small entourage broke away and launched their startup here in the east. Mostly New York City and parts of New Jersey, but drugs had been spilling over into eastern PA for decades, mostly ice and bath salts. Not a huge surprise; I knew of a few small, struggling ex-coal towns locally who dealt to stay financially afloat.

I closed my phone, tucked the unicorn folder away, and drove to the shop to open up—several hours later than I should have. Thankfully, Morgana wasn't there to scold me. I did find a note on the door that read "When you finally read this, move the new stock to the floor. ~M"

"Yes, ma'am," I said, unlocking the door and flicking on the lights. It was a little before noon and I had lost the morning to that little excursion in the mountains, but since this was a Sunday, that was okay. Blackwater is a devoutly religious little town. Everyone was still in church, being good little Christians. After they had stuffed themselves at one of the many steakhouses on the Strip, they would drop by our shop to buy their tarot cards and herbal remedies and pretend to be good pagans. It was the hypocrisy that kept us alive and running in an otherwise rather orthodox little town.

I was perched on a stool behind the counter, laptop on my knee while I did due diligence on Papa Lacroix, when the first of the locals in their Sunday bests began pouring into the shop.

A few of our regulars gravitated to the front and discreetly requested their usuals—potions for sexual potency, money, or just regular old arthritis relief. The teens ogled the glass display case. I had dutifully unboxed the shipment from our media distributor as Morgana had requested. We never really knew what the company was going to send us, but this month, it was the complete *Dark Shadows* TV series box set, which came with a cool little coffin to slot the DVDs in. Some of the kids asked me what the show was about. I tried not to roll my eyes as I explained the premise while chewing a Red Vine.

When they had finished, a cocky-looking young guy in a nice suit came up to me and started witnessing about the gospels of Jesus Christ. "You know, mister," he said very somberly, "the devil prowls around like a roaring lion, seeking someone to devour."

I stopped taking notes and pointed my pen at him. "That's a really good idea, kid. I'm starving and these Vines aren't doing it for me."

"Excuse me?"

I picked up the paper menu for the pizza shop down the street. "Should I get the penne in vodka sauce or the fettuccini alfredo?"

Around six in the evening, Morgana texted me to tell me she was on her way home. I texted her back and told her everything was cool and she was free to make an evening of it if she wanted. I was happy to take the shop till ten when we closed. I figured she deserved a night to herself.

Why? she texted back. *What did you do now?*

I felt a spike of outrage that she would suspect me of ulterior movies, but if I was being perfectly honest, I think I was just bitter that she hadn't said anything about my birthday. Then I forced myself to laugh it off. I'd always hated my B-day, and she probably remembered that, but the truth was, the surprise party this morning was nice. I liked that the coven had taken the time and seemed to genuinely care about my special day. The little gifts had kind of choked me up.

I looked at my phone and mourned the loss of our friendship—we'd been solid once in the time before we became lovers and then bitter, angry exes—but then decided to let Morgana off the hook. I had a lot to answer for.

I've got nothing going on. I can take the shop.

If you're sure, she said.

Yep. Go have some fun.

Thx, Nick. Happy birthday.

She texted me an animated gif of kittens in witch hats holding orange and black birthday balloons.

That was nice.

Thx. Cya, I texted back and then, with a sigh, put the phone face down on the counter.

***

When I got back to the coven house, Henry, who was busy winterizing the bushes in the front of the house with burlap wraps, stood up, knocked the dirt from his hands, and told me that Juliette was here and had called an esbat. I figured it was because it was my special day. I was, after all, the one these young witches worshiped—I was still getting used to that.

The day had warmed up considerably in that weird way that late fall in PA can, and Henry had taken off his T-shirt to work and was now using it to wipe down the sweat on his chest, which was kind of distracting. But I heard him well enough. He didn't say as much, but I knew if he was giving me this information, it was a hint they wanted me to officiate the esbat.

They asked, but they never forced me. I think that would have been a breach of etiquette or something. We'd had a sabbat the night before for All Hollow's Eve, so probably I could have gotten out of this gathering, but it felt important somehow, so I told him I'd be there.

I went upstairs and took another shower, a cold one this time, and then put on my official Satan suit. I mean, no one but you knows I call it that, but I do. Black leather trousers and a matching suit jacket, no shirt. I had tall, sexy, lace-up boots that went with the outfit, but all the hiking today had left my feet sore, so I slid them into the blue Cookie Monster slippers I'd gotten at Wal-Mart. If the nice Satanists noticed, they never commented. I tied my hair into a tall ponytail and went downstairs to attend to my worshipers.

On entering the common room where we normally held our meetings, I saw the coven was already assembled. They were naked and holding hands in a large circle. It had taken me a bit to get used to all that vulnerable flesh on display, but after living with the Children of Endor for over a year, it didn't bother me now. Amber and Henry, holding hands, called the corners, then opened the circle for me to enter, swiftly sealing it after me.

I went to sit down in the chair they had provided me in the center of the circle and manifested the bident, laying it across my lap. That was another thing that had taken some getting used to—being the center of attention. I was used to being low-key and practically invisible, but after over a dozen ceremonies, my stage fright wasn't as bad as it was when I began.

They began to chant and called down praises and prayers upon me. As something of an idiot craft savant, I listened and tried to accommodate them. My control over magick was tenuous at best, but I could make things happen through sheer will if I focused enough. If I'd been in their place, I wouldn't have trusted me to change a light bulb, but they seemed to have an endless stream of faith in my ability to do things without fucking them up.

Every few seconds, they shifted the circle a few feet along so I was continually looking at someone new. Juliette was here, as was Sada, and even David, who had yet to miss an important ceremony. But Antonia couldn't be here because she wasn't yet one of them and not privy to our workings.

"Lord Lucifer, you've risen and fallen a thousand times. Michael drove you down into the pit, but you rose again, great dragon.

Gabriel sent you into the mountains, but you returned stronger than ever."

Their words rang in my head like a bell, and their devotion and worship enlivened me and made my heart beat faster and faster. The magicks of the living "Well" we created here began to gather and fill the room. My head began to swim, and slowly, only over the next few minutes, I became aware that my chair was hovering several inches above the floor...

Those of my bloodline acted as sort of psychic vampires. Like many of the Old Ones, we gain most of our power from the Well—the power given to us by our believers. My believers' Well was pretty deep, and as the power—their worship—flowed over and around me, I felt it infuse my blood and bones with an extra layer of pure power. It was a little like putting a layer of armor over an already, but thinner, existing layer of armor. Layer after layer building up. You got stronger the more you did it, building up a magickal shell that was well-nigh impossible for most other magicks to penetrate.

Their chanting grew stronger, louder. Bolder. At the height of it, I felt my back stiffen in an almost orgasmic way, and I threw back my head as my wings manifested, shushing gently at the air. Now, this was definitely the best birthday gift of the day, I thought.

It didn't last long, and after it was over, the coven went from a bunch of somber-eyed, Satan worshippers to a giggly group of young people wanting pizza, sex, and control of what Netflix movie to stream. Some paired off and went off to have fun—that, too, would feed my power late into the night. David brushed my shoulder in passing and said he'd be upstairs in his room if I needed him.

Juliette, however, remained. She threw on her official robes, grabbed a chair from a corner of the room where most of the furniture had been shoved out of the way for the ceremony, and sat down opposite me. She looked at me with great wisdom and concern.

"You're growing in power," she told me. "You've gotten stronger. I can feel it."

"I hope so," I told her. "I've been practicing. Doing those exercises you suggested, even though most of them are boring as hell."

Juliette smiled and I realized I'd made a funny without realizing it.

Because of her, my own personal Mr. Miyagi, I spent a lot of time sitting in chairs, visualizing things, which didn't feel all that special to me, but she told me they would help me focus and refine my craft—which was a mess, frankly.

Juliette nodded sagely. "It's paying off. Your craft is still chaotic and unfocused most of the time, but at least you have a measure of control over that chaos. It may even be your forte as a witch."

I saluted her like a good soldier. "If you're going to be a mess, be a hot mess."

"Something like that," she laughed. "I've known a few Chaos Witches in my time. They are not to be underestimated."

Over the past year, Juliette had taught me a form of mental and spiritual yoga meant to strengthen my "relationship with the craft," as she called it. Back in the old days, I wouldn't have bothered. I would have even laughed her off. But not too long ago, the Arcana had gotten a hold of me, kept me locked up in a church for days, zapped me of my power, and beat the living hell out of me. It almost killed me. Juliette said if I'd been in better shape, craft-wise, I never would have been taken so easily by such a low-ranking member of that group of angel-eating psychos. It wasn't even the first time the Arcana had almost bested me. And it all proved how much of an amateur witch I was. Well, I was determined to never let that happen again.

"But...you're not a mess," she told me more seriously. "You just haven't been schooled well, and you have time to make up. And, being a Chaos With isn't the worst thing."

"It sounds dire."

"Not necessarily. Controlled chaos can be quite useful, Nick. If you're naturally erratic or unpredictable, your enemies may have a lot of trouble entrapping or controlling you. Remember what I said some time back? Everything is—"

"—a tool," I finished her mantra with a nod.

She smiled, then looked me over critically. "You look well. Strong. How are you?" She quickly added, "I don't mean craft-wise."

I ran my hand through my hair. "Good. I'm good. And you?"

She tilted her head. "You always do that."

"What?"

"Deflect the conversation away from how you're feeling. You never really open up with anyone."

"I don't—"

"You do. It's instinctual for you. It's how you've survived. No judgment." She held up her hand. "But I want to know how *you* are. Are you sleeping well?"

Did I mention that Juliette is also a therapist by profession? Yeah. "Well enough."

"But you have nightmares."

I didn't like that she knew that. Probably her followers who warmed my bed told her everything I said in my sleep over the course of the night. I might need to start sleeping alone.

"Everyone has nightmares, Juliette."

She gave me a poignant look, so I sat up straighter. "I'm fine. I'm good. I'm your little lord of hell, remember? Nothing beats the Devil."

She smirked at that and nodded. "You're resilient. Willful. That's the source of your strength more than anything else."

"Correct."

"Just remember that I'm always here for you, Nick. We can talk about anything."

| 4 |

How to Save the World (In Ten Steps or Less)

THE FIRST THING I did the next morning was ring Morgana.

"I need a few personal days," I told her while I pulled on my clothes.

I expected her to bitch me out the way she usually did. She probably knew I was hip-deep in some angel/demon/monster nonsense. She always did. But this time, she surprised me.

"How many days, Nick?"

I thought about that as I sat there on the side of my bed. I was mostly dressed but I needed to do something with my hair. "I'm not sure. A week?"

A pause. Then: "That's fine. You helped me out yesterday."

"You mean you're okay with that?" Maybe I hadn't heard right.

"Is it important?"

"Kind of." I stood up, trying to pull my jeans up with one hand. I considered a moment, then decided to go for it.

"You remember Cassie Berger, right? The missing girl from a few years back? Well, the Archangel Michael visited her a few days ago and threatened her life. Malach's, too. So he asked me to hunt him down so Malach and I can knock some sense into him. He's gotten it into his head that he wants to take the throne and subjugate the world, which would be really bad. Despite what you might have heard in church, Michael's not exactly a saint or the merciful kind and will probably kill every human on the planet in a massive Armageddon orgy because the Holy Host is sick of our shit. Someone needs to stop him. That's about the size of it."

A beat.

Then: "Hunt down the Archangel Michael. Stop him from killing everyone. Save the world. Got it." Morgana hung up.

* * *

Downstairs, the kids were making breakfast and talking at the long, communal trestle table. When they saw me, they gave me smiles, waves, and plenty of "good mornings," but I was glad they had done away with the whole "my lord" business because that was creepy as fuck and I never did get used to it.

Juliette had taken off for Philly, where she and her brother ran their multi-billion-dollar corporation that paid to keep the Children of Endor going, but Sada brought me over a mug of tea sweetened just the way I like it. In the beginning, I'd insisted on making my own morning tea, and I rarely ate breakfast. Then I realized it made the kids sad that they couldn't do anything for me when I got up, so I let them do this one thing.

I nodded a thanks to her as I leaned my butt against the kitchen counters and sipped my breakfast with both hands. It was a frosty morning, and the hot tea tasted good.

"Road trip?" Sada asked. She nodded at my windbreaker, which I had draped over one arm.

"I gotta see a man about a drug," I told her honestly.

"I can be ready in five."

"It's not anything dangerous," I explained to my bodyguard. I mean, I didn't think it would be.

Lying in bed last night, I'd had time to think about my next move. In years past, I would have jumped in with both feet and let fate have me. But I was a year older, and—I hoped—a year wiser. I had a plan. I didn't want to make any mistakes.

"I believe you," Sada told me. She folded her arms and her long fingernails, detailed with glyphs, ticked against her bare upper arms. "But I don't want my mom angry with me for abandoning you."

It was smart of her to guilt me into taking her. She was hitting below the belt, but I could respect that. Juliette was tough on her only child and expected a lot of her.

Once we were in the Monaco and on our way, I explained about my encounter with Malach and Cassiel, which had her curling her upper lip. Like me, the kids of the coven were no fans of angels. Couldn't blame them. "Michael's been associating with this drug kingpin in New York named Papa Lacroix. I traced a bunch of drugs back to him, including some pretty nasty bath salts I recognized as popular around these parts." I shrugged as we drove out of town. "It's not a big lead, but I want to check out this low-level dealer and see what he knows about Lacroix before I confront the dude. I've decided *not* to go in half-cocked this time."

Like Juliette, Sada nodded sagely at me. "I'm happy you took me."

I smiled nicely at her. "I don't need a chaperone."

"Then think of me as backup. In case things get nasty."

"I know Sean," I said, referring to the low-level drug dealer in question. He and I had a history. Not a long one, but it was there. "He's not nasty. Bit of an idiot, actually."

"Sean," Sada said. "He's Kara's ex, right?"

I winced. Sean, Kara, Vivian, and I used to party back in the day. But last year, when everything took a turn and Vivian and I broke up, something happened between Sean and Kara and they went their separate ways. Sada, when she first arrived in Blackwater, crushed hard on Kara. They went out a few times, but nothing seemed to come of it—maybe because Kara was a traditional Wiccan and didn't believe in the Devil the way Sada did. But I hadn't asked for details; I'd felt it wasn't my place to probe into Sada's romantic life.

Sada stared out of the windshield for a full minute while she rubbed at her arms with those long nails. Then she glanced up and said, "I have a bad feeling about this, Nick. Watch your back."

An intuitive witch, I took Sada's warning very seriously and nodded as we drove toward Riverdale, which everyone in northern PA secretly called Drugdale. Sada was busy on her phone, so I dug out my own and rang up Vivian.

"Nick…" she said, sounding out of breath. "Happy belated birthday! Sorry I didn't ring. I was…occupied."

Vivian runs the sweet shop Confessions on Broad Street in the roiling heart of Philadelphia. She's a talented maker of confections and fine chocolates. She's also my step-sister (on my dad's side) and a fire witch who makes charms for people with little to no hope left. The "on my dad's side" thing means she's also a Daemon like me and a damned fine witch. Probably better, seeing how she actually knows what she's doing most of the time.

We have always had a strong connection, and my heart beat once very hard. Just hearing her voice could do that to me.

We'd had a deep and tumultuous relationship as lovers once (don't judge; I didn't know about the step-sister thing at the time) and now we maintained a sibling connection that had us calling each other at least two or three times a week just to make sure we were both still alive. As a fellow Lucifer, Vivian gets herself into some pretty hot messes—not that I'm judging. You've seen how my life goes.

I turned onto Route 209 going toward the mountains. This being a weekday, the traffic was particularly egregious.

"Thanks, Viv. I was just call—" The sound of breaking glass made me sit up straight in my seat and I had to serve to avoid hitting a vintage truck. "Did I get you at a bad time?"

Vivian muffled a cry and then said, "Oh, you know. Stuff's been happening in the city."

Another crash—louder this time.

I was about to ask what was going on when she offered the information, "Did you know Philly has vampires? Well, they might actually be CHUDS. I'm not sure."

"CHUDS?"

"Cannibalistic Humanoid Underground Dwellers—like in the movie." There was a pause wherein I heard some motion going on. Vivian was on the move. Then another thing smashed to the floor of her shop and something not quite human cried out.

"No," said Vivian, "I'm pretty sure they're vampires."

Her partner Sebastian must have taken the phone from her because I heard him say clearly in that weird accent of his, "Aye. Most definitely vampires."

Then he gave it back to her, because Vivian said to him, "Go over there. Don't let them in!"

"How am I s'posed to do that? They're a bunch of bloody wankers!"

"Get the fire ax."

"Yes, mum," came Sebastian's voice from farther away.

I juggled the phone, almost running a red light as I drove the snaky road around the mountain that led to Drugdale, the town that Sean dealt out of. "Viv, do you need me up there? I'm on the road. I can turn off and come help you."

Another glassy smash, teeth-rattlingly loud this time. Something not quite human screamed in pain, and then I heard nothing but silence. Finally, Vivian said clearly and cheerily into the phone, "Handled! We caught him before he got away!"

"You caught a vampire?"

"Yep—the rat. Well, Sebastian caught him because I'm talking to you."

At this point, I was very confused, but said, "Uh...I called about something else, but it's not really important if you have a vampire and all..."

"I'm good. Seb's tying him up. Shoot."

I imagined her leaning on the glass display case of her shop, probably nodding to Sebastian to get a rope for the vampire they'd caught.

"Uh...okay, um...do you remember Sean? Sean and Kara?"

"Sure. What about him? Did something happen to Sean?"

"Not that I know of. I just need to get in touch with him. Is he still living in that big Victorian in Lansford with all the roommates and shit?"

"No, Sean moved out some time ago. I ran into him once or twice down at the Turkey Hill. He's over in Nesquehoning, at the Methodist church."

"What's he doing there?"

"Youth pastor is what I heard."

I had to stop and absorb that. The dude Vivian and I used to party with, the one who supplied half the designer drugs in this area, was working with kids now. "You're kidding me."

"I kid you not," Viv said. "He had a big reform or some such. Went total Holy Roller. But if you see him, tell him he still owes me a couple of kilos. Hey, I gotta go. The vampire is getting antsy and I think Sebastian needs help."

"Thanks, Vivian," I told her. "I'll talk to you soon."

"Tell me how your crisis is going, and I'll tell you all about mine," she said just before she hung up.

***

I was glad I'd called Vivian. It saved me from having to double back from Coaldale to Nesquehoning, which was on my way. Ten minutes later, I pulled into the parking lot of the Methodist Church in question, cut the motor on the Monaco, and got out with Sada in tow. But I didn't immediately approach the church. Instead, I leaned against the ticking hood, lit a smoke, and took stock of my options.

"Yes," Sada said without me having to say a word. "That's going to be a problem."

If I went inside, I would be severely weakened. It didn't matter the type of church; they all took it out of me like a sucker punch. Once, I wouldn't have even blinked, just gone inside, did what I needed to do, and endured the consequences. No more. Being virtually powerless didn't appeal to me these days.

"Do you want me to go in for you?" Sada asked.

I was about to say that wasn't a bad idea when a large, late-model SUV pulled up and a blonde woman with just the right rouge and three preteen kids got out. She was carrying food in Tupperware and looked at me oddly as she passed and went toward the rectory door.

"I have a better idea." I crushed out my cigarette and called to her.

She stopped, turned to look at me, and cowered slightly as I approached. As I grew closer, she shooed her children inside the building even though I've always thought I looked pretty harmless.

"Do you know Sean Miller?" I asked.

She gave me some serious side-eye and looked toward her purse. I wondered if she was carrying mace and was considering using it on me. I wasn't *that* scary, was I? "Why? Does he owe you money or something?"

I held up my hands. "No, nothing like that. Sean and I...well, we're old friends, and—"

"Get lost, creepy. You'll have to go somewhere else to get your fix. Sean doesn't deal anymore."

Creepy?

My posture must have said it all, because Sada sidled up beside me, looking tough. It didn't take much. She was tall and liked short leather jackets, concert T-shirts, and torn-up jeans. Plus, she was a Black woman, and I wasn't such an ignoramus as to believe that alone didn't scare this Karen half to death.

"What did you call him?" Sada asked, eyes narrowed.

Ut-oh...

I was about to say something to break up the tension between the two women when Sean suddenly stepped out of the rectory and said, "Stephie, honey?"

Stephie suddenly turned about-face and, spotting Sean, hurried toward him, her candy-pink high heels clicking on the asphalt. They exchanged a few words—presumably about me and my scary bodyguard—and then Sean ushered her inside.

Sada rolled her eyes at the display.

Closing the door behind his girlfriend, Sean turned to face me. He looked different. And worried.

Viv said he was a youth pastor these days, but I had to assume he hadn't been doing it long. He wasn't dressed in the typical black suit or cleric's collar, just a humble dark blue suit and black shirt. He watched me nervously as I approached. Despite the changes and the annoying perfect Stephie, I was buoyed to see him out here. It meant I wouldn't have to go into the church that would make me as sick as a dog.

"Nick," Sean said nervously, rubbing his hands together even though it wasn't that cold. He didn't sound greatly pleased to see me.

I nodded toward the rectory. "You have a cute girl. Calls people names, though."

"Stephie's okay. She knows who I was and doesn't give me shit about it." He looked past me to Sada and flinched a little.

"But she doesn't like your friends too much."

Sean held up his hands. "I don't keep *those* kinds of friends anymore. I'm clean, man. On a new path. And if you're looking for tabs, man, I can't help you."

Back in the day, Sean dealt weak acid, shrooms, and cheap Mexican weed. He used to sell those button candies you usually buy on white ribbon, except these would help you see music. Real petty shit. Viv and I used to get our spliffs from him.

I looked him over. He was a short man gone to paunch, now balding. I was extremely tall, so I sort of towered over him in a way that was probably making him nervous. "Reformed, eh? A man of God?"

"You could say that."

I cut to the chase. "I'm looking into something for someone, not buying. The story I heard is you were dealing bath salts for a while out of Drugdale."

He held up his hands defensively. "The important word there, pal, is *were*. I wanted to move up, man, and I did. Salts, gravel. Really stupid shit. But I don't do that anymore. Not since I met Stephie and took on her kids. And not since I made a pact with Him." He pulled the little silver cross out of his shirt to show me who *Him* was. "He saved me, man. Got me clean and out of all that shit."

Sean looked up at me defiantly, which I could respect. "I dunno what you're looking to find, Nick, but I can't help you, man. I left all that shit behind."

I held up a picture of Papa Lacroix—not the pic that Malach and Cassiel had given me. One I'd printed off the internet. "I don't want you. I want to talk to *him*."

Sean, cowering slightly away from me, squinted at the pic. Then his eyes widened. I thought maybe he was myopic. He rubbed his little cross like a good luck charm. "Him? Hell. I don't do biz with that dude no more, man. Not after Moon."

Still holding the pic in two fingers, I said, "Who's Moon?"

"Moonie. Moondog." Sean looked down at his feet sadly. "He—"

Stephie had stepped outside the rectory, sans kids, but now she was carrying a yellow plastic whiffle bat. She watched us carefully, and when Sada stiffened, I whispered, "Down girl." And she did. I guess she really didn't trust her guy because she looked like she wanted to bonk him with the bat. I had a feeling they were going to have a lot to talk about once Sada and I were gone. So much for being cool with Sean's past...

I flicked the pic, which made Sean flinch. "Who's Moondog?"

"M-Moondog...Brian, his name is," Sean choked out. He looked on the verge of hysterics suddenly and was clutching his cross like he was facing down a vampire. "He bought some gravel off me this one time, but it was a bad batch, man, and he went off his head. I mean, really bad. I think...I think he fucking died, man. I dunno. Died and maybe came back—y'know like in those stories you see on TV? Got institutionalized and all." Tears were now streaming down Sean's face and plinking to the asphalt at his feet. "It was Papa's shit, man. After that, I went straight as an arrow, man. I don't ever want to see sumthin' like that again!"

It took a little coaching to get Sean to calm the hell down and get Moondog's full name. Brian Salsa. After that, I let little Scaredy Sean go. He quickly scurried back to Stephie and started crying in her arms, and I don't think he was doing it for show, either. After a few seconds, he looked me up and down and seemed to see me finally for what I was. He grabbed his cross again.

"Let's get out of here," I suggested and we started back to the car.

But Stephie called after us. "Don't come around here no more, creepy!" To Sada, "You neither, coon. He's done with that life, and I don't want your kind 'round my kids!"

Sada, steaming, started back toward Stephie, but I grabbed her gently around the shoulders and whispered in her ear, "Three words: Fucking racist police."

She just stood there, vibrating with rage. "I know," she whispered after a few rapid heartbeats. "All these damned towns are alike…"

"C'mon, darling. I'll buy you a milkshake."

We got in the car. As I screeched out of the parking lot, Sean added, "Leave me alone, Nick! Everywhere you go, trouble follows. And I got souls to save!"

* * *

I stopped at the local Burger King to get two large milkshakes. I asked them for extra whipped cream on Sada's and bought her some onion rings on the side, her favorite.

Sada slurped in silence, so I knew it wasn't working all that well.

The truth was, I was angry too. It was stupid to be taking this so personally—especially from a lowlife like Sean—but, damn. A part of me wanted to turn the car around, march up to the rectory, grab Sean, and…do something to him. What, I didn't know. But definitely something dramatic. But I didn't. These mountains had produced conservative Christian towns. If it got back that the Children of Endor were involved in an altercation, the police would raid the coven house and make Juliette and her people feel the heat. There would be consequences.

I just clutched the wheel and breathed until most of the really bad rage had passed.

The little shit's not worth it.

I must have said that last bit aloud because Sada said around her straw, "I know. I'm sorry I lost it back there. I just found it very triggering. Not my first rodeo."

I had no words for that, so I just put my hand on her knee in commiseration.

* * *

That evening, I decided I needed some alone time, so I made my way downstairs to the basement of the coven house. The Children of Endor had converted what was once a storage space into an English-style study for me. It sported nicely paneled walls, a dozen bookcases containing some of the most important volumes on the craft in the world, a big oaken desk where I often did my research and craft exercises, and a scattering of different tools and weapons on the walls. Under the large Oriental carpet was a huge glyph made of different colored stones that could be arranged in specific patterns so I could perform difficult but important craft rituals. I had used it a few times with varying success—mostly as a "recall station." That is, when I visited Dis or the very few other planes of existence I could reach, I used the glyph like a tether to safely drag myself back to this world.

When I'd left it the day before, the desk had been piled high with books for a spell I'd been trying my hand at, but the kids had done their housekeeping duties and put all the books and tools back where they belonged. Everything in the room was dusted and orderly.

I sat down in the executive chair behind the desk and flipped open my work computer—a super-fast prototype that Justin had sent me. I needed to do my due diligence on the drug gravel, but all I learned was that it was a Haitian drug—synthetic cocaine, actually—and that it could fuck you up, make your heart beat too fast, or, in some cases, too slow. People were thought to have died of it before reviving in their coffins during their funerals. They made that movie *The Serpent and the Rainbow* about it. There was even a YouTube video where a Voudon priest used the drug to control another man and made him do stupid things, but it all looked pretty staged to me.

I texted Vivian since I was afraid to call her. I didn't know if she was still dealing with vampires. Or CHUDs. Or whatever had infested Philly. Hopefully, though, she could help me. I knew her partner, Sebastian, was pretty tight with the drug scene down there.

Does your partner know anything about gravel? Flakka?

That was its other name.

I felt a little bad about sending that text. I was basically telling Viv that her partner was a drug bunny—though I knew he was, and so did most of the Poconos.

She texted me back pretty quickly. *He said they don't call it that here. It's slightly different. They call it Z-Quil.*

Z-Quil?

That's what Seb said. Helps you get your zombie Zs.

I snorted. *Thanx.*

"Z-Quil." I popped that into Google and got some pretty messed-up results.

| 5 |

Royal Rumble

THE NEXT MORNING, I put the Monaco into drive and drove out to The Ranch in downtown Allentown, the place where Brian "Moondog" Salsa's parents had incarcerated him after he took some Z-Quil and lost his mind. I knew all that because I'd spent half the night Facebook stalking Sean's small circle of friends, most of whom were stoners and creeps, and I'd gotten some good info on Moonie, as his friends called him. As I tapped along, good little stalker-investigator that I was, I wondered if Stephie knew Sean still had a profile and his small circle of junkhead friends that he had supposedly dropped.

On Sada's behalf, I decided to anonymously email Stephie a link to Sean's Facebook profile so she could see who he was still friends with, including all the hot girls he messaged regularly. It was petty but I felt they both deserved it.

Back to the present. So, today, I decided to go it alone. I mean, Moondog had had a complete nervous breakdown with intense paranoia. He'd believed everyone in the world had been replaced by robots controlled by lizard men and wouldn't take his meds because he believed someone had been putting tracking technologies in it.

It was pretty intense stuff, but I was pretty sure I could handle him if he got too rowdy.

I found the hulking, miserable grey building that looked nothing like a ranch easily enough and parked in the visitor's parking lot. There were two checkpoints, and I knew there was no way the orderlies at The Ranch were going to let me waltz around, so before I went into the rambling cement brick building that looked about as welcoming as a prison, I grabbed my gig bag from the back.

Normally, I carry my tools of the craft in it—a large pink duffle bag with Hello Kitty on it because no one can ever be bothered to peek inside such a bag—but I've been known to carry much more in there, including my piece, my athame, backup bullets, and other suspicious things. I pulled out my old rig, clicked it on under my open jacket, and slid the badge that one of my friends-in-low-places in Philly had counterfeited for me many moons ago onto my belt. Impersonating a cop is a federal offense, by the way. But since I really was a cop (once), I figured I was only half-breaking the law.

Or that's what I told myself as I ambled inside all cowboy-like.

I must have really put off an aura of "cop" because all I did was introduce myself as Officer Wodehouse (my mom's maiden name) and move the jacket aside to reach for the badge when the receptionist stood up. I didn't even need to pull it out.

"We took care of all the violations already," she said, whatever that meant. "But I can get the manager…"

I had no idea what she was going on about but decided to roll with it. Unfortunately, my plan hinged on not getting the manager or any other people in authority involved. "I'm happy to hear that, ma'am, but I'm not here for that. I just want to speak to Brian Salsa about a case I'm working on."

"About what?"

I made shit up real fast. "He's a material witness in a case I'm investigating."

Maybe that was too much conflicting info because a deep dent formed between the pretty girl's eyes. So I leaned forward and gave her a slightly perverted smile and her face instantly relaxed, her eyes became all sparkly, and she immediately sat down and tapped at her keyboard. I didn't even need to use magick.

A bank of computer monitor cameras lit up behind her. "He's in the common room. I can get an orderly to escort you, Officer Wodehouse."

I waved her offer away. "That's okay. I'll find my way." I wrote a phone number on the back of a pamphlet and slid it across to her, which made her smile grow hungrily. 867-5309.

The place was like a damned maze, one depressing, nondescript corridor feeding into another. Most of the heavy grey security doors on both sides were locked, and there were a lot of warnings about where you could go and what you could bring with you. I was pretty much breaking all the rules.

I got lost pretty fast, so I decided to follow a few shuffling patients to the common room, which was vast and lighted with harsh overhead lights to chase back the miserable November glare coming through the tall windows that lined one full wall. Tables were scattered around the room with people playing board games, doing puzzles, or just staring sightlessly up at the large-screen TV hanging on the wall. An old episode of *Bonanza* was playing. Hoss had lost a valuable racehorse in a wager and was scheming with his brother to buy it back.

Glancing around, I spotted Moondog right away. He was the younger, slinky-looking dude sitting by himself. He had paper-grey skin and thinning black hair. He was seated at a table by the window, staring down at a half-finished puzzle, but not doing anything with it. Several boxes of other unfinished puzzles surrounded him, the pieces all over the table and the floor.

As I headed toward him, I noticed his eyes didn't seem to blink very often, though they did slowly shift my way as I approached, just not the way eyes usually did. Instead of sliding, they seemed to tick toward me like one of those old-fashioned dolls with the eyes that move around in that creepy, unanchored way. His shoulders tensed as I reached him.

"Brian Salsa?" I said. But he didn't react. So I tried, "Moondog? I'm here to ask you a few questions—but you're not in any trouble."

Nothing.

I noticed an orderly pushing a cart on the other side of the room. He looked my way but I raised my hand to keep him from approaching and turned my attention back on the man in the dull grey pajamas.

"My name is Nick. I'm Sean's friend."

Nothing. Not a reaction, even when several guns went off on the TV.

"Moondog?" I tried again. "Moonie?" A little bit desperate, I put my hand on his rounded shoulder.

Moondog's eyes suddenly jumped in his head to meet mine.

I quickly removed my hand but watched him carefully. He'd seemed to have seized up on me and wasn't even blinking now.

I didn't want the orderly coming over to throw me out, so I decided to take a seat across from Moondog as if he and I were old pals. I glanced at his puzzle but couldn't make heads or tails of it. "I talked to Sean," I explained, trying to keep my voice soft and modulated. I had no idea how far gone Moondog was, but this wasn't looking good. "He told me about what happened to you. I also know about the Z-Quil. Is that the drug you took?"

Nothing.

Something about the colors in the puzzle bothered me. I studied it for a long second. It looked a mess of different colors and shapes but there seemed to be something there...

Refocusing on Moondog, I tried honestly. "Look, man. I know that stuff messed you up. I'm trying to learn everything I can about Z-Quil. Did Sean ever tell you where he got it?"

Moondog glared at me almost as if he recognized me, which was ridiculous. I had never met the guy in my life. After a few seconds of uncomfortable silence, the man raised a shaking hand. In it, he had a medium-sized puzzle piece that he clicked down into the puzzle. He grunted as he pressed it home.

Random factoids often make their way into my head. One is the fact that most puzzles are die-cut along the same pattern of pieces. That means you can combine two or more puzzles of the same size and make some weird, Dali-inspired picture if you are inclined to such things. Which Moondog was, though I had to stand up and turn my head to see the puzzle from his perspective.

It was only half-done, but I could make out a man on his knees before another man. The one kneeling looked blond and had a sword running through his body. The second man had driven the blade through the first, but I couldn't make out the second man's identity because the whole top of his body wasn't yet complete.

I got a real bad feeling then—one similar to that hair-rising-on-the-back-of-your-neck thing I'd experienced the other day.

Moondog suddenly looked up at me, opened his dry lips, and said something, but not in English. It sounded like a cross between archaic Russian and a buzz saw.

Divine. He was speaking in the language of the angels.

It took me a moment to realize what he had said. I was still getting used to the hang of angel-speak and knew some but not all of the words.

Son of the Morning Star. You will be ended.

"Shit..." I started to say and then said no more as Moondog stood up and, very casually, grabbed me by the upper arm and used his incredible, angel-infused strength to throw me halfway across the room.

* * *

I landed hard and awkwardly upon the orderly's cart, which broke my fall in the worst way possible.

It was a large stainless steel contraption covered in trays containing dozens of small paper cups full of pills. A couple of clipboards were attached to the front. Despite its size and durability, I pretty much destroyed it as I fell upon the surface, scattering pills everywhere. My impact pushed it into the plaster of the nearest wall, and my shoulder took the brunt of that impact. The whole cart then flipped sideways, dumping me to the floor. It was about that time, while I was down on my face, my whole body was smarting like a mother, that I realized it would have been smarter to have taken Sada with me.

Nothing I could do about it now.

The orderly, a small, waifish guy, had been thrown into the wall and now lay against it, deep in la-la land, which was good, I figured, considering what came next.

I had just barely gotten to my shaky feet when I spotted Moondog flying at me. And I don't mean that metaphorically. As he closed in on me, I recognized he had wings. A lot of them. He was basically a mass of wings pointing in different directions with a head in there somewhere. I immediately recognized his shape as that of a Virtue, which are like worker bee angels. They do a lot of the boots-on-the-ground stuff.

A soldier angel.

If the blow hadn't stunned me, I would have done something spectacular like punched him or manifested the bident and run him through. Later, when it was all over, I thought about how I could have handled things better. But I hadn't expected Moondog to turn into a freakin' angel, and I just reacted, doing the first thing that came to mind. I grabbed the dented-up cart and blindly threw it at the Virtue.

Mostly, I don't care for being a Daemon. It means a lot of things are out to get you. But the super-strength sure comes in handy sometimes.

The Virtue collided with the cart in mid-air and both pinged off in opposite directions. The cart crunched down atop a table where some inmates were playing cards, flattening it. The Virtue hit the wall and was crushed into the plaster but rebounded in record time and came at me again.

Motherf— I thought just as it hit me, driving me back into the wall, and then right through the wall—the studs, the plaster, everything!—and into a room adjacent to the common room where there were tall racks of cleaning equipment. The racks snapped under us as we went down, mops and buckets flying everywhere. I fell flat on my back with an *oof*, the Virtue on top of me, muttering in that wretched language about how he was going to destroy me, the charmer.

My first instinct was to go for my gun, which I still had in the pancake holster on my side, but then I remembered I'd strapped it on as a prop and hadn't put any bullets in it because I hadn't expected to *wind up in a life-or-death struggle with a human-angel hybrid, thank you very much...*

But I had my athame, bathed in the blood of angels and gods...

As it reared up over me, hissing and spitting, I wiggled the athame from my belt, brought it around in a whooshing arc, and drove it into its side. It roared in surprise, beating savagely at my face with its wings, but the weapon hardly seemed to faze the creature.

I grunted and snarled as it pummeled me for a full ten seconds before another rack full of heavy cleaning supplies fell over, crashing atop the Virtue, which knocked it sideways off me. I wasted no time taking advantage of the situation and sliding out from under the mangled mass of twisted metal, boxes, and bottles. While the creatures struggled to right itself, I lurched to my feet amidst the debris. I was dizzy, almost seeing double, and there was blood obscuring my vision from some serious cuts above my eye, but now I knew how fast the bastard was. I needed to stay levelheaded but act fast.

The Virtue was stuck down on the floor, trying to level a fallen rack off its back. I stepped over some industrial-sized bottles of Clorox and Mr. Clean, grabbed the angel by a wing, and ripped it loose. With a grunt of effort, I turned and swung it out of the storage room and back into the common room. It slid across the well-waxed floor and crashed into a table, upending it, then kept going. It didn't stop until it hit the bank of windows opposite us.

The (presumably) shatterproof window spiderwebbed when the angel's head hit it. Then all of the glass fell out of the frame and chattered to the floor all around the creature. Beyond the broken glass, I spied the security bars over the window—the only thing that had kept the angel from falling out the window and into the parking lot.

By now, the patients were running from the room, but a few too high on drugs or simply too far gone to react were weaving in place, watching us with big, vacant Belladonna eyes. One woman pointed at me and made weird monkey-like noises.

"It's a hallucination," I told those who remained as I stepped out of the storage room, wiped the blood out of my eyes from the multiple cuts on my face, and manifested my wings, which are large, feathered black, and demonic as hell.

The Virtue, spotting me, recognized I meant business. It started scrabbling to get up amidst all the broken glass, but its wings were twisted at odd angles and it was having trouble finding its balance.

Good. Because I was going to beat the ever-loving feathers out of it with my bare hands.

"Lucifer...!" The angel, realizing its dilemma, raised its hands to ward me back. It had four of them. Its eyes went wide at the sight of my rampage. "No!"

"Yes," I said, coming upon it. I reached for the angel.

It slashed at me with its wings—tipped in metal, I now saw. No wonder it had scratched my face up so badly back in the storage room. I leaped back, but also kind of *up*, flapping my wings to keep myself at a safe distance. The force manifested by my lift drove me up and against the ceiling. It creature, having untangled its many wings, followed, meeting me head on.

We clenched and rolled around on the ceiling. I punched it. It took the blow like a champ and hissed at me, trying to bite me with what looked like sharp, bullet-like metal teeth. So I punched it again. Didn't do a damned thing to it. Whatever it now was—human, angel, some weird hybrid—it sure was well-nigh invulnerable. And strong. As I got on top of it, it wrapped its wiry, powerful arms around me and flipped me over on the ceiling. I hit it hard, wrecking the drop ceiling and breaking a couple of light fixtures. Then it suddenly changed its trajectory and drove me to the floor on my back, then up to the ceiling, then back down again.

The ping pong impacts knocked the breath out of me. I groaned, almost seeing little birdies at this point, but I still had enough presence of mind to raise my forearms before it started scratching at me like a wildcat. Its claws razored up my arms and over my sweater and puffy jacket, just barely missing my throat and face. It hurt like hell but I kept my forearms in place to protect my face. At the same thing, my wings shushed wildly at the floor, trying to give me the leverage I needed to throw the feral hybrid off me, but the two of us stacked on top of one another were too heavy, and I was shit at this flying crap anyway.

I was close to panicking when, out of nowhere, someone ripped the angel off me. It took me a few seconds to realize it, and a few more to gain the courage to drop my arms. But when I did, I recognized a man standing over me, wrestling with the angel he was trying to restrain.

The creature, hissing and snapping like a rabid animal, turned to assault the newcomer, but the man was having none of it. He was also clearly experienced in hand-to-hand combat because as the angel whipped around to loosen his hold and slash at him with those metal wings, he deftly blocked its blows one after another, precise and controlled. No panic. He had hardcore military training, I decided. Plus, he was damned strong himself.

"Hashmal, get thee done!" the man proclaimed, his voice deep and powerful so the room virtually vibrated with it.

But when the angel Hashmal didn't obey and landed a blow across the man's face, he snarled and, in a badass move right out of some action (or possibly horror) movie, ripped a wing clear off Hashmal. The sound was sickening, like tearing a drumstick off a turkey, and it was accompanied by the crunchy snap of bone. All at once, the Virtue's bluish, otherworldly blood flecked us both, the floor, and the walls. Even the ceiling got a repainting.

My savior turned and threw the angel away from him, but not before following it up with a series of knives that came almost mystically out of his long leather motorcycle coat. The knives found their home in various parts of the angel's anatomy and made it smoke like a barbeque. The angel floundered on the floor, knives sticking out of it, clearly off-balanced by the loss of its wing and enraged by the pain of its injuries, while the man threw the severed wing away. It flopped down next to me, still wiggling and bleeding.

Christ!

The man turned to me. I recognized him, though it had been decades since I had last seen him.

He was tall like me—most angels are—but young looking like an eighteen-year-old boy. Dusky skin and black hair done up in dozens of intricate braids that seemed to shiver and move around his shoulders. He had black eyes and at least seven earrings in each ear. He was dressed in jeans and an Anthrax T-shirt under the ankle-length black leather coat.

He said only two words to me: "Nicky. Bident."

I nodded and did as he asked, manifesting my bident, which filled my left hand with its considerable weight.

By now, security was filtering into the room, telling everyone to freeze and get down on the floor, but the newcomer seemed unperturbed by that. He turned, almost dancing in the air, and raised a hand, freezing the room in a Time-lock. I'd experienced this before and felt the very molecules freezing around us. Everyone went into that weird freeze-frame that I will never, ever get used to. All but the three of us—me, the newcomer, and the injured angel.

The Virtue had partially recovered and was getting back on its feet, though it wobbled badly and blood was bubbling up from its wounds like blue ink out of a broken pen. With such grievous wounds, I had no idea how it had managed to not pass out, but I wasn't about to ask it.

I got to my feet too and turned to face the angel. I had the bident, so now I was armed to the teeth, Satan-style.

The angel growled at me, pulled a smoking knife right out of its chest, and threw it at me underhand-style. I was still half-blind from the blood running into my eyes and the hybrid had really good aim. Only the newcomer sliding in front of the knife stopped it from finding a home inside me.

My savior deftly stopped the blade by clapping his hands together, then let the blade fall to the floor. "Bident, Nicky, bident!"

I nodded.

"Get 'im, my boy!"

As the angel charged my savior, I turned, aimed, and let the silvery Morning Star with its incredibly sharp, soul-eating tines fly. The angel was already on the move, and it more or less impaled itself on them.

I didn't do anything. I knew the Morning Star would seek out and find the creature's angel heart, located deep in its belly. The Morning Star had the wicked ability to find any living thing's heart.

That stopped it. The hybrid howled at the weapon sank deep into its belly-heart, staggered back, then sleekly and efficiently turned to grey stone, its hands scrabbling at the weapon that was its undoing. Once it was a solid stone statue, it swiftly manifested cracks and began to crumble to the floor. Did I mention angels don't do particularly well impaled on the Morning Star?

Once the Virtue had disintegrated into a pile of rubble on the once sterile floor of the common room, my savior went to retrieve the Morning Star that had fallen into the pile of ash. He admired it a moment and then turned to face me. "Hi, Nicky."

I staggered back against a wall as I sought my balance, my whole body aching. "Hi, Grampa."

| 6 |

Grampa Monster

I WAITED BY the car while Grampa Lucifer did cleanup in the clinic—which was mostly getting everyone to forget about the battle that had torn up the common room. On my way out of the building, I spied the kitchen and checked the freezer. Finding a frozen bag of peas, I took it with me to put on the big bruise under my left eye. Since everyone on the premises was still stuck in a time-lock, I didn't need to worry about anyone stopping me.

Ten minutes later, Grampa stepped out of the facility and headed for the car. He was still carrying the Morning Star, which winked in the noontime light. "Thanks, Nicky. It was nice to have her back again in my hands," he said as he reached me. He rubbed the shaft familiarly before placing the weapon in the backseat of the Monaco.

"You can hang onto her if you want." It was his weapon, after all.

"Oh no. You're the current Lucifer. She's your birthright. Anyway, I have a feeling you'll be needing her soon."

"No kidding. I still have a lot to learn in handling her, though," I sighed. "By the way, I should be thanking you for the intervention. That was brutal—and unexpected."

"Being the current Lucifer is brutal and unexpected." He smiled at me over the hood of the car.

Unlike my dad, I have always gotten along with Grampa Lucifer. Ha-Shaitan. He is super chill. My dad has mentioned in the past that I'm way more like Grampa than I am like him, which I can see.

He looked me over, throwing a few heavy braids off his shoulder. "He did a good number on you, my boy."

"I'll live. I think."

"C'mere."

I was reluctant to let him look, but after he gave me a "don't be a stubborn schmuck" look, I lowered the frozen bag of peas and he examined my eye.

He turned my face slightly so he could get a good look at the scratches on my face. "Angel claws. That's gonna take a bit to heal. You may even have scars."

"Great."

"It'll make you sexier."

"I don't know about that."

He grinned. "You know how to take some knocks, son. I'll give you that."

"Yeah, I'm a regular punching bag, don'tcha know?"

"I think you'll live."

"Heh." Didn't feel like it. I put the frozen peas back on my swollen eye. "Can you drive? I can't see shit."

"Gladly." He rubbed the hood of the Monaco. "It's a nice car."

I liked that Grampa approved of my wheels. I threw him my keys and we got in, me on the passenger side for a change.

"I need a coffee," Grandpa said, sounding tired and maybe a little grumpy as he put the car into gear. "It's been a long day."

"Take me to lunch and then explain what the hell *that* was all about."

"You got it."

He drove us to a little greasy spoon called the Jubilee. The building was a converted railway car with a lot of shiny chrome, red leather booths had little jukeboxes on the table, and pleasant-looking, smiling wait staff. I could see why Grampa liked it. As we were sitting down, Grampa said, "I've been here before. Their pirogues are fire."

The waitress gave me a concerned look while we ordered and got our coffees. I knew the swelling was rapidly going down in my face, but there were still scratches all over it from whatever the Virtue had at the tips of its wings. I probably looked as if I'd wrestled a raccoon in a Dumpster.

Grampa waved his hand in her face. "This is my grandson Nicholas. Isn't he the most handsome devil you've ever seen?"

He must have done something to her because she suddenly stopped looking concerned and smiled broadly for me before running off to fetch our lunch.

I turned back to my grandfather, who was playing with the jukebox. "So what the hell was that all about?" And then I added, "And what are you doing here in NEPA anyway? I thought you were retired."

"I was," Grampa said, abandoning the jukebox to look over the ice cream menu. Grampa loves his ice cream. "But then the trouble started. All this violence."

I didn't know if he meant violence in general or something specific. The world has always been plenty violent. "You mean like Moondog? What happened to him?"

"Yes." He put the menu down. "He's not the first. Probably not going to be the last, either. I've been hunting them down all over the east coast—or trying to, anyway." He frowned with concern. "It can be difficult to differentiate between regular human violence and angelic possession violence."

I sat there and absorbed what he was saying. It was absurd, but I knew Grampa always knew what he was talking about. "You mean Moondog was possessed. By an angel." As far as I knew, that was impossible. Angels lived in a state of Grace—the ones who didn't fall, anyway—and they couldn't turn humans into meat puppets. That was strictly a demon-type thing. But then I recalled there was no God and no Grace. So maybe the rules had changed?

Grampa nodded as if he had read my thoughts. "Exactly. Humans are turning up all over possessed by members of the Holy Host. Demonic possession is one thing—the victim usually invites it in. But this is entirely different. As far as I can tell, the angels aren't being invited in. They're just taking over." He paused. "Ah, here we are."

The pirogues had arrived and we ate in silence for a few minutes while I worked on mentally digesting everything he was telling me. The pirogues were good, as Grampa had stated. After a few bites, I said, "Angelic possession. People being possessed by angels."

He pointed his fork at me. "Strange, is it not?"

"I mean...how exactly does *that* work?"

Grampa chewed for a few moments before saying, "I'm not sure, Nicky. Nothing like this has ever happened before in the history of the world. But I have a feeling you'll figure it out, what with that big brain of yours."

I felt a little flattered by Grampa's backhanded compliment. I'd been called smart by two different people over two days. It truly was a red-letter day for ol' Nick.

Grampa went on to explain that he'd been going up and down the coast, hunting down the human-angel hybrids—a kind of personal military duty, if you will. He even discreetly lifted his coat to show me the array of angel-killing knives he carried. He said they were created after he melted down the nails that crucified the Son of

God. They would kill damned near anything and the angels seemed to be particularly vulnerable to them.

"Yours worked way better than my athame," I pointed out. The hybrid had just ignored the big hole I'd put in it.

"Trial and error," he said with a nod. "I've already killed a large number of hybrids, but more keep popping up. It's sort of turning into whack-a-mole." After a few more bites, he showed me the map he'd drawn of various attacks and outbreaks of violence. There was definitely a pattern there.

"How long has this been happening?"

He thought about that. "A few weeks at least. I was hoping you might be able to shed some light on why it's happening or where this is coming from."

Since Grampa was being so open with his intel, I decided to tell about what Sean said about Moondog losing his mind after taking some of Papa Lacroix's Z-Quil, and how the kid's family had put him away for violent behavior. I also told him Sean thought his friend had died and come back from the dead.

I spooned some more sour cream over my pirogues. "Sean thought he imagined Moondog dying, but maybe he really did die. Maybe that's when it happened."

Grampa nodded thoughtfully at the information.

"How did you know to show up today?" I asked.

He indicated the map. "I wrote an app for my phone that can approximate the next attack based on the emerging pattern here."

I almost choked on my food. "You wrote an app?"

He looked surprised, then smiled and leaned over to tap the side of my head. "Where do you think you get your smarts from? It's not your dad."

I snorted at that. He laughed companionably.

"He says I'm all you, Grampa."

"John's a bit of a half-wit. But don't tell him I said that." Sitting back, Grampa added, "Actually, you remind me of your grandmother. She was a Jotunn. A Frost Giant. Gorgeous woman, brave, and smart as a whip. You have her eyes—and her humor."

All this stuff was getting to be too much. I was going into information overload and needed a break. Excusing myself, I visited the men's washroom, where I checked my scratches, splashed some cold water on my face, and dried off with a scratchy brown paper towel. When I got back to our booth, I spotted my grandfather filming himself with his phone and talking candidly about the incident at The Ranch.

"What are you doing?"

Grampa put down his phone and said, "I need to update my YouTube Channel."

"You have a YouTube Channel?"

He gave me a pleased look. "Twenty-K followers and counting." He shrugged. "My followers keep me updated on the little outbreaks of violence. They are how I was able to write the algorithm for my app."

I thought about that—my grampa the YouTube star. "Isn't that a little dangerous? Telling people who you are?"

"It's not like they believe me or anything."

I shook my head in disbelief. Back to business. "Do you think Sean is onto something with this drug?"

"It's certainly possible. Perhaps the angelic possession is linked to the Z-Quil. We don't know what's in the stuff."

I got a bad feeling about that suddenly. It didn't take a genius to put two and two together. Swallowing hard, I said, "Angel parts."

Grampa narrowed his eyes with interest.

"The drug is made from parts of angels." I knew it was true the moment I said it. I wasn't planning to tell Grampa about the stuff with Malach and Cassiel, but it fit too well together, so I told him about my mission and how I'd been tasked to look for the missing Michael.

Grampa nodded at that too—but to his credit, he didn't tell me not to do it, that it was too dangerous. Maybe he too sensed how important this was. "I'd heard Michael was missing. You think Michael's behind the synthetic drug."

"Why not? Maybe that's why he's working with Papa Lacroix. Maybe he wants to make the hybrids and Lacroix is distributing the stuff. Growing an army on Earth, if you will. Hell, I don't know. But my gut tells me Michael's behind these hybrids somehow."

Grampa leaned an arm over the back of the booth and tapped his fingers. "You're probably right. Michael has always been overly ambitious."

"You would know," I pointed out. "You fought with him."

"I fought *beside* him," Grampa clarified. "We had a common enemy. But we were never friends. Michael was too much like our Lord Ha-Shem. Too..." He seemed to be searching for the right word and a shadow passed across his face, making it appear older. "...too bloodthirsty."

I wasn't super up on what had transpired between Grampa and the God he had put on the throne of the world, but I knew there was a lot of bad blood between them. Grampa and the other angels had fought legions of Old Ones to secure the throne for their chosen god, Ha-Shem. But somewhere along the line, Ha-Shem abandoned his beloved Ha-Shaitan's counsel and went his own way, resenting his general's suggestions on how to rule. Maybe Grampa overstepped, or maybe God was a jerk. I wasn't sure. But in a fit of temper, Ha-Shem sent the Angel of the Morning down into hell...or, more precisely, exiled him and his followers to the Hell Planet that I was now supposedly in charge of. That was the story

I'd been told. But I never really understood the details of their break-up, or how things had come to be so bitter between them.

I thought about asking, but then decided it might be too personal and painful for my grandfather to get into.

As if sensing what I was thinking, he changed the subject. "What's your next move?"

I nodded as I thought about that. "I think I need to pay Papa Lacroix a visit. If he really is tied up in all of this, Michael won't be too far. I'm hoping I can smoke him out."

My grandfather suddenly looked reserved. "Nicky, do you think you're ready to take on Archangel Michael?"

I told the truth. "Absolutely fucking not. But then, I probably will never be."

"But you're going to do it anyway."

"Fucking absolutely."

He laughed. "You really are like your grandma." He looked down at the ice cream menu. "Do you want the Pineapple Express Sundae or the Cherry Jubilee?"

After ice cream, we made our way out of the diner.

Back in the parking lot, Grampa made me stand next to the Monaco while he vlogged us together, singing my praises to his YouTube followers. At least by then, my scratches had mostly healed and I had wiped the blood off my jacket, so I didn't look like a homeless bum who'd gotten rolled in an alley. He told everyone how handsome I was, and how proud of me he was. It was pretty embarrassing.

When he was done, he put his phone away. "Well, I'm off."

I felt a pang. "Not coming with?" I looked dejectedly at the car.

He held up his phone, which was pinging a new location for a possible hybrid. "I need to take care of this pronto. A good devil's work is never done."

"A devil's gotta do what a devil's gotta do."

We both laughed.

Before he left, he put on his Ray-Bans, then reached into his coat and offered me one of his special knives, handing it to me hilt-first. "It's not as powerful as the Morning Star, but it's good if you get in a tight spot. And, most importantly, it's an angel-eater, so, obviously, you need to be careful. Handle it accordingly."

"Got it. Thanks." I took the athame carefully from him. I planned on putting it in the sheath on my jeans in the place where my original had been but now was lost. It had melted after being stuck in the hybrid too long.

But before I tucked it away, I looked at the long, thin, age-blackened weapon that was shaped more like a switchblade than a traditional athame. "I wonder why my athame didn't work—what makes the hybrids different."

Grampa shrugged. "They're hybrids, so the normal rules no longer apply. Everything is upside down now. Everything has changed. Keep that in mind."

"I will. Thanks again, Grampa. And thanks for the backup."

He leaned in and pinched my cheek. "You stay safe, my boy. I'll see you soon." He swiftly spread his wings—they were black and god, really beautiful—and rocketed upward into the sky.

I waved my grandfather off, then got back in the Monaco for the ride home.

| 7 |

Coitus Interruptus

IT WAS LATE afternoon by the time I got back to the house, too late to make the long drive into NYC. Besides, I wanted to pack an overnight bag and pick up a few weapons. Ten years ago, I would have rushed right into the maelstrom like an enthusiastic numbskull and probably gotten myself slaughtered, but these days, I like to think I'm wiser as well as older.

It had cooled considerably. As I got out and went inside, it almost felt like a dusting of snow might happen overnight. My face was still smarting from the rumble at the funny farm, and I got a few odd looks from the Children of Endor as I passed them and went upstairs to pack my bag.

Someone knocked on my open door, and I turned to find Sada standing there. She did not look pleased that I had essentially dumped her, and when she saw my injuries, I could feel the "I told you so" she was working to keep in. To her credit, she only said, "The others said you're injured. Do you need my craft, Nick?"

In addition to Sada's skills as a bodyguard, she is also an excellent healer. Juliette had assigned her to me to keep me from getting myself killed doing something stupid, but when I managed to do stupid shit anyway, she was always on call to heal my most grievous injuries. Last year, she had her work cut out for her.

After tossing one of my pullovers into my overnight bag, I reached up and touched the deepest scratch just below my right eye. "This is nothing. Doesn't even hurt."

She folded her arms and gave me a "right, sure" look.

"I'll take some of that healing ointment if you've got it." I didn't want Sada to think I didn't need her.

"I'll get the first aid kit. Oh, your pet FBI girl is waiting for you down in the study. She says she has something for you. A file?"

"Antonia?"

"Is that the little witch's name?"

I gave her a look. I had a distinct feeling that something more was going on here. I wondered if Sada was upset with my hanging out with Antonia, even though I knew she wasn't into guys at all. "Jealous?"

I'd meant it as a joke, but Sada suddenly looked angry. "No. I just don't like occult groupies."

"She's not an occult groupie," I insisted, getting angry in return. "She wants to be one of us."

Sada pursed her lips no-nonsense-style. "So make her one of us."

I didn't know where this was coming from. It wasn't as if Antonia was hoarding in on me. I didn't spend more time with her than with the members of the coven. But maybe Sada's breakup with Kara had been rougher on her than I thought.

Wanting to make it up to Sada, I went to her and put my hand on her shoulder, then slid up her neck to her cheek. Leaning down, I kissed Sada's forehead. "I am sorry I went out without you...without considering the consequences or how this might affect you. I shouldn't have done that."

She sighed. "I suppose you are what you are."

That stung.

"If your mom is on your case, let me know and I'll talk to her."

Sada squirmed and I knew I was right.

"I'll go talk to Antonia."

As I headed downstairs, I wondered what I was going to do with that girl. I mean, Antonia knew everything about me—everything I was—and hadn't run off screaming into the night. That was good. She had even been to Hell with me. But I'd been avoiding making her one of my brides for the better part of a year now.

It just…it didn't seem right. I'd known her since she was in high school. She had a bright future ahead of her. I couldn't see her getting involved in all my demon shit and it not changing her—for the worst.

She was in the study as Sada had said, clutching a file and talking to Juliette, who was leaning against the desk. "Nick," Antonia said, turning to me with a smile. "I'm glad you're back…" Her smile fell when she saw my face. "What happened to you?"

I rubbed at one of the few remaining, crusted-over cuts on my cheek. "That's a really good story."

Juliette gave me a disapproving glare. I grinned back at her. As usual, I could not charm her the way I could most. "Are you okay, Nick?"

Nodding, I said, "I am. The other guy? Not so much."

"Do you need the corp to do clean up?"

"It's handled," I told her. "I'll brief you after I talk to Antonia."

She looked between us, sensing the fission in the air. "I'll leave you two alone, then," she stated as she waltzed past.

I expected the usual tongue-lashing, a "What have you gotten yourself into this time, Nick?" speech from Antonia, but she just watched me earnestly and clutched the file she had brought. I liked that she was treating me like an adult.

I went to shut the door. "Sada said you have something for me."

She stared at me a long moment before seemingly coming alive. "Y-yeah. I got you this."

I took the folder from her. Inside, I found a whole dossier on Papa Lacroix, his cartel, and his known cronies—names, places, events, the whole shebang. Most of it looked exhumed by strict, inside FBI protocols.

"How did you know…?" I started asking the obvious question, then recalled that Antonia was pretend-dating one of the nice Satanists. He must have informed her that I was on the prowl. I nodded over her findings. "You're not going to get in trouble over this?"

Antonia lifted her chin defiantly. "As part of my training, I'm allowed to research one of the FBI's persons of interest. So I chose him." She nodded toward the folder. "The fact that you can benefit from my intel is strictly coincidental."

I grinned at her. She grinned back, and we shared a moment.

"Thank you," I told her, holding the folder up before moving to my desk.

While my back was turned, she said, "I talked to the magus about the requirements for joining the Children of Endor. She gave me all the important information I needed, but she said only you can initiate postulants."

I could appreciate that Antonia was being this forward. I liked a woman who knew what she wanted. I just didn't want to have this conversation right now.

Turning, I leaned against the desk and watched her intently, then realized I probably looked like I was trying to seduce her and stood up a little straighter. "And you want me to initiate you."

She was still dressed in her FBI uniform, which reminded me a little of military armor, but her white shirt was open a couple of buttons, showing off her lovely brown cleavage. She'd undone her bun and her hair—it was straight and had that fiery streak in it—swept her shoulders like a cloak of darkness. She formed words and then stopped and looked down at her feet shyly. "I think I made a mistake. I assumed this was the natural outcome of our...relationship. It never occurred to me that you wouldn't want me for one of your brides."

I wanted to tell her the truth—that people got hurt around me. That my whole life was a hot mess full of demons, monsters, and now human-angel hybrids. Hardly anyone got away unscathed. Not to mention my track record was pretty sketchy when it came to keeping commitments. "I guess I'm wondering why this is so important to you."

She looked up and I could see the disappointment in her eyes.

My shoulders slumped. "What would Sheriff Ben think?"

Antonia wrinkled her nose in the way she did when she was upset. "My dad doesn't control me, Nick. If he can't deal with my religion, the type of life I'm leading, or who I sleep with, then that's on him, not me."

"I didn't mean—"

"Oh, my god!" Antonia suddenly shouted, throwing up her arms. "Please don't do that whole 'you're such a good girl' shit to me, Nick! I'm twenty-three. I've had two boyfriends, and, yes, I've had sex. Multiple times. I'm not a fucking Disney princess who doesn't know what she wants. I'm not star-struck with you or just trying to get into your pants."

I hung on a response.

Antonia, not particularly given to sudden outbursts, suddenly seemed ashamed of her reaction. She ran her hand through her hair, then sat down in a nearby chair, took a deep breath, and looked me in the eyes. "I'm a witch, Nick. A Luciferian witch. I chose this path...and I want this path. This is *my* path. I know my destiny is to be with you. To be *your* witch."

I squirmed around uncomfortably, not knowing what to say to that.

She watched me for some time before getting up and taking a step toward me, her eyes pinning me where I slumped against the desk. I smelled the cocoa butter on her skin, her shampoo. It made my cheeks burn in a not-so-adult way.

"You're shy," Antonia said, sounding surprised. Her eyes dropped to my greatly tented jeans, then moved back up to my face. "I didn't expect that from you."

I shrugged. "The rumors of my exploits are great—"

I never got a chance to finish because she took another step, putting her soft, rounded breasts right against me. We stared into each other's eyes for a long moment before she reached up to snag my shirt and pull my head down so she could kiss me. Actually, she stuck her tongue down my throat until I groaned and started clawing at her shirt, practically ripping the buttons from it.

"No…I think they're exactly right about you," she laughed as she yanked at my pullover. I helped her roll it over my shoulders.

The coolness of the room made me shiver. I took one look at Antonia—god, she was beautiful like a goddess sent to Earth, her clothes all twisted on her now.

"I haven't had great luck when it comes to relationships," I warned her. "Everyone I fall for winds up angry with me over one thing or another." I didn't add that I wanted her anyway, that I was practically sore from wanting her all the time.

But she seemed to know. She looked up at me very seriously when she said, "I'm not looking for that. Haven't you figured that out yet?"

I frowned, confused.

Again, she laughed. "I have a boyfriend, Nick. Maybe it isn't this wild, destructive Romeo and Juliet love story going on between us, but I genuinely care about Jeremy, and we get along. We have a lot of common interests. I don't want to replace him, Nick. I just want to be your witch."

Reaching out, I stroked my fingers down the side of her cheek. She really was amazing. She grabbed my hand, still grinning. "Besides, I hear the whispers around here. I want to know what makes the others go all swoony on you."

"They don't 'go swoony,'" I laughed. "'Swoony' seems like a bit of an exagger—"

But she grabbed me and pulled me down for another round of tonsil hockey.

There is only so much a man can take. I grabbed her, swinging her around so she was sitting on the edge of my desk. She squeaked at the sudden motion, but then I clamped a hand in all that hair of hers and kissed her again, which stopped the noises she was making. I kissed her savagely, with all the bottled-up fear, desire, and frustration I felt. I dragged my mouth down her chin and throat to parts more northern. I tongued the pit of her cleavage, then sank to the floor while I worked on getting serious about this witch business.

Antonia whimpered as I teased her up and down with my lips and tongue—quick little kisses and bites that left her jumping and cooing in a way that made me wish my office was soundproofed. She wrapped her arms around my neck and skated her fingers through my hair, pulling it in great swaths from the thick yellow Scandinavian braid I'd put it in this morning.

"Christ, you are a beautiful man, Nick," she said, kissing a handful of my hair. "And you even smell good."

I laughed at that. It was probably pine sap still in my hair from my little jaunt through the forest yesterday. Grabbing her chin, I forced her face up and placed a long, lingering kiss on the corner of her mouth. When she smiled, I forced her legs apart and slid one hand up the inseam of her black trousers. Snagging the waistband, I yanked them down with a little wiggle work from her. She groaned and writhed against me as I went down on her, licking her through her light blue cotton boy shorts.

"Oh, god, yes…right there…" she hissed through her teeth.

I thought how this could have had a very happy ending, except that a crashing noise from upstairs made me stop. I stiffened and both of us instantly went on alert. Putting my hands on Antonia's knees, I stood up.

Another crash. Antonia's large brown eyes had gone even larger at the sounds of the struggling upstairs.

"Stay here," I told her, liberating the athame from my belt, "Don't come up."

I started up the stairs, the knife pointing downward in my hand military-style. A smash of glass and someone crying out in pain or surprise made me flinch as I reached the kitchen. It sounded like a full-on war going on in the living room.

As I made my way to the entrance, I sensed a presence behind me and glanced behind. Antonia was standing at my back. Her shirt was open and she was only in her underpants, but she didn't seem to even mind. She was packing the heat the FBI had given her. I almost told her to go back but then realized I needed to stop infantizing her at some point.

She was Quantico-trained. I could trust her to have my back.

I indicated with my finger that I wanted to circle around and come in through the connecting hallway. She signaled she knew and would back me up from here.

I went around and slid my back down the corridor that led to the common room. I wish I had my gun, but that was upstairs. Grampa's angel-eating knife would have to do.

Someone was shouting from the room in a deep, disturbing baritone, demanding they bring "the angel-breaker" to him. That was me, by the way. And, truly, this is my shocked voice. Juliette responded, telling the intruder she would do no such thing. The creature bellowed in response, and I heard the kids in the house squeak in fearful response. Juliette then tried to talk the intruder down like he was some manic patient from her practice. He shouted at her to shut up or he'd gut her like the pig she was. That pissed me off.

I moved casually into the doorway, the knife hidden against my wrist (and burning me a little, if I'm being honest), and stood there to address the creature who had broken right through the large picture window in the front of the house and was now standing in the glass, the drapes fluttering around him and a light snow swirling around its fugly head.

The Children of Endor shifted back, most of them in poses that looked unsure. They had been watching TV or playing board games when the monster dropped in.

I immediately recognized the invader as a cherub—and not the cute little baby kind, either. It stood at least nine feet tall and had four faces, those of a man, an ox, a lion, and a hawk, and four white wings, two raised toward the ceiling threateningly, the other two covering its naked body down to the floor, where I could see its hooves shifting in a lot of broken glass, Jenga blocks, and Monopoly pieces Its eight beady eyes surveyed the room analytically, passing over the humans trying to shift away from it, but they quickly came to rest on me, leaning in the doorway.

"You!" it bellowed in delight.

"Looking for me, ugly? How did you get in here?" The house was warded so no Otherkin could enter it without permission. But, somehow, this thing had made it through.

The cherub shifted its stance, all its attention on me now. "Lord Lucifer," it intoned, extending its incredibly muscular arms and offering its hands to me. "Star of the Morning…"

"Just Nick," I said and took a step into the room. "Save the proselytizing, bub."

"I am he who stands at the door...I am the agent of your destruction..."

"Blah, blah, blah...whatever. Get the fuck out before I cut your angel heart out and make you eat it." I showed him the athame I carried.

It lurched slightly at the sight of the knife. "You mock me."

"Oh, I'm gonna do a lot more than that to you, bitch." I extended my four archangel wings as I took another step toward the abomination. The witty comebacks were entirely staged, by the way. I mean, yeah, I can be a pretty funny guy when I want to be. But their real purpose was to give Juliette the time she needed to quietly and efficiently escort the kids out of the room before the creature and I tore it apart around them.

By the time I had crossed half the room, only Sada remained. She stood against the wall, almost invisible and entirely immobile, eyes closed as she called up a powerful protection spell. I could smell the magic on the air.

The creature, seeing me approach, lunged, but it was big and heavy and awkward, so I had time to slide backward and out of the reach of its grip. At the same time, Antonia moved into the doorway, expertly raised and aimed the gun, and calmly squeezed off a series of shots that penetrated its heads and shoulders. The angel absorbed them, jerking as each bullet fucked into its flesh, but it hardly seemed fazed by the impact. It simply turned its heads—multiple ones were bleeding—to her and bellowed in rage.

Antonia stuttered and had to reassure her grip on the gun. I could feel the fear pouring off her and couldn't blame her for the lapse. It's one thing to know about the existence of angels; quite another to confront one that means to end you. Angels are fucking scary even when they are trying to be nice. To her credit, she didn't drop the gun or run away. She simply emptied the remaining bullets into the creature's chest as it moved toward her.

It was a good distraction. But I didn't want it grabbing Antonia.

"Oh no, you don't." I jumped on the angel—that was hard, given the angle of its wings, but I was stupid and brave—and tried to wrap my forearm around its neck. My goal was to use the knife to cut its throat (throats)? But it was much larger than I was, way stronger, and one of its heads was facing backward. That one—the bull—snorted and snapped at me with its unnaturally pointed teeth.

I lost my nerve and slid down its back. The cherub flapped its wings with irritation and that knocked me back. I fell onto the large glass coffee table where the kids and I played our board games, crushing it.

The impact stunned me, but only for a moment. I got up, meaning to jump back on the angel, but I was suddenly so dizzy I could barely stand up. Maybe that fight at The Ranch had hurt me more than I'd thought. There was also a bitter, almost metallic, taste in the back of my mouth. I had never experienced that before. I took a step forward, then lurched back to find my balance.

"Nick!" Antonia called to me. The thing was quickly closing in on her.

I shook my head to clear it, but I was aware of a ringing in my ears that was growing louder and louder. "What in the actual fuck?" I said, slapping at myself so I focused. That didn't help, so I stood still for a moment to compose myself.

This fucking little knife was useless, I thought, throwing it aside. I raised my hand and tried to manifest my bident. It took two tries because I couldn't seem to focus at all on the spell. Plus, the lights in the room were brighter than they should be, almost blindingly so.

The cherub was on Antonia, who was kicking at it, using all the training she had learned in the FBI to get it to back off. And she was doing a pretty damned fine job of it too. But there were limits to what she could do against one of the Holy Host.

Meanwhile, I realized I was really, truly fucking this up. Only whatever Sada was doing was helping as she seemed to be trying her hand at a kind of time-lock, only slower and weaker than an angel can wield. It was causing the cherub to move in slow motion rather than freezing everyone up entirely. That was good, but the angel still had Antonia by the arm and was in the process of lifting her so it could bite her face.

Even though it felt like I was moving through syrup, I swallowed hard, focused, and lifted the bident, aiming the tines outward. Problem was, I didn't think I had enough oomph to charge the cherub without falling on my face. So I turned to Sada and jerked my head back, hoping she understood.

She did. Turning back, she motioned with both hands. Her long, thin, dark hands were tipped in even longer gold nails with both holy and sacrilegious symbols carved into them, her version of a blessed athame. I had seen them in action and they were incredibly powerful.

Motioning to the angel, she managed to ensnare it and pull it in super slow-mo a few feet away from Antonia as if it was caught in an invisible fishnet. I knew that wouldn't last very long, though. Angels are very good at breaking enchantments. But it didn't have the time to do that, because, with a snap of fiery, ozone-smelling magick, Sada drew her arms back, doubling her already considerably powerful spell. That jerked the angel backward and off Antonia—not as fast as I would have liked it, but enough that I was able to stumble forward, get behind it, and slide the bident into the small of its back.

It bellowed as it fell backward and onto me, but by the time it had knocked me down, it was already turning to stone and falling apart as Moondog had, though that didn't make it hurt any less. Basically, I was pummeled by small, heavy rocks as I dropped like a sack of potatoes to the floor.

There was silence for several seconds.

Then: "Nick!" Antonia raced to help me up. She grabbed my hand and pulled me up. But by then, whatever was wrong with me had amped up a notch and I became aware that my entire body had stiffened up like an electrical charge was passing through it. My hands had clenched into tight fists at my sides and I fell back, my heels beating a thunderous tattoo on the floor as a spastic fit took me over.

I slumped back, watching Antonia stand over me, her face pale and terror-stricken, a hand over her mouth. I thought how incredibly fucked up this was. And then, thankfully, everything went black for a while.

| 8 |

Hybrids

I WOKE UP in bed feeling like someone had dragged me backward through a picket fence. Literally, no part of my body didn't hurt, and that horrible taste lingered in my mouth. I was also dry. So much so that I could barely speak after I came to.

Juliette sat in a chair next to my bed, legs crossed as she consulted a tablet in her lap. "You're back with us."

I tried to sit up but moaned as a wave of nausea swept through me.

"Don't move too much," she insisted. "You're not well enough yet."

I looked at the magus of my little coven, trying to convey the questions I had with my eyes.

"You'll be all right, Nick. Just give yourself a little time to recover." Juliette smiled encouragingly. "You've had a rough night."

Amber came in carrying a glass of water. Eyes bright, she helped me drink it down. I choked a little, then slid back against the pillow, blinking through muzzy eyes while she tenderly wiped my mouth for me. I was aware my hair was all tangled around my head and shoulders and sticking to the sweat on my bare chest. I moved my fingers slowly at my sides, surprised I could unclench them.

I had to swallow hard before I could speak. "W…what happened?"

Juliette got up and checked my pulse by pressing two fingers against my neck. She was a therapist, but I knew she had some rudimentary medical training. She looked over at Amber. "My dear, can you give me a little privacy to speak to Nick, please?"

"Of course, magus." Amber bowed to Juliette, gave me another sweet little smile that seemed to say *everything will be fine*, and then exited the room.

Once we were alone and the door closed, Juliette picked up the tablet sitting on the bedside table and sat down on the edge of the mattress. "Nick, I want you to look at this."

Even though I had a headache, I made myself squint at the image on the tablet. My eyes were still a little bleary and it took a second. After blinking a few times, I realized I was looking at one of a series of full-body X-rays—but for the life of me, I couldn't tell which way was up on the tablet.

"We have a portable CT machine," Juliette explained. "Alexander bought it for us when we realized that you were going to be a…challenge." She'd meant "a problem" but was being diplomatic. "We couldn't have you going off to the hospital every time something came for you."

She shrugged. "I mean, it's true we have members of our group in administration at Pocono Medical, but things get messy when X-rays like this turn up. Staff all the way down to the technicians start to ask uncomfortable questions that we don't want to have to answer."

In her subtle, motherly way, Juliette was telling me I was a royal pain in the coven's ass. Not that I disagreed.

I'd finally got the tablet the right way...I think. "This is...this isn't me?"

She nodded.

Holy hell. Literally.

Though I'd been injured plenty in the past, I normally relied on the coven's magic or my own to heal me. As a result, I haven't had many occasions to visit the local hospital. And I'd never had a full-body X-ray before. I gaped. The image was pretty messed up. There were bones where I didn't think bones were supposed to be in a human skeleton. And organs crammed into odd places. It looked like the X-ray of some alien autopsy.

"Jesus Christ," I uttered.

Juliette suppressed a smile. "He probably looks something like this too."

I flipped the tablet over before it made me sick to look at it. I swallowed hard, then I looked up. "Why the X-ray? Am I dying?"

She maintained her smile in a way that told me she was about to drop a really bad truth bomb on me. "Can I ask you a very personal, medical-related, question, Nick?"

Her tone of voice petrified me. "I guess?"

"How long have you had untreated epilepsy?"

It took me a very long moment to even register her words. Then: "What?"

She took the tablet, turned it back over, and started scrolling through the images until she reached the one that was presumably of my brain. She pointed out some blurry images I couldn't decipher. "You have scars on your brain, which happens to patients with untreated epilepsy. Not a lot, but enough that they are noticeable. You've never been diagnosed or treated, have you?"

"Uh...no," I looked stupidly at the scars. "Epilepsy?"

In a thousand years, I'd never have believed I was having this conversation with anyone. How could I possibly have epilepsy? I'd never even had a sniffle.

"And you've never had a seizure?"

I almost said no, but then remembered that last year, I'd had seized while the Arcana agent, Kip Murphy, was beating the tar out of me. Naturally, I thought it was because I had taken some hard knocks to the head over the long hours of my imprisonment and subsequent torture. She seemed to pick up on that in that intuitive way she had. Juliette could almost read your mind at times, though whether that was because she was a powerful witch or a talented therapist, I've never figured out.

She asked another uncomfortable question. "Nick, when you were in school, did the teachers claim you spaced out or didn't pay attention in class?"

I snorted because that one was easy to answer. "They were always complaining about my behavior or failing me for one thing or another. None of them liked me much. But...epilepsy?"

Juliette nodded. "It's as I suspected. Absence seizures. Not all epilepsy manifests itself in grand mal seizures, Nick. Some look more like daydreaming or acting out." With another nod, she announced, "You were having absent seizures all through your youth, but because of your...special situation...no one noticed."

It was nice of her to say it in such a way that it didn't sound sad or dispiriting. I'd spent most of my childhood in foster care, and no one, not my teachers and caseworkers and none of my various foster families, had given a shit about me. I was a foster kid—thus, I was a troublemaker, a bad egg that would surely come to no good end.

"But your last seizure—the one you had last night—that one was definitely a grand mal," she announced.

I swallowed hard at that and tried to wrap my brain around the fact that I had this terrifying and embarrassing medical condition.

I'd never been sick a day in my life, so this all seemed so…strange and awful. I'd seen seizures in real life and depicted on TV. Didn't people sometimes wet themselves? Oh Christ, had I embarrassed myself last night? I was too afraid to ask.

I glanced up at Juliette, who was watching me sympathetically. "You mean I've been like this my whole life? I was born this way?"

Juliette nodded. "Yes. I think you were, which seems horrible, I know, Nick. But try not to get too upset. Considering your physiology…" She scrolled through the horror show that was my anatomy. "…I think you got away pretty lucky. There are things on here…well, I don't think there are names for them."

No shit.

Over the next hour, Juliette showed me some other really disturbing things, including the fact that I had two hearts, a human one in just about the same place as a human, and a second one I wasn't aware of located deep in my belly, where I knew full-blooded angels had them.

"As I see it," she explained when she was done showing me the nightmarish images of my insides, "you could get down about your condition or just appreciate that your physiology managed to accommodate a bunch of genes that don't belong in the human body. I mean, Nick, the fact that you are alive and functional is essentially a miracle. Besides…" She pulled an amber pill bottle out of her pocket and showed it to me. "If you take one of these each night before bed, you shouldn't have any more seizures."

I looked at the bottle and its label. Phenobarbital. I felt a little like crying. Maybe I was just tired.

Setting the bottle down on the table, I looked at it and muttered a half-hearted "Thanks."

Juliette put her hand on my shoulder. "I'll let you rest now."

Before she left, something came to me through the muddied haze of my wounded, scarred-up brain. "Is everyone all right? Is Antonia—?"

She patted my shoulder. "Everyone is fine, Nick. We've taken care of it all." Then her face darkened. "But we have to talk about what happened. It's pretty obvious that something is going on, and I think we deserve to know what it is."

"I know what happening." I gave her a quick rundown on what I'd learned on the road, and then I told her I needed to make a trip into New York tomorrow first thing.

"I'm not sure that's wise. I don't think you're strong enough, but I won't stop you," she said as she gathered her tablet and prepared to leave. "I will caution you, though. You should bring backup with you—at least until you know the medication is working and you won't seize up in the middle of an angel fight."

She made a good point, one I agreed with. "I guess I could take Sada."

"I'd like that, but she's recovering from that spell last night and is not at her best." When she saw my worry, she added, "She's fine. Resting. But I don't want her out in the field right now. That spell overextended her."

Shit. I'd have to find someone else to take. "About last night," I said as she walked to the door. I sat up in concern. "Do we know how the angel got in?"

She turned and looked at me in a disturbing way. "The angel...was one of us, Nick. I mean, he was before he took that drug you talked about and was...changed."

Shit. Shit shit shit!

"We believe that's what caused him to...well, to become that thing. And why he was able to breach the coven's house."

My heart skipped and I tried to get up, which didn't work. My head swam and I had to lie back down. "Who was it, Juliette?"

"That's not important, Nick. We'll discuss it later. Shall I send Amber and Henry in shortly?"

"I...I guess."

She ducked out before I could beg her to come back and explain things. With nothing else to do, I took the time to rest, but that got on my nerves pretty quickly. So I made a call to Malach and gave him an update on my leads. I sounded tired and croaky even to me, but he thankfully never asked me what was wrong with me.

I took my medication and tried to sleep.

Near morning, I woke up with Amber and Henry spooning me on both sides of the bed. Both of them were naked, their arms wrapped around me as they fed me their healing sex magick.

Juliette had given the twins to me as sex bunnies, which I should have found insulting, I know, but their magick was incredibly potent and their worship helped me in a variety of ways. I'd resisted at first, but soon enough, I'd come to genuinely care for them. Henry woke first, kissed me good morning, and got up to get the special witch's first aid kit they kept around just for me.

Henry climbed into my lap and put special, peppermint-smelling healing ointment on the scratches on my face while Amber brushed the knots out of my hair and started to braid it back for me. As powerful witches with extensive sex magic talents, just having them close buoyed my powers and my healing. The ointment was probably a placebo, not that it wasn't nice. It felt good to snuggle with them, like human-sized teddy bears.

When they finished putting me back together, they fetched me breakfast—pancakes and bacon with a lot of maple syrup. I was tired by the time I finished eating, but my spirits were up and my stomach wasn't rumbling and sore from emptiness. Breakfast in bed with the beautiful sex bunnies was a good way to start the day.

After I'd eaten and my companions had licked up the maple syrup wherever it had dripped, they begged me to make love to them. Best I could do was a good snuggle with some heavy petting. At the moment, I was too sore for those kinds of gymnastics.

I fell asleep again, my body working overtime to heal itself, then woke around four in the afternoon according to my phone. I lay alone for a while in the deepening twilight pouring through the bank of windows opposite the bed, watched the first serious snow of the season flutter against the windowpanes, and (for a little while, at least) felt pretty sorry for myself. I thought about the epilepsy that had dogged me my entire life, felt angry with all the people who never noticed or cared, and then told myself to toughen up and let it go. Those thoughts would take me nowhere, and, anyway, it wasn't the end of the world. I had a hell of a lot more to worry about than my completely treatable medical condition.

That was the second human-angel hybrid I had encountered. And things weren't getting any better.

I was feeling stronger and a little less depressed, so I got out of bed, showered, shaved, put on fresh clothes, and had a pep talk with the tired, raccoon-eyed image of myself in the mirror. Then I went downstairs to see what was shaking.

The Children of Endor looked a little surprised to see me up and about so soon, but I smiled nicely and nodded to them as I went about looking for Juliette. I found her in the kitchen, talking to Antonia. They seemed to be having a heated conversation, but when I entered, they stopped and turned to look at me with concern.

"Are you sure you should be up, Nick?" Juliette inquired.

"I'm fine," I told her. "Amber and Henry fixed me up." I recalled my walk through the house, all the kids I had passed, and then said, "Where's David?" I hadn't noticed him, and I was pretty sure he'd be here tonight, fretting over me. He had always been a little overprotective of me, both as my lover and as my disciple.

That's when Juliette gave me an odd look and put her hand on my arm, rubbing it. Meanwhile, all the little pieces fell together in my wounded, scarred-up brain.

My heart fell. Both of them. "Oh...oh, no," I said, and the tone of my voice caused Juliette to quickly remove her hand. "Oh, no...no no no..."

I was muttering incomprehensively, and the room suddenly felt too hot and small for my liking. I felt claustrophobic, and I couldn't stand the way the two of them were looking at me with such pity...

Antonia said, "Nick, Nick...I'm so sorry..."

I never heard the rest of her statement. I pushed past them and went to the back door, letting myself out into the chilly, snowy early evening air. A stone path was cut through the property behind the house. The rickety, leafless black trees lined the path on both sides, white birch and acorn, with more and deeper woods at the end. During the summer, I walked in the woods with various members of the coven. Sometimes we did rituals back here. But all the trees were naked and covered in a fine fluff of white now...

I started to walk down the stone path, moving blindly. Mechanically. It was almost fully dark now.

I went faster and faster until I was running full tilt for the forest. It was pitch black, not dark like a horror movie with a large, gravid spotlight moon above to guide me. Completely lightless, the kind of black that can kill you, but I cut through the trees and the darkness like a bullet, instinctively picking my way over the icy stone path. At one point, my long hair caught on a branch. I ripped the braid out of the tangle of branches, snow falling down the back of my shirt, and kept running until I was almost to the end of the four acres of woodland that crouched protectively behind the house.

Slowly, I went from a run to a slow jog. I knew a short but dangerously vertical washout was here. I wasn't running through the woods atop the tallest cliff you've ever seen, but it was significant enough that if you rolled down it, you'd wind up breaking an arm or leg. A highway lay at the bottom, and the few cars that passed splashed their headlights across the reflective yellow sign with the familiar leaping deer on it. The one at the bottom of the mountain had been Rudolphed—that is, someone had affixed a red dot to the deer's nose. I don't know why I recalled that, but it was the way my brain was processing now.

I stopped just short of sliding off the mountain. Panting, I bent over, my hands on my knees, and tried to catch my breath, which was hard, given I was still recovering, the air was icy in my lungs, and I'd covered a lot of ground in a hard run. It rasped in and out of my lungs like cat claws. Feeling sick and dizzy, I crouched down in the fallen branches and leaf litter—and suddenly threw up on the hard, icy ground.

God, it hurt. It felt like someone had their hand on my heart and was squeezing the muscle tight, trying to end me. I put my hand on my chest as if I could stop or slow it. The sob that escaped my throat made me ashamed, and I moved my hand upward, clamping it over my mouth so no one heard me scream while I stumbled around stupidly in the frozen dark.

Antonia found me like that, crouched over, sobbing into the dirt. She too was panting as she worked to catch up to me, but I ignored her. She stopped some twenty feet away as if she was afraid to spook me.

"Nick," she said. "God, Nick, I'm so sorry about David!"

I stood up slowly and slid the hand off my mouth. It was covered in the tears and snot that was running freely down my face. Shit, I thought. Shit. Last night, while I was caught up in defending the coven's house and killing an angel, I was also killing David. I had no idea how he had come to be wrapped up with the Z-Quil. Maybe a friend had given it to him. Maybe he'd been tired and frustrated after getting off his shift. Maybe he'd always been into recreational drugs and I never noticed. Or, hell, maybe my shitty treatment of him had caused it.

Regardless, David was dead, and I'd killed him. Me. The man who was supposed to protect and love him.

I swallowed the hard knot in my throat before turning to face Antonia. Cars continued to pass below, and their light splashed upward briefly, lighting different angles of her beautiful face, which was splashed with tears.

A thought occurred to me, so I said it. "Why in hell do you want to be with me?"

She looked confused, stuttered on a response, then said, "I care about you, Nick About what you're trying to do here." She indicated the woods, the coven house, the Children of Endor.

"No, why do *you* want to be with me?"

"I…I love you, Nick."

Her words made me groan and I held my head as I sank down on a deadfall. "I am going to get you killed, Antonia." I ran my hands through my now-tangled hair. "I'm going to bury you the way I bury everyone. Is that what you want? To live your life being hunted by monsters, angels…hybrids?"

She didn't answer. And when I finally pushed my hair out of my eyes, I saw the outrage in her eyes. I could feel her vibrating with her anger, which surprised and puzzled me. It took her a moment to respond to that. "You have a lot of fucking nerve, you know that, Nick? I'm a Black woman. I've been in danger my whole life, but I think I held my own pretty well last night."

Antonia turned to face the cliff and screamed into the night, a sound so raw it made the little hairs on my bare arms stand up. Then she turned to glare at me, tears falling from her eyes. "You're not Jesus, Nick, and I don't need you to save me. So, fuck you!"

Swinging around, she started marching back down the path that led to the house.

I sat there for a long while, just absorbing her words, the night and the cold, and made a series of important decisions about my life. I barely felt the freezing temperature—maybe that was the Jotunn in me, I don't know.

Near morning, when I finally walked into the house, I told Juliette I would be upstairs packing for my road trip to New York City if she needed me, and I would be taking Antonia with me as my bodyguard.

| 9 |

Going Down

WE WERE HEADING down I-80, a little over an hour into the drive, when the silence finally got to me. I was tired of counting willow trees in the median. Tired of Antonia giving me the cold soldier while she studied her phone.

"I'm sorry," I told her. "About last night."

She didn't look up, so I continued. "I disrespected you, I know. I had my reasons, but that doesn't excuse my shitty behavior." We passed a Stop & Go, which made me wonder about where my gummy candy population was in the car, but I didn't feel like stopping.

Time ticked by. I counted some more trees. When that got boring, I found the Swedish fish in the pocket of my coat that I'd bought at Wawa before I left Blackwater.

Finally, Antonia's head came up and she looked over at me. "Thanks. I appreciate that." She put the phone down. "I'm not deliberating ignoring you. I'm studying a spell."

I nodded.

"Can I have a fish?"

I handed her the bag and listened to it crinkle. Then: "Sorry, I ate all of your fish."

When we came upon the next rest stop, we got out to stretch our legs, use the loo, and hit the vending machines. I studied my options. Planters Trail Mix or Cheez-its. It was a tough decision.

Antonia stepped out of the ladies' room, drying her hands on a brown paper towel. "Cheez-its."

Back in the car, I took a long slurp of the Dr. Pepper I'd gotten and set the can inside the cup holder that I think Antonia had installed in the car because my old one never had such swag.

"How is she handling?" Antonia asked as she bit down on a milk chocolate Raisinet.

"Like a dream," I answered. "You had her serviced just before you gave her to me, didn't you?"

A long pause. "Are you all right, Nick?"

I looked at the gummy worms I'd bought along with the Cheez-its, but I had no appetite suddenly. I had the oddest feeling. The pieces of my life felt like they were separating with parts falling away, leaving me more and more isolated with each disaster. I didn't know what I was going to do about that.

"No," I told her truthfully. "I don't think I am. I don't think I'll be all right for a while. Maybe I'll never be all right. But I'll live." It wasn't like I had a choice in the matter.

She nodded as if she understood. "I liked David. He was really good at Scrabble."

A smile ticked the corner of my mouth at the memory. "Yeah, he was."

Just before we hit the Holland Tunnel, I had a thought. "You said you've been studying spells. Do you practice craft?"

"I do," Antonia affirmed. "Not officially with your coven, of course, but on my own. And the magus has been giving me some tips. She's not supposed to do that, but..."

"Yeah, Juliette is cool that way. So that's why I'd found them together more often than usual. "Could you research some spells for me?"

"What kind?" She picked up her phone, and I suddenly realized she must use it to study the craft. I knew the Children of Endor had a huge database of e-spell books. Juliette had probably given her access to their cloud library.

It took me a few seconds to express my thoughts. "When all that went down the other day, I thought the only way to separate a victim from the angel possessing them was the bident. And I was right. But the bident is like a nuclear warhead, you know? It just destroys the angel *and* the victim. I want a way to separate them without hurting the victim."

"Like an exorcism spell."

"Something like that, yeah. But more delicate." I tapped the wheel. "I want a way to peel the angel off the victim and destroy it, but leave the victim intact. Does that make sense?"

Antonia nodded. "On it."

At least we weren't hating on each other when we got to the city. Before I left Blackwater, Juliette had informed me that, yes, the Children of Endor had holdings in New York City—they owned a whole brownstone on W51st Street in Hell's Kitchen. Most of the flats were rented out year-round, but the modest penthouse was deliberately kept empty for when the members of the coven needed a place to crash in the city. She'd given me the necessary keycards. Antonia read off the GPS directions while I navigated the newly gentrified, almost unrecognizable streets.

It had been almost a decade since I'd been back to New York. So much had changed.

We found the brownstone all right, and there was even an empty, renovated coach house in the back for the Monaco, which was nice. I mean, the car wasn't exactly a classic, but it was just vintage enough to attract the wrong kind of attention on the streets. I could imagine a kid like I had been taking her for a joyride.

We got out, and I carried my and Antonia's overnight bags to the back of the building where Juliette said there was a private lift. Antonia had the keycard and swiped it. We got in and it took us to the top floor of a posh little penthouse. Not one of those sprawling, all-glass flats with the in-ground swimming pool you see in movies. This was a cozy, renovated flat done in all neutral greys and beiges with only one large bay window facing the street (for coven privacy, I assumed), a nice-sized modern kitchen, a small bathroom, and one bedroom on the main level with a second one located in a loft upstairs. The place looked like an expensive hotel room.

Antonia immediately rushed upstairs and confirmed that, yes, all of the coven's magickal paraphernalia was locked away up there and we needed the keycard to access it as Juliette said we would. I thought about how the coven's tools could aid us in our mission and vowed to check it out after we got something to eat and maybe some much-needed shuteye

"Could you unload our stuff and order something to eat?" Antonia asked.

"Sure."

Antonia asked to be excused and went up to the magic loft, presumably to track down a spell that could help us. Meanwhile, I ordered a pizza and then some Thai (I wasn't sure what Antonia was in the mood for) and then set the table in the little corner dining room space while I waited for the food to the delivered. I found the plates and glasses in the cupboards, and even some candles and holders, which I also set on the table. The refrigerator and freezer were fully stocked, and I found some bottles of wine in a bar fridge in the living room. I chose a rose and set it on the table between the lit candles.

When the food arrived a half hour later, I tried to space it out nicely on the table between us and tried to make it look as nice as fast food can look, anyway—and then went to tap on the loft door to tell Antonia there was dinner.

Antonia said she'd be right out and I went back downstairs to pour the wine.

About two minutes later, Antonia emerged wearing a long red dress that was exceptionally thin—little more than a nightgown, really—and chandelier earrings. The dress contrasted beautifully against her dark skin and set off the streak of bright red in her hair. I felt woefully underdressed in my jeans and pullover as I pulled the chair out for my companion and then sat down opposite her. I wish I had showered and put something nice on, but now it was too late to do that without making it look obvious.

"This is nice," she said, looking over everything approvingly. "It feels almost like a date."

"Does it?" I handed her the Thai. I hadn't realized how romantic it all felt with the candles and everything, but she was right.

As Antonia unwrapped some chopsticks, she asked, "I think I may have a spell, but I'll need to practice it. I'll need some time to perfect it so I don't mess it up."

I nodded. "I have complete confidence in you. Tell me what I can do to help." I picked up my own chopsticks to dig in. I'd meant in terms of what tools she needed, or anything else I could help her with, but she surprised me.

"Make me your bride tonight."

I almost choked on a noodle.

She sighed and gave me a longsuffering look. "I can see we've made no progress on that front."

"No." I coughed out the errant noodle. *Great going, Nick.* Just what I needed during my romantic date meal—the Heimlich. I swallowed again and decided to tackle the issue head-on. "No, I've decided it's time, and I want you to be my witch, Antonia. I just didn't think tonight was the right night with everything going on. I didn't want to rush you into it."

"You're not rushing me. And if not tonight, then when?" she challenged.

I pointed my chopsticks at her. "New coven members are usually initiated during a Sabbat with an elaborate ceremony and everything. You would be missing out on all the pageantry."

The last member I had initiated into the coven was David. We'd...well, to put it bluntly, we'd had ceremonial sex in the presence of the whole coven. I think I was more embarrassed than he was. I wasn't much into exhibitionism, but the Children of Endor treated it as de rigueur. Afterward, we'd had a bit of a welcoming orgy to seal the deal, a lot of food, and we'd all gotten a bit tipsy. It was a good night.

"You won't have the benefit of the whole fancy setup," I added. "All the ceremonial bells and whistles."

But Antonia shook her head. "I don't need anything fancy. And it's not as if you need a ceremony to do it, right? I mean...you just have sex with someone and they become yours."

"More or less. Maybe a little more."

Antonia nodded. "And if the shit hits the fan tomorrow and you need to face Michael, you'll need as much of your Well as you can access. I'm here. I could contribute a lot of power to that."

I looked at her for a long moment, then nodded. "You're right."

"Good," she said with a satisfied smile and tapped her sticks against the plate. "It's settled, then. We'll do it right after dinner."

"I don't get a say in the matter," I joked.

"No," Antonia asserted. "You have to do exactly as I say tonight, Nick."

I laughed. "What about Jeremy? Does he know about this initiation?"

And she nodded. "Yes. I explained everything to him before I left. He understands." Then she gave me a pointed look. "Since he's part of the Children of Endor, he understands the importance of ceremonial sex. Besides, we're not exactly monogamous."

That surprised me. "Oh."

"Yes," she affirmed. "Oh." Then she added, "Like the other Children of Endor, we have an open relationship. So, you see, you and I aren't doing anything wrong. We aren't 'cheating.'"

I watched her in wonder. "So you have everything planned out."

"Yep." She smiled. "I plan to seduce you tonight, Nick. And then you'll take me to bed and make me your witch." Her smile turned saucy. "You should know I've already put a spell on you. You won't get away from me. You're quite doomed."

Her words gave me a tingle of anticipation. I liked the idea of her putting a spell on me. I wondered about the possibility of putting handcuffs on her at some point later tonight...

Dinner seemed to go on forever. I could barely eat and was as nervous as a high-schooler copping his first feel in the backseat of his car. "This is ridiculous," I said under my breath several times. I was a grown man almost twice her age. But every time I looked up and met Antonia's eyes, I felt my carnal appetite for her grow, and the food was doing nothing to help satisfy that.

I felt like some randy teenager experiencing his first time when Antonia took my hand and led me into the large, posh bedroom adjacent to the kitchen. It was done in all dove grey and mauve. It should have felt generic, but I found it extremely soothing, which was good. I was already almost too nervous to kiss her. She asked me to sit on the edge of the bed while she undressed for me.

"I used to fantasize about you, you know," she told me as she slipped out of her dress so she was just in her lacy black bra and boy shorts. "I mean, long before I knew what you were, I kind of had a crush on you." Her cheeks pinkened with her words, which charmed me in a way nothing else could. It also saddened me. "I always thought you should be a movie star or a celebrity."

I shook my head. "Not my cup of tea."

"What is your cup of tea?" she asked as she removed her bra and stepped boldly out of her shorts. She was curvy and solid. I could tell she worked out and could probably Karate throw me if she wanted to. And that turned me on. I admired her lovely, apple-shaped breasts and her nipples a deep purplish color. She hadn't shaved under her arms or at her groin, and though I knew some guys were pretty psychotic about that, it didn't bother me at all. It told me she was in charge of her life.

"You are," I told her truthfully. "You're my cup of tea."

She tilted her chin up and observed me sadly. "What's bothering you, Nick? You look so sad."

"Besides the obvious? You are so young and so...untouched." She didn't say anything to that; I knew she was growing tired of that argument. So I told the truth. "I murdered one of my lovers a couple of days ago. I'm still having some trouble wrapping my brain around that."

"And you saved me in the process," she added. "Or did you not think about that? The hybrid would have killed me if it wasn't for you. Any way you look at it, you would have lost one of us."

I looked down. "You're right."

"So what else is bothering you? Because I know something is."

I felt self-conscious suddenly. Juliette was right when she said I didn't open up to...well, anyone. I never really had. Maybe to Vivian, once, but even then, I'd kept things from her that were too personal, or too painful. But, I had decided I wanted Antonia to really know me. And that included knowing about my condition. I didn't want her to see me as this perfect, angelic savior, even if she said she didn't think of me that way. So, I asked her to sit beside me and told her about the epilepsy.

She gave me big, sympathetic eyes while she listened. When I had finished, she asked, "Are you okay? Do you need your meds?"

I shook my head. "No, I'll take them before bed."

"Well, I'll make sure you don't forget."

I bit my lip. "It doesn't bother you?"

She smiled and shook her head. "Since we're bearing out medical souls, you should know something about me." She went to her overnight bag and showed me a small grey kit bag. "I have to take insulin. I inherited Diabetes Type 1 from my dad." She went about the process of displaying her pen and the cartridges that fit into it. All these years, and I'd had no idea Sheriff Ben was diabetic. Antonia showed me how to load the pen and where she injected it into her thigh or abdomen.

"That looks like it hurt," I remarked.

She shrugged. "Welcome to being human." She pointed out the scar tissue that had built up around her middle from the long-term use of the needle.

My condition suddenly didn't seem so dire. At least I didn't need to stick a steel needle into my body every morning. I reached for Antonia, took her hand, and pulled her close. She blushed as I drew her down so she was sitting in my lap. She wiggled a little, wetting my jeans with her excitement. I still had my clothes on, and I think that embarrassed her. After pushing the hair out of her eyes, I lifted her up and laid her gently down on the bed.

I stood there a long moment just looking down at her soft brown curves. Then I undressed while she watched me intently—enjoying the show, I suppose. She looked me up and down, her eyes tracing over every inch of me. When she got to my goodies, her eyes widened. Not wanting her to be afraid, I lay down beside her, palmed her cheek, and kissed her lips. She enjoyed that very much.

It wasn't long before I started moving down her body. I touched her scar tissue with my fingertips, then with my lips. Her scars were a little tougher than the rest of her soft skin.

She watched me, purring at the close attention I was giving her. Reaching out, she took my hand and brought my fingers to her lips to kiss. "I really love your hands, Nick, do you know that? You have such beautiful, long, tapered fingers."

Her words saddened me, not sure why.

No, I did. I'd done some terrible things with these hands…

She must have been reading my thoughts because she tangled her brown fingers in my much whiter ones, then said, "But you've never hurt anyone who didn't deserve it. You've protected a lot of people with these hands."

I didn't know what to say to that. I didn't have her kind of faith that I was that good of a person. I'd driven my father's weapon through the bodies of gods and monsters. I'd use my hands to rip a man apart—and eat him. I'd hurt a lot of my past lovers. I didn't think all that made me such a great guy. Frankly, even before I learned how screwed up my physiology was, I already knew I was a monster.

I stopped ruminating on useless philosophical stuff that would never be answered to concentrate on Antonia. When I would make love to Vivian in the time before it all fell apart, we often attacked each other like animals, buttons and torn clothes everywhere. We liked it fast and rough. But I didn't feel that way with Antonia. I wanted to go slow; I wanted to show her such tenderness.

"Antonia," I said. "Look at me."

She did. Her eyes were dark and bright and seemed to be full of stars tonight. I pinched her chin and kissed her with the barely restrained urgency I felt. I enjoyed the sweet and slightly spicy taste of her mouth. As for Antonia, she was hardly passive. She ran her fingernails over the shivery muscles of my chest, then skated them downward, tickling me in all the right places. Her light, moth-like touch was doing all kinds of things to me.

I lay flat on my back and positioned my lover atop me. She continued to trickle her fingers over my super-sensitive skin. I captured her beautiful face in my hands and rubbed my thumbs over her cheeks while I watched her body bloom and respond to my touch.

"You don't have to be gentle," Antonia told me. "I'm not glass, you know."

"I want to be," I told her truthfully before kissing her again. But her impatient whimpers caused me to move my mouth downward. I kissed and then sucked at her throat, then her breasts, squeezing the exposed nipples hard, which made her moan with something like relief. When she was comfortable enough, I moved her into position and thrust upward, allowing her to impale herself on me at her leisure. Her eyes narrowed to slits and she gripped the headboard—black iron and resembling twisting vines—so she could control our rhythm. As far as I was concerned, there was nothing in the world sexier than a woman taking over—the sound and smell of her, the heaving of her breasts.

Our gentle but urgent rut seemed to knock the breath from my throat—and hers. Antonia rode me hard, fast, then slow, then fast again. She possessed beautifully untapped sex magic, and soon I felt like I was drowning in her.

After a few minutes, we were both panting and I felt like I was sliding away.

"Harder, Nick," she begged.

I groaned, sank my fingernails into her hips, and gave her all of my unrestrained desire. She cried out in surprise and delight and discomfort. Our magick grew around us, weaving a tight net over our heads—her witchery, my natural Daemon talents. Juliette once said the craft loved me, but because I did not love it back, I had hobbled it. I could only tap into a small percentage of what I could do. But in the months since I had become part of her circle, I had endeavored to give the craft free reign. I had put in the work and the effort.

And it had grown inside me.

The magick I naturally possessed—that given to me by my mother the witch—was stronger than I had ever anticipated. It felt so primal...as wild and unstoppable as a storm. As the beautiful woman riding me. I grunted as it was pulled from me by our lovemaking, and soon my wings manifested, huge raven-black things that shushed across the white sheets and filled the entire bed and most of the bedroom from wall to wall.

Antonia stuttered at the sight and then cried out in surprise.

"Sorry," I managed. That was my version of a premature ejaculation. Get me too excited and I get all angel-y on you.

"Don't be," she told me. "They really are beautiful." She even ran her fingers over the long primary feathers before leaning down to whisper her desire, her fantasy, into my ear.

My eyes grew wide at her request. "Are you sure?"

She nodded. "It's been a fantasy of mine for a long time. I mean...if you want to, of course."

"Of course. Yes." I flipped her over and started giving every bit of myself to her. She tangled her arms in the iron headboard so hang on, which only accentuated the sweat droplets glistening on her breasts. The magic around us grew dense and sweet. It filled the room as it began to bind us and make her one of my brides. We moved as one, harder, faster. Antonia made sweet little mewing noises. Leaning down, I kissed and nibbled the skin at the side of her neck. She moaned and released the headboard so she could trickle her fingers through my feathers while I took us up to the edge of release and then over it, my teeth in her neck. I hoped the walls were soundproofed because the way she cried out made me worry we'd bring the police.

As soon as she'd come for me, I began again. Call it my secret talent.

"Oh, my god, Nick..." she cried out as she wrapped her legs around my waist and fell into the rhythm I was setting for us this time. "Now," she begged after I began building toward a second climax. "Do it now."

I wasn't exactly a prodigy when it came to most magic, and I had only a tentative grasp on spells, but I could do this well enough. I willed us...down. Down to the place of my origins, to my home away from home, if you will. And since my father's world is as much a part of me as my grey eyes or my blond hair, I didn't have to try very hard. It even called to me at times. It was like falling and not falling at the same time. I simply had to hang onto Antonia while I did it.

We dropped through the bed, the floor, the world. Everything rushed by us until we landed in the throne room of the Watchtower, somewhere in Dis—don't ask me where because I've never been able to figure that out. You know it better as Hell, though I had learned long ago it wasn't a lake of fire or even all that terrible a place. Just some other dimension or a parallel world in the multiverse or an as-yet-undiscovered planet. I haven't figured that one out yet.

The throne room is vast and moldable. When my father commanded the place, it used to look like a fancy mansion from out of old Hollywood. But since it had become mine, it had grown more modern, with a lot of conveniences. It looked more like a posh hotel these days. The walls of the throne room went so far back that I could never quite see them. The place also shifted around a lot. But we landed in the place where I always wound up—upon the throne, which was large enough for both of us to lay sideways upon it. It was a massive structure made of angel bones and covered in what I suspected was angel skin and feathers. I never not found it creepy as fuck, but it was the one thing I seemed incapable of changing. When we were here last, Antonia had been fascinated by it. She even asked me if she could sit on it, which I told her sure if she was brave enough.

She was.

"Oh," she said as we continued to make love on the royal seat. It made her fiercer in her demands, and soon we were scratching and biting and teasing and tormenting each other to ever-higher levels of passion even as the heat from the contemporary white marble fireplace spilled over us and the feathers of the dead angels on the throne tickled us in different places.

Antonia sighed in relief when we finally lay side by side sometime later. She cuddled into me and played with my hair, and I thought about how incredibly soft and tender and wild our encounter had been. It made the creepy throne feel less creepy. And, oh, it had been a long time since I had experienced anything like this.

David and I used to have encounters like this—sweet, sexy, sometimes funny. I waited until Antonia had fallen asleep in my arms, her head tucked under my chin, then I gave into my bottled-up grief and cried over David until I fell asleep.

| 10 |

Black Buddha

THE FOLLOWING DAY found us cruising down a well-maintained street in Smithtown, a family-friendly suburb of Long Island. I studied the cookie-cutter houses, pristine landscaping, and honest-to-god picket fences as we passed. We were looking for the house that belonged to Papa Lacroix.

Antonia kept checking the material in her folder that she wouldn't show me. She said she'd "borrowed" the dossier on our fellow from her FBI field office and, in good faith, she couldn't show it to a citizen—even if that was me. I admired how she was willing to steal (rather, borrow) the info, and yet she wanted to keep the rule-breaking to a minimum. A woman after my own heart.

I hadn't totally corrupted her yet. In fact, this morning, after she got out of bed, she told me in a shy tone of voice that she needed to shower and get ready. I told her I could help her with the showering part, but she glanced down and her cheeks darkened at the idea. She even used my shirt to cover herself on her way to the bathroom. It was sweet.

"Turn here, Nick."

I did and we rumbled down a long, dead-end road. Near the end of it, we encountered a tall, fancy iron gate. Beyond it was a curvy driveway that led to a house almost hidden among tall trees. From what I could see, it was huge, with an impressive number of turrets and balconies. It looked like a fortress. I leaned out the window and hit the call button on the high-tech intercom system.

"Amazon Prime delivery," I said.

A low, menacing voice stated, "Do you have an appointment?"

"No," I told Mr. Menace. I'd prepared for this. "But I want to speak with Papa Lacroix all the same. Go get him."

"We don't know who that is."

"Your boss. The drug dealer."

A pause. And then: "I'm afraid I can't help you, mister. Now get the fuck outta here."

I was undeterred. I didn't expect this would go smoothly.

"Relax, Rover. I'm not a cop," I told Lacroix's watchdog. "My name is Nick Englebrecht. I'm here on important business. I need to warn Lacroix about the Z-Quil he's dealing in eastern Pennsylvania. It's laced with angel dust. I mean dust from actual angels. It's why his customers are losing it, turning into monsters, and dying. Now, let me the fuck in if you want to know more."

I let go of the talk button and sat back in my seat.

Antonia turned to stare at me. "You don't fool around, do you?"

"I know these types from my time on the beat. Direct is best."

"But do you think he'll buy it? Do you think he even knows?"

As if in answer, the big iron gates swung open. Ahh, yiss. We drove through and up the drive to the house. I parked the Monaco near a tall, Grecian fountain with beautifully rendered stone goats surrounding a woman with a large urn on her shoulder, maybe Amalthea.

Before I got out, I turned to Antonia, grabbed her somewhat aggressively, and gave her a hungry kiss while I ran a hand up the inside of her thigh and pressed against the seam of her pants between her legs. Antonia cried out.

"What was that for?" she asked.

I pressed my forehead against hers. "I want you to know I'll be spending the whole day thinking about last night. And thinking about tonight."

She smiled. "Me too."

Antonia and I got out and climbed the impressive stairs to the massive front door of the manse. But before we even reached it, the door swung open, and there stood Rover, aka Mr. Menace.

He was a huge wrestler-type bruiser in a nice Brooks Brothers suit. He had a neatly trimmed goatee and his hair was done in twists and beads that fell down his back. He wore the angry look of a bouncer asked to do a task he didn't approve of. "I'm only lettin' you in 'cause the boss says so, aight? Your weapons."

I gave the man my grandfather's athame. That's all I had on me. At my request, Antonia hadn't brought her piece.

Rover looked at my weapon. "Weird knife."

"It's an athame. Don't lose it. It kills human-angel hybrids."

He grunted. "Anything else?"

"I have a magic pitchfork. Do you want that?"

He looked confused. "Follow me, but no funny shit."

Antonia gave me a sidelong look that said, "Can you believe it's that easy?"

I shook my head because I knew it wasn't going to be easy at all.

While Rover led us through the house, I glanced into each room we passed. It was filled with posh, antique furniture and what looked like classic paintings on the walls. The library was well-stocked. Rover stopped and lowered his head a little when we reached the study. "Sir?"

A deep voice echoed out. "Send them in, Charles."

Charles gestured to us to enter the study.

The room was comfortable and warm, fitted with bookshelves and a brown leather smoking couch. An older man, a man I suspected was Papa Lacroix, was sitting behind a large oak desk. Behind him was a marble fireplace, flames crackling in it. Several small statues rested on the top of the mantel—a painted antique horse figurine, a crystal oyster that was open with a huge pearl inside it, and an onyx Buddha. Pictures of a younger Papa Lacroix, his arm around various family members and friends, dotted the walls.

The man stood up as Antonia and I stepped into the room, but he didn't immediately say anything. Assessing me, I suppose.

Papa Lacroix wasn't what I expected in a high-end New York City gangland crime boss. I figured he'd be a huge, tattooed Haitian with beaded long hair like Charles, his suit barely containing his bulging muscles, and maybe some blood under his fingernails from last night's Fight Club incident or something. But he was an older gent in his seventies, of average height, with a balding pate, a white beard, and a nice suit.

His eyes, though, passed over us keenly, and I saw a dangerous young man inside the dangerously powerful elderly man. "Charles told me you have important information." He spoke with only the vaguely ghost of an accent. "Be aware that if you are lying, young man, you won't walk out of here. I may be old, but I am not above putting you into the ground." He glanced at Antonia. "Either of you."

I didn't appreciate him threatening a lady, but I held my temper in check. "He told you what I told him?"

"Correct. But I want to hear it from you."

The little old man moved out from behind his desk and sauntered up to me, eyeing me in that wizened way that said he took no shit from anyone no matter how tall or young they were. After a moment's consideration, he added, "Whoever you are."

He was requesting my credentials, but I planned to be a bit cagier than that. He wouldn't believe me anyway. "I'm nobody," I told him. "Just a concerned citizen."

Squinting up at me, he said, "Is that so, boy?"

I started to say something to that, but for some reason, my attention went past him and up toward the mantel. I forgot what I was going to say.

After a moment of uncomfortable silence, he held up a shaky finger. "Be aware that the only reason I am even entertaining this audience is that you have the *kouraj* to tell me such a ludicrous story."

I didn't believe him. If he didn't believe me, he would have thrown us out already. Or killed us.

But I decided to humor him. Tearing my eyes away from his collection of chachkis, I said, "Your alliance with the Archangel Michael..." That made him start "...that was an exceedingly bad idea, Mr. Lacroix. It's a losing proposition. He's only using you to help him distribute that poison you call a drug."

I saw in his rheumy, yellowing eyes that he believed me. He knew I knew.

He put a hand in his pocket where he probably had a knife. Maybe even an athame that Michael had given him. I wouldn't put it past him. I glared at his hand, then up at his face. He took it out like he was embarrassed.

"I have an athame, too. Charles took it," I explained. I made a circuit of the room, studying his things. All under the watchful eye of Charles, of course. "And I would like it back before I leave. It was a gift from my granddad, Ha-Shaitan."

"Your granddad," he said, sounding incredulous. Then he laughed. "Ha-Shaitan? You playin' me, boy?"

I shook my head. "I'm the current guy in charge of the Lake of Fire and all that happy crappy. Which is why I know what you're playing with is dangerous..." As I neared the mantel, I stumbled on what I was saying and it took me a moment to get my attention back to what I was saying. I hoped I wasn't having a seizure. I did take my meds the night before. "What you're distributing is going to bite you on the ass, man. All you're doing is helping Michael distribute displaced angel souls and..."

My eyes went up again and settled on the trinkets on the mantel. I had the oddest feeling of déjà vu...

Papa Lacroix ignored my lapse. He looked flustered. "Who the hell *are* you, boy?"

Again, I forced my attention back to the man. But before I could answer, he called out for Charles.

"Take this playa out back and ice him, will you? We're finished here."

Charles, plus three others, suddenly poured into the room and surrounded us on all sides. Three of them grabbed me by the arms, pinning them to my back, while one grabbed Antonia. Since my companion was Quantico-trained and knew a fair amount of mixed martial arts, I knew one guy on her was definitely underestimating her, but she didn't resist. She just looked at me for the signal to do something.

I shook my head. I didn't want her resisting just yet. I was afraid they would just shoot her on the spot, especially if they rifled through her coat and discovered she was with the FBI...

The other three guys hauled me back toward the door. I started to struggle, which made it hard for them all to hang on. I look pretty strong, but I'm even stronger than I look. All those human and angel genes had mixed down in such a way that I was capable of quick bursts of tremendous strength. They didn't last, but I didn't usually need them to. Turning, I flung one guy off me. He hit the smoking couch so hard he bounced off and slammed to the floor. One arm free, I turned and decked the second guy right in the face. He flew all the way across the room and hit an antique curio cabinet, smashing it to bits. The items inside—they looked like a combination of glass and porcelain—imploded and then vomited out of the cabinet in a glass-and-porcelain slurry.

"Holy fuck!" the third guy said in my ear, which was pretty funny when you thought about it.

Clenching my hands into fists, I swung around to face him, simultaneously breaking his hold on my arm. I almost punched him through a wall before I saw his face and stopped dead in my tracks. He was a young kid in his early twenties. He was wearing a baggy sports shirt, basketball shorts, and designer sneakers. His hat was twisted sideways on his head, partly obscuring his face, which is why I hadn't recognized him until I was staring him straight in the eye.

"Troy?" I said.

He looked at me funny as he came to fully realize who I was. Then he withdrew his hands like he was touching fire and backed up a step. "Nick! Oh, hell no!"

Before he got too far, I reached out and grabbed a bunch of his shirt, hauling him closer. The toes of his sneakers dragged along the hardwood floor with a loud squeak. "What the hell are you doing here? Does Althea know you work for this chump?" I cocked my head back toward the Big Kahuna.

Troy scrunched up his face. "Fuck no she doesn't! You crazy?"

I pushed him back against a wall where he bounced and gave him a stern look. "Stay."

"Fuck off, man."

"Stay or I tell Aunt Althea."

That stopped Troy. The last thing he needed was Auntie on his case.

Papa Lacroix, now thoroughly confused, looked back and forth between us before barking orders at Troy. "Take him, boy! Take that motherfucka outta here!"

But Troy stayed where I'd put him.

I swung around and approached the man, my fists aching to turn his face into soup. "You have *Troy* working for you, old man?"

Troy, meanwhile, was trying to edge around the doorway.

I turned back and snapped, "Stay!"

He stopped and glowered at me. He knew Aunt Althea's wrath all too well.

In the meantime, I went up to Papa Lacroix, put him in a restraining hold, thanks to my training by the NYC PD, and pushed his face down on his desk. "Tell Charlie Brown over there to let Antonia go."

He muttered something into his blotter. I shook him. He repeated what I'd said.

Charles, looking unsure but at a loss as to what to do, let Antonia go, who slid away from him and joined me at my side.

I leaned down to whisper savagely in Lacroix's ear. "I came here as a courtesy, but now I'm not feeling so charitable. Listen up, chump. Stop your production of Z-Quil immediately. Get it off the streets and out of Pennsylvania. And after you finish doing that, tell Michael I was here and he can take it up with me if he doesn't like the new plan. If you don't do those things, I will return, and I will fuck up this whole nice house of yours." I shook him again so he understood, then stood up and marched through the debris to the door, Antonia in tow.

On my way out, I grabbed my cousin Troy by the back of the collar and dragged him from the room. "*You* are coming with me."

"Fuck off, man!"

So I stopped and glared at him and reminded him of my promise to tell Aunt Althea. That shut him up. I walked him down the hallway to the front door. When he tried to resist going down the stairs, I squeezed the back of his neck. He saw what I'd done to that dude. He was suddenly very compliant.

When the three of us got safely back to the car, I told Troy to get in the backseat.

Antonia, brows knitted, said, "Is he really your cousin?" She looked at the young Black man sulking in the back seat of the Monaco. I mean, I got it. There wasn't a whole lot of family resemblance between us—except, maybe, Troy's penchant for being in the absolute wrong place at the wrong time. That was definitely a family attribute.

"My idiot cousin Troy, yeah," I said, adjusting the review mirror so I could keep an eye on him. "Let's get the hell out of here."

| 11 |

All in the Family

THINGS HAD NOT gone to plan. Then again, with me, they seldom do. Man plans and God laughs, as my Yiddish friends say. David used to say that.

"You have a lot of fucking nerve, Nick," Troy grumbled from the backseat. "I was working, man."

"Working with Papa Lacroix, a known gangster?"

"What do you care?"

I snorted. "I suppose you never considered how this would break Aunt Althea's heart?"

"Like you care about Nana."

I ignored his jab. "Working for a criminal, Troy? Really?"

"It's not Troy. It's T-Dawg."

I rolled my eyes.

Antonia, looking uncomfortable, asked that I drop her off at the coven's apartment in Hell's Kitchen so she could work on perfecting the spell she had found. I really couldn't blame her for not wanting to get in the middle of my stupid family drama, so I told her I would.

After we were back on the road, and Troy and I were alone, my cousin said, "Where we goin'?"

"I should take you to jail," I joked. "But that's too soft. We're going to see Aunt Althea."

I expected him to give me shit about that, but he grunted instead. Then he kicked my seat. After that, he took out his phone and seemed glued to the game he was playing the whole time. Criminals and cops were one thing. Weathering Aunt Althea's wrath was a whole other ball of wax.

My aunt, who ran a café on Restaurant Row for years, lived in a posh little two-bedroom unit on Eighth Avenue in Harlem. It wasn't huge but she had raised two kids and one grandkid (Troy) in it after Troy's parents died in a car crash many years ago. When I got to the brownstone, I got out, opened the back seat, and told Troy to let us in.

"Nana's not in, you know. She's working today," Troy insisted, sticking his lip out at me childishly.

"Then we'll wait for her." I indicated the door to the building's lobby.

Looking upset but unwilling to push his luck, Troy used his keycard and we took the curvy, rainbow-painted stairwell up to his floor. Before we even reached the door, my first cousin Kiara poked her head out.

"Troy, where you been, boy?" she hollered at him, then stopped when she saw me walking behind him. "Nick. Weren't expecting *you*, sugar."

"I didn't expect to be here," I told her as I reached her. I gave her a hug and she held on for several seconds. Then she ushered us both in but put a finger to her lips. "Lil' Nick's down for his nap."

I nodded as I closed the door. I'd heard Kiara had a boy about six months ago. She'd spent most of her young life in graphic design, got married about a year ago, then divorced six months later. She was closer to my age, so hers was definitely a late-in-life baby, but she'd gotten through it with flying colors from what my Facebook stalking told me. I'd sent her a congratulations card and a dreamcatcher I'd enchanted, but otherwise, I hadn't spoken to her in years.

Truthfully, I hadn't spoken to any of my family on this side for what seemed forever. Five years ago, Kiara arranged a family reunion, the first one in decades. She held it on the patio out back and insisted—nay, commanded—that I show up "at least for an hour."

I'd dutifully dropped in, spoken briefly to Aunt Althea and a couple of my cousins, and then vamoosed when I figured I could get away without anyone noticing. I'm not one for being self-conscious, but it just felt strange to be the only white guy hanging in the corner, trying hard to be invisible, though I knew my passing for white wasn't all of it.

There was a lot of stuff between me and my family. A lot of unresolved issues.

Now, Kiara, who had always liked me for reasons unknown to me, insisted in a whisper that I sit down and have a coffee with her. She was using that same voice she'd used to invite me to the family reunion—less an invite and more a command. I watched Troy sulk his way down the hallway to his room, then joined Kiara at the kitchen counter bar.

She was still the lanky tall girl I remembered playing with when I was nine years old. She had a flurry of cornrows and her makeup was on point, including a lot of gold eye shadow and silver lipstick. She hardly seemed to have aged, which was good because I figured I could use genes to explain why I never seemed to change much.

Putting a coffee cup down in front of me, she said, "Mama will be back in an hour. She just went to work to handle some business. Something about a stove breaking. She's retired now, you know."

"Oh," I said, taking a sip. "I didn't know."

"Still has her hands full with you-know-who." She tossed her head back to indicate the closed bedroom door at the end of the hallway. "What he do now?"

"Do you really want to know?"

"No," she said, sipping her own coffee. "Hell no."

The baby started crying, and Kiara rushed to get him. "Nick," she said, coming back out, "meet Lil Nick." She waved Lil Nick's tiny hand at me.

Nick is an old family name—our great-grandfather's. So no, Kiara didn't name him after me.

For the next hour, I got to play with Lil' Nick and Kiara caught me up on family gossip. Who was having a baby, who was on their way out. New diagnoses. And a lot of the same old.

When Aunt Althea bustled into the flat, I started to get up.

"Nick," she said in surprise when she saw me. Then she wiped all the emotion from her face and asked noncommittally, "How you been, chile?"

She looked strangely shrunken and beaten down, which surprised me. She used to be such a powerfully built woman, keen of mind and strong of opinion.

Aunt Althea was my mom's and my Aunt Josephine's sister. All three girls had been born with a fair amount of talent in the craft, but my mom quickly outpaced her two sisters. I think it scared them both—or maybe their jealousy got in the way. I never quite figured that out, but there was definitely bitter blood between them.

Then my mom met my father. Neither my Aunt Jo nor my Aunt Althea liked him (no surprise there). And when my mom disappeared when I was six, they blamed him, naturally—not that I could blame them. The police did nothing, of course. My mom was Black and no one cared that a young Black woman had disappeared, leaving behind a five-year-old boy.

That was a scary period. I remembered missing my mom and thinking she would return—or that my dad would show up to take me away to be reunited with her, which never happened. I remember my two grief-stricken aunts fighting about what would happen to me and who would take me in. Aunt Althea was getting married at the time and was reluctant to take on a child, so my Aunt Jo stepped in, though she vowed never to speak to Aunt Althea again. They had a terrific row about it. Then Aunt Jo died a year later—a bad heart—and I went into foster care.

For years afterward, I waited for someone to come for me. No one ever did.

"Hi, Aunt Althea," I told her. I kept my voice level as I stood up. I had Lil Nicky half-asleep on my shoulder, where he seemed right at home. "I just swung by to drop off Troy. I was just leaving."

"Troy's in trouble again. Don't ask," Kiara put in as she cleared the counter of cups.

Althea looked at me long and hard for a full ten seconds before saying, "Stay, Nick. Please."

Things were getting awkward, and I wanted to get out of there. I had nothing to discuss with my aunt and I figured Antonia was probably hoping I'd get back so we could work on her spell. But Kiara, a natural peacekeeper, leaned across the counter and grabbed my hand. "Mama will make you one fine dinner if you stay." She looked over. "Right, Mama?"

Althea nodded. "Sure will."

I hated being pressured, but I always did everything Kiara asked me to do. I'd even showed up at that stupid family reunion. So I gave them a brief nod, then turned to Kiara. "You want me to put Lil Nicky back down? He looks tired."

"Sure! Follow me." Kiara walked me back to her room.

After I put Lil Nicky back in his crib for a snooze, I noticed an easel set up in the corner with an extra-large board and pictures and documents pinned all over it. I thought it was a vision board until I looked at it more closely in the dimness of the room.

"That's my pet project," Kiara whispered as she shoved some baby clothes back into a highboy. "I've been tracing our people back to where we were taken." She pointed to some printed documents she'd pinned up. "So far, I've traced our family back to the Massachusetts Bay Colony. We were house servants there, mostly, but some of the men worked the fields, too."

"Huh," I said, squinting at the ship documents. "Slaves to the Puritans."

"Yeah," she said, folding her arms. "Figures, eh? So much for their high Christian ideas. I think they took us from Barbados, but I haven't gotten that far yet."

I looked over the work that Kiara had done. It was impressive. "This is so cool. You missed your calling, Ki."

"I can keep you up on what I find. I'll invite you to the private Facebook group I created for the fam."

I felt flattered but shrugged. I didn't want her to think I was looking to reconnect with too many of my family members. "I mean, if you want..."

She grabbed my arm and looked up at me sternly as she walked me out of the nursery. "I know this family's been hard on you, Nick, but you're still a Wodehouse. You are still one of us—whether *they* like it or not."

I smiled down at her. "Thanks." That meant a lot to me.

Back in the kitchen, Aunt Althea was cooking up a storm. I knew her café specialized in Creole and Caribbean food and that it was a passion of hers. She was making Louisiana-style fried chicken, red beans and rice, and Southern biscuits. I told her she didn't have to put herself out, but she insisted she had to make dinner, so why not add "a lil' sumin-sumin," as she liked to say.

She turned to Kiara and asked if Lil' Nicky was down.

"For the count!" she proclaimed in victory. "I think Nick wore him out."

"Can you get me some seasonings from down the street, chile? I'll watch the baby."

"Sure, Mama," my cousin said and grabbed her coat and purse. She winked at me in encouragement.

Since I knew Auntie always kept a stocked pantry, I had a feeling she just wanted a few moments alone with me, which made me nervous.

Once Kiara was gone, Aunt Althea said, "What he do now?" just the same as Kiara, regarding Troy.

I might have been a cop, but I was never a snitch. Feeling a pang of loyalty for my idiot cousin—I'd been young once and done some pretty fucking stupid things, too—I folded my arms, leaned against the pantry door, and said, "I found him wandering around Long Island like some lost sheep. Didn't want him getting into anything."

"Mmm-hmm..." said Aunt Althea. It was pretty obvious she didn't believe me, but to her credit, she didn't push for more.

Then she looked up from the biscuits she was cutting out and said, "It's good to see you, Nicky. Been too long."

I sort of smiled. "Want me to talk to Troy? Put the fear of God into him?"

She thought about that. "Yeah. I knows you can. You good at that."

I nodded and started off to his room, but she surprised me by turning and saying, "I knows I owe you an apology, Nicky."

That stopped me dead in my tracks. The kitchen was filling up with some great aromas, which relaxed me. I wasn't quite as stiff and on alert as I was when I first stepped into the flat. "What do you mean?" I asked, turning around

She wiped her hands on her apron and stared down at her biscuits for a long moment. I could tell this made her uncomfortable. That, in turn, made me uncomfortable. But before I could shrug it off, she suddenly piped up. "I shoulda been there for you. And for Willa. I wasn't. It's been bothering me sumthin' awful lately."

Meeting my eyes, she added, "I know it was Willa who had the sight, but I'm not without. This whole family comes from a long line of cunning folk. You know that, right?"

"I do." I waited to let her explain.

Her eyes moved analytically. "Sumthin' bad comin', Nick, and I been thinking a lot about the past, some stuff I coulda done better. A lot of my mistakes was family shit. Neither Aunt Jo or I did right by Willa."

"It's all water under the bridge, Auntie."

"Is it?" She bit her lips and stared at her feet. "Because you ain't never said nothin' 'bout it. Even during the reunion…"

I thought about her words before saying, "I know you had your reasons. And things were pretty jacked up back then. Hell, you were practically a kid at the time."

"Still." Her eyes went back up and refocused on me. "You was family. I shoulda done more." I saw tears forming in her eyes, which upset me. She turned away quickly to pat her eyes with her apron, then put her biscuits in the oven. "I shouldna put all that on Jo."

"No one knew Aunt Jo was sick. Not even Jo," I argued. "Anyway, it all worked out."

"Did it?"

I spread my arms. "Here I am. Alive and talking to you. I made it through."

"Still…"

I knew what she meant. I'd had a problematic upbringing and had gotten into trouble. A lot of it. She expected me to blame her for that. But I wasn't a grudgey kind of guy. Anyway, I have always felt I was captain of my own boat. Yeah, I'd sailed it onto some sharp rocks from time to time, but I always found my way out in the end.

I think I was still feeling raw from my loss of David. I didn't want to leave this place with bad blood between the two of us. I didn't want another long lapse of avoiding reunions, parties, and invitations. So I approached Aunt Althea. She only flinched a little when I wrapped my arms around her and kissed the top of her head. "I really am happy to see you, Auntie."

She grabbed my arm with both hands. "Me, too. And I need you to know it was never 'cause you passed for White. That weren't it." She hesitated and I drew back to look at her distraught face. She was playing with the little gold cross around her neck. I'd seen several of them throughout the place. "It weren't that at all. I was just so afraid of *him*, Nick. Your daddy…well, let's just say he scared the Jesus out of me. That ain't an excuse, but it's an explanation."

I smiled at that. "I know." I gave her another kiss before going down the hall to talk to Troy.

* * *

My cousin was playing video games at his desk when I tapped his door open.

He told me to go away. I went inside, instead.

His was a small room but packed with his stuff. A narrow bed, his desk, and a basket of folded laundry in one corner. He had a lot of old retro posters on the walls—movies from the 1970s with Sonny Chiba and Bruce Lee in them. I knew he'd taken Taekwondo some years ago.

"Man, get the fuck out!" he growled, throwing an old action figure at me. "I don't need you making shit bad between me and Nana..."

I caught the action figure before it collided with my head, then put a finger to my lips and closed his door. "She doesn't know about Papa Lacroix," I explained when we were alone. "If you don't want her knowing, I suggest you lower your voice."

He looked at me suspiciously.

I leaned against the door and looked at the figure in my hands. It was the classic WWE wrestler Junkyard Dog—one of my favorite old-school wrestlers. It made me think. Admittedly, I'd never had kids, so I knew jack-all about talking to them, but I'd been a kid once. I'd been on the path that Troy was on now. I figured I could use that.

But before I could even open my mouth, Troy started in on me.

"Man, I know!" he said in a loud whisper. "Don't mess with Lacroix. He gonna get you plugged, boy. Message received. I got it. Now you can fuckin' leave, man."

I slowly let out my breath. "Got it all figured out, huh? I was going to say don't mess with Lacroix. But not because he's gonna get you killed. Not *him*."

Troy went back to his shoot-em-up game, then swiveled back around. "Then who?"

I pointed to a poster on his wall. It was for some old martial arts movie with a cop taking down a bunch of ninjas.

"What, ninjas?"

I gave him a droll look. "You know I was a cop, so you know I know what I'm talking about, Troy."

"The pigs? Well, shit, I know that. I don't need no white bread preaching me down."

I wondered if he was using that term because it was back in vogue or if he'd seen too many old movies. "If you knew that," I pointed out, "then you wouldn't have been there."

Troy opened his mouth, closed it. For the moment, he was out of quippy one-liners and insults.

I went to put Junkyard Dog back on the shelf over his bed. "Papa Lacroix is allying himself with some pretty bad dudes, Troy, and his expiration date is due. It's only a matter of time before the Feds take him down. Or his own people. You wanna be in that house when a bunch of jacked-up uniforms kick in the door? Because I guarantee you that you'll be on the floor with a cop's knee in your neck."

Troy swallowed. I let that sink it a moment before delivering the coup de gras. "You want that shit on a body cam for your nana to watch over and over again? You want Kiara to see that? You want a memorial? To be some statistic on the internet? Because you're heading that way."

Slowly, Troy got to his feet. He was sweating and he glared at me like he wanted to hit me. His hands slowly balled into tight fists.

I held my ground. I knew I was right. So did he.

Little by little, Troy's posture relaxed. He relaxed his fists.

I hoped I'd done enough. Put the fear of God into him, at least.

"Just think about it," I told him before I left his room.

* * *

I went out back and called Antonia, but she said she needed a few more hours to perfect the spell she was working on and hoped I'd take a little time to hang with my fam (her words exactly). I didn't know if she telling the truth or not, but I assured her I would.

When I went back in, I told Aunt Althea I was taking her up on her offer for dinner—which was amazing.

It was a nice family meal, accompanied only by small talk. We didn't broach any more uncomfortable subjects. Kiara asked me who I'd phoned, and I told them about Antonia. Both women were ecstatic about that. Aunt Althea promised to send me home with plenty of vittles for "my girl."

Halfway through dinner, Troy crept out of his room to sit with us briefly before taking dessert—one of my Auntie's key lime pie slices—back to his room. Aunt Althea watched him slink off.

"Whatever you said to him—thanks, Nick," she told me.

I stuck a bite of key lime pie in my mouth and chewed slowly to savor it before telling her, "He's a good kid. He's just missing his mom and dad."

There were tears in her eyes. She knew I knew what I was talking about.

She gave me a tight hug when I told her I had to run. Kiara hugged me even tighter and reminded me to check my FB so I could join her private Wodehouse Family group. And she said to not be such a stranger.

I promised her I would not.

"I will send you more info about the ancestors," she promised.

I told her I couldn't wait, got into my car, waved to my fam, and drove away with a little more hope in my heart than I'd had when I arrived.

| 12 |

Cluster**ck

I HAD DECIDED I wanted to buy Antonia a little something for all the hard work had been putting into this. I felt she had more than earned it, putting up with me. The problem was, I didn't know her well enough to know what she'd want, and I was adamantly against getting her some random thing for the sake of presenting something. The challenge dogged me as I drove back toward Hell's Kitchen.

Then I spotted the occult shop near Union Square. It was squished between a Spirit's Halloween and an adult bookshop. I parked in the lot behind and went in.

It was huge but dimly lit. Shelves and shelves of gifts and magic paraphernalia surrounded me in a large labyrinth that led to the vast display cases that made up the checkout counter. It certainly made our little shop on Main Street in Blackwater look like amateur hour. But I didn't feel too bad when I spotted the guy manning the cash register. He was a dumpy little fellow with a goatee and a balding pate dressed in some kind of cheap black robe, a large rhinestone pentacle hanging around his neck. He didn't even look twice while

I perused the jewelry under the glass, which told him he wasn't just a poseur witch, but one with no real interest in selling anything.

The trinkets they were selling were lame costume junk, but when I got to the display spinner where some books, games, and divination tools were on display, I spotted a set of Tarot cards with an African Orisha theme, and even though they weren't expensive, they spoke to me. I felt it was something Antonia, as a budding witch, would appreciate.

I was on my way back to the car when the call came in.

Unknown number.

"Englebrecht," I said and was rewarded with several seconds of uncomfortable silence.

Then a nauseatingly familiar basso said into my ear, "Greetings, Spawn of Ha-Shaitan."

I felt a cold finger go up my back. I slid into the car while all the hair on my body stood at sudden attention. The sound of that voice scared the shit out of me, no lie. But I was determined not to wuss out now that I'd come this far.

"Michael," I said in a steady voice. "You're a hard man to find."

"I am not a man."

Leave it to an archangel to have zero sense of humor.

With a tinge of surprise in his voice, Michael said, "You're afraid."

"You put me through a wall the last time we met, so, sure. I'm not stupid."

"I should have ended you then. But I had my orders."

I laughed nervously at that. "Are you telling me your boss told you to spare me?"

He ignored my question and answered with only a long, breathy pause. "Why are you, half-creature, threatening my servants? Why are you asking to see me?"

"Why are you putting your angel cronies into human beings?"

Another long pause. "None of this concerns you, child. In honor of your grandfather, whom I fought behind, I will let you live if you stay out of it."

I thought about that a long, hard moment. I could walk away. Let Malach handle this clusterfuck of his. But that would mean abandoning Cassie. And I just couldn't do that and call myself a man.

"No. You woke the hellhound. Now I'm on your trail, bud."

Michael laughed uproariously at that. "You are full of fear of me, and yet you are ready to fight me." He muttered something in Divine that I couldn't quite follow. "I think I like you! You are brave, Daemon. Foolish, but very, very brave."

I started to say something, but Michael quickly added, "If you meet me at my servant's house tomorrow night, I will entertain whatever it is you have to say. If you entertain me *enough*, I may not even kill you. We shall see."

The line went dead in my ear.

***

I felt a great heaviness when I got back to the apartment in Hell's Kitchen.

"Nick." Antonia swept toward me and gave me a brief hug before pecking me on the cheek in greeting. "I'm glad you're back. I want to show you..."

She stopped when she saw how concerned I was. "What's wrong?"

I moved to the sofa, sat down, and told her about my conversation with Michael.

"That's good news, isn't it?" she said, sitting on the arm of the sofa. "I mean, you'll be able to get this nasty business over with, and then we can get back to Blackwater."

I nodded. "It is." I didn't want to add that Michael would most likely kill me tomorrow night, but I felt I owed her the whole story. So I told her about my first run-in with the creep, and what he said during our conversation.

She looked down upon me, her face pale. "Can he do that? I mean, isn't that going to unbalance the universe or something? I thought you were the sentinel of free will?"

I thought about that. "I'm not sure he really cares about that anymore. I can feel in my bones he has this great big scheme going. He's making hybrids for a reason. And honestly, I think he just wants me out of his way." I didn't add that he'd given me the option of running because I was already regretting my rash decision to take him head-on—and that made me ashamed. It made me feel like a coward.

Simply put, I was more than a little afraid of Michael ending me, and I was pretty sure he could. I didn't know what would happen if the current Lucifer was destroyed with no one to pass his legacy on to, and, more profoundly, I had no idea what would happen to me. I didn't even know if I had a soul or not.

I didn't know what it was like to be told you had a terminal disease, but I figured it probably felt like this.

Antonia bit her bottom lip. "What can I do?"

I put my hand on her knee. "I'd like to spend some time with you later, but right now, is it okay if I have a little time to myself?"

"Of course." She looked at me, fraught with worry. "I'll be upstairs."

After she was gone, I thought about what was important. Then I thought about what I wanted.

I wanted to talk to my friends and family. I wanted that very much.

The first person I called was Morgana. She was a little harried from working the shop by herself, but she did inquire as to whether

I was all right. I didn't tell her about Michael's threat or what was going down tomorrow night. We passed some nice pleasantries, and I told her about the shop I'd visited near Union Square. I told her about some ideas I had for our business. I knew the deli next door was going up for sale. She was intrigued by the idea of expanding, buying up more space, and offering more merchandise and services. "You mean an interconnected shop where I could do readings and seances?" she asked, intrigued. I knew it was something she'd dreamed of for a while now.

"Yeah. I could run the shop and you can prey on desperate widows," I joked, and she actually laughed at that, because she knew I didn't mean it the way I'd stated it. She really was talented.

"I'll think about it and look into the details of the sale next door," she told me before she signed off.

The next one I called was Vivian, asking about her vampire problem.

"Well, that got complicated, but I figured it out. You're in for some surprises when you visit," she said, not-so-subtlety reminding me that I did indeed promise to come up and see her soon.

"Let me guess. You're now Queen of the Vampires."

"Something like that," she laughed.

Finally, I gave Aunt Althea a call and told her that I would like to come up for Thanksgiving in a few weeks if that would be all right with her. She was ecstatic and gave me a rundown of the menu she had already begun constructing. I didn't think I'd be around for it, frankly, but it was fun to talk about it. She said Lil' Nicky missed me already.

The last call I made was to Malach. I told him to get ready. We would be facing Michael tomorrow night. He said he would be there, and that he was impressed with the work I had done on this case.

"He's coming in hot," I warned the soldier angel. "Be on your toes."

"We will take him together, Nick. No worries," he said before he hung up.

* * *

Antonia came down the spiral stairs, the tools she needed to complete her spell jostling around in the duffle bag at her side. I was waiting for her at the bottom. I didn't have any tools or weapons to take. The Morning Star was the only thing that could destroy an angel. By hook or by crook, I was going to give it the best shot I could.

She set the bag on the floor and let out her breath.

"Okay?" I asked.

Another deep breath and she nodded. She was dressed in her FBI uniform, her hair scraped back into a tight bun on the back of her head. Her eyes were dire and a little red-rimmed. I thought she might have been crying.

When she'd taken her deep breath, her jacket had moved and I'd noted her piece. She saw me looking and swept her hand over her holster. "I know it won't hurt an angel, but it could prove useful if Lacroix or that big bruiser stands in our way."

"You can hang back, you know," I told her, wanting her to have the opportunity to walk away without any shame or hard feelings. "It won't change the way I feel about you. This shit is dangerous on a level even I'm not used to."

To her credit, I saw her thinking about it. "I could. But this is the life I've chosen. If I hang back now, I'll do it later, too, when I'm a fully-fledged agent. And what good will I be then?"

I wanted to say *at least you'll be alive*, but I got what she was saying.

She put a hand on my wrist. "I'll be careful. If I'm out of my league, you'll see my dust. Promise."

I nodded, and we loaded everything into the Monaco. I drove automatically and in total silence to Long Island and stopped the car at the gates of Papa Lacroix's house. The estate was lit with a series of security lights, including several floodlights over the gates. I noticed they were partly slid back on their track, obviously unlocked.

"Huh," I said, looking around. "That's very odd."

I tried the intercom but got only static. No menacing voice. No one answered at all.

Antonia scanned the grounds. "I'd say they weren't home, but I'm pretty sure Lacroix doesn't leave his gate unlocked."

"Noticed that, huh?"

I had a bad feeling already. Getting out of the idling vehicle, I slid the gate back with no resistance.

Antonia got out, too. She had her gun in her hand and cased the property in the front. "It's probably a trap."

"Maybe. But Michael would anticipate I'd know that, so it seems counterproductive."

"We going in?"

"Not yet." I didn't care for the feel of this. It felt…off. I'd had a sudden revelation. Picking up my phone, I dialed a familiar number.

It only rang twice before Grampa picked up.

"Doing anything special today?" I asked.

"What's come up, my boy?"

I caught him up on my sitch, including Michael's thinly-veiled threat to murderize me. "If you're not busy, I'd like a little backup."

"I can be there in ten minutes."

Antonia and I waited, keeping our eye on the house. But nothing on the property moved and there were only a few lights on. Not even a shadow stirred.

Grampa suddenly appeared near the Monaco. He was dressed in his leather coat with all of the fancy knives on the inside, but this time, he wore leather trousers and a Slayer T-shirt, which was different. I assumed he'd flown.

As he walked up to us, he threw a knife up in the air repeatedly, catching it expertly each time. He indicated the long drive with the point of it. "Lead the way, grandson."

"Michael is going to try and end us," I warned.

But Grampa smiled. "He can try."

I liked how ballsy he was being. It gave me the confidence I needed to turn and face the manse. I led the charge, with Antonia just behind me and Grampa bringing up the rear. I felt so much stronger, having my family with us.

Antonia said, "Is that kid really your grandfather?"

I nodded as we approached the house and went up the wide, sweeping staircase to the front door. "But don't call him a kid. He's…well, I don't know how you calculate infinity." I tried the doorknob and found it unlocked.

"That's not good," Antonia said.

Grampa said, "I'm going to go around back."

"That's a good idea," I told him. "I'll see you inside."

He saluted me, spread his wings, and shot upward and out of sight.

It took Antonia a moment to gather her bearings. "Wow," she said, then shook her head. After a second, she moved in front of me, which surprised me.

"You are so much taller than me," she explained. "If you let me case, you can use your pokey stick to draw fire. Michael will be looking for you. Aiming high, amiright?"

Her plan impressed me. "Sounds good." I manifested the bident, reassured my hold on it, and indicated that Antonia should go ahead of me. Being shorter, she was naturally less of a target.

We moved as silently as possible through the manor, passing through room after room. When we reached the study, I took the lead and went inside, the bident pointing outward. But it was curiously empty. The curio cabinet was still in a heap, and no one had bothered to pick up the debris. I scanned the room for any presence, human or otherwise, but it was dead silent. Too soon, my gaze was drawn to the mantel, now cold, the fire having long gone to ash. The black Buddha was still there, and that gave me a sense of relief for some reason.

"Nick!"

I turned just in time to spy a shadow moving through the corridor behind us, but the quick glimpse I'd had of it wasn't enough for me to determine if it was human or not. It disappeared around a corner and into the foyer. Turning, I pursued it down the hall, but it stayed just on the periphery of my vision.

I came out of the corridor and into the foyer, fully expecting to see something. To the right was a sweeping staircase that went all the way up into the darkness of the second story. Ahead of me was the front door. The shadow had flickered up the stairs, I was sure. I started going up but spied Grampa emerging from one of the other rooms. He was faintly frightening with his glowy eyes, but as soon as he stepped out and into the muted uplights of the foyer, I saw he had a wry smile on his face. "See that?"

"Yeah, I did." I started up the stairs, the bident at the ready. In retrospect, it was a really stupid mistake on my part. I should have taken one of the others as a backup because before I even reached the top, I caught a flicker of movement from the corner of my eye, and then something leaped catlike at me from the darkness of one of the side rooms.

The thing was roaring, its tongue sticking out, and I realized in that split second that it was some kind of half-creature with the head of a man—that man being Charles, Papa Lacroix's heavy—the body of a large golden cat, and four wings going in opposite directions. A creature in transition. Mutating. Charles—possessed by a cherubim. My mind processed all that in a matter of microseconds. I didn't want to kill him, so I did something very dangerous and stupid and shifted the bident back so Charles wouldn't fall upon the tines.

That left me open, and the hybrid collided with my shoulder instead. I yelped; it roared. Both of us went backward, my legs folding underneath me. The world went topsy-turvy as we wheeled down the long, curved staircase, the angel's claws in my shirt and the flesh of my shoulder, its foul breath in my face, and my back hitting the wall, the stairs, and the railing as we tumbled down. The pain was sudden and startling. Thankfully, at the bottom, I fell on top of the creature, which broke my fall. I'm not flyweight, so that seemed to stun it, and for several struggling seconds, it failed to attack me with its claws. I was able to roll off it and to the stone floor of the foyer.

A lot of stuff happened after that. I was in too much pain to get up immediately, but the angel had crawled to its feet, its head hanging. It was pretty banged up. It started limping toward the front door, but Antonia got there first and locked and bolted it, then sprang away before it could reach her and swipe a paw at her. Her eyes were bright and horrified, but to her credit, she didn't scream or lose it, though I wouldn't have blamed her if she had.

Grampa moved into a position behind the cherubim to box it in, knives in both hands, but the creature suddenly sprang back to life and turned on him, roaring and lashing out with its claws. Its human teeth couldn't do a lot of damage, but those huge, hooked, black claws could make mincemeat of even Grampa. Thankfully, he was pretty battle-hardened and lunged out of the way, cursing at it.

"Hold it!" I dragged my sorry ass up, but my knee was seriously screwed and wouldn't hold my weight. I had to drop the bident to grab the banister to haul myself up. Antonia, who had circled back to my side, bent to retrieve it, but I shouted, "Don't!"

She listened and snatched her hand back.

"It'll burn you if you touch it," I groaned through gritted teeth. I was in pain and didn't feel like explaining that only those of the Lucifer line can handle the Morning Star, but I think she understood.

She slid backward and said, "What can I do?" Then, before I could answer, she got an idea, pulled off her coat, and threw it on the bident, carefully picking it up with the fabric wrapped around the staff.

I was surprised by how well we were working together. No screaming or shouting. Grampa was holding the hybrid at bay with his knives. Antonia was getting me armed. We were working like a well-oiled, angel-defeating machine.

"Good idea." I took a step and almost crumpled but caught myself. There was something seriously wrong with my knee. I got in front of Antonia and grabbed the bident. I wasn't too steady, but I was determined to walk it off. "Can you support the back end?"

"Yeah, but this thing's fucking heavy."

"I know. Do your best."

She held up the back of the Morning Star while I got both hands wrapped around the silvery staff near the head of the weapon. This was going to be awkward.

"On three, we lunge."

We took off on three, me more limping mummy-movie-style than anything else. We crossed the foyer and closed in on the cherubim, still near the door.

Grampa saw us coming and sidestepped. In the last seconds, the cherubim spun around, roaring. It was freaky as hell, but I used all of my strength to drive the tines of the Morning Star at it, praying my aim wasn't crap.

And that's how we got the tines into the door to either side of the cherubim's neck, trapping it. I must have been stronger than I felt, because the door was one of those banded oaken things with the rounded tops and the rivets that you see decorating some of the fancier manses, and I'd driven the sharp tines halfway into the dense wood. The small blade that protruded between the two long tines of the Morning Star had stopped perilously close to Charles's Adam's apple.

Almost immediately, the hybrid began to struggle, wiggling like a worm on a hook as it tried to free itself. It both screamed and roared. I had to put my shoulder into the work of keeping it trapped. Antonia, meanwhile, stepped backward with a squeak of surprise.

I realized pretty quickly that my bum leg wasn't going to hold. We were either going to get the angel out of Charles or I was going to have to kill the hybrid. "Antonia...the spell!" I managed through clenched teeth.

"Y-yeah." She moved back where she would have more room to cast and stood there a second, breathing in and out. Once she had stopped trembling in absolute terror, she raised her hands and covered her eyes. I guessed it was part of the spell.

Grampa watched from a safe distance, interested.

The hybrid began to hiss and spat up this greenish gook onto my arms and the front of my sweater. It felt hot like acid. Some got on my face on the left side, but I dared not let go of the Morning Star to wipe it away. It smelled like sulfur and crackled on my skin. Ugh.

Antonia, meanwhile, was chanting in Divine, her hands still over her eyes—slowly at first, but soon with an increasing tempo. And the faster she chanted, the more agitated the hybrid became. Pretty soon, the thing was rocking and rolling against the front door, and its strength was so great, I found I was having trouble keeping it pinned. Each time it bucked, the tines of the Morning Star loosened and I lurched more than a little.

"Y'ai 'ng'ngah, cherubim, h'ee...L'geb f'ai throdog uaaah..." Antonia chanted, and then again, faster.

The spell grew, swirling around us like a cool breeze.

The hybrid began to scream and spit. Smoke poured off its weird, slimy golden skin. Its muscles twitched and *twisted* in unnatural ways like the world's worst Charley horse. It still had Charles's eyes, though, and they were round and full of pain and terror...

"Ogthrod ai'f geb'l...Ee'h cherubim 'ngah'ng ai'y zhro..." Antonia's chanting grew faster and faster, almost inhumanely so.

Pretty soon, the spell was less of a breeze and more of an arctic wind. The whole room dropped to sub-zero temperatures and a blast of cold air almost froze me on the spot.

Antonia continued to change in Angel-speak, but now great plumes of warm air were exiting her mouth, and I thought I spied a few snowflakes swirling around us.

Suddenly, the hybrid lurched so hard, I was almost thrown backward. The only thing that saved me was Grampa getting behind me and using his weight and considerable strength to hold me in place. My bad leg took the impact and I saw red for a second with the pain of it all.

"Hey," I whined through gritted teeth, "can you fast-forward this spell...?"

"I'm doing the best I can, Nick!" Antonia said and immediately went back to chanting.

Grampa leaned forward and whispered, "Hang in there, grandson. I think it's working."

"Awesomesauce," I said in absolute agony, tears flowing from my eyes with the pain. And now I was freezing on top of it all as the snowstorm raged around the three of us.

Another lurch, this one harder. The Morning Star was almost pushed from the door. The spell wasn't going fast enough, or the two of us just weren't strong enough.

"Stand back," I told Grampa, and he did. I manifested my wings and let the updraft from the spell drag me upward. I didn't know if it would work, but with one giant flap of all four wings, I shoved the bident deeper into the door—and almost beheaded poor Charles, who was wailing even as the spell, which had finally begun to work, was stripping the angel off of him in large and small pieces.

Charles looked like a cracked vase, the golden bits shedding off his skin to reveal his dark human skin underneath. I realized I was seeing parts of the cherubim being ripped off him and swirling around us all in a small, wintry cyclone. The bits of angel were screaming, though, and the sound of the angel's frustration was so loud I could barely hear Antonia's spell over it all. I did my best though, keeping the bident in place until the last of the angel was stripped away.

Only then—only after Charles stopped fighting me—did I relax my hold and float to the floor. Meanwhile, the cyclone of angel parts whirled around us, perhaps seeking a new host.

But my Grampa had that covered. He went down on his knees, spread his wings, and raised the knives in both of his hands, chanting something in angel-speak that I didn't understand. The screaming bits of angel did one more circuit around the room before burning up in the spell.

As soon as it was gone, the winds settled, the room warmed up, and Antonia dropped to the floor like a sack of flour.

| 13 |

The Angry Red Planet

I ASKED GRAMPA to take care of Antonia first, make sure she was comfortable and not in any distress, then come back to the study for me. He took her off to a sofa in the living room before returning to the study to scoot down the wall beside me.

"She's resting, but he's awake."

That was a huge relief to me. I nodded a thanks to him.

I was sitting on the floor behind the desk, my back to the mantel, the black Buddha in my hands. Sometime during the battle, it had fallen and cracked in half. I don't even know why I cared, but I cradled it in my lap, trying to keep the Buddha from crumbling. I was holding onto it as if it were a beloved childhood toy I'd once had.

Charles, who was passed out, was lying a few feet away. I kept checking his breathing and his pulse, and he seemed to be alive. I just didn't think he'd be coming around anytime soon.

Grampa said, "Let's see what happened." He reached for my injured leg, but I flinched and clutched the Buddha closer. For one dreadful moment, I thought he was going to take it from me.

"It's not broke, Nicky," he told me in a sibilant voice.

I told myself to stop acting like this and opened my hands. As I did so, the pieces of the Buddha fell away. Inside it was a perfectly round object that resembled a black pearl or a perfectly round onyx stone. It felt warm in my hands, almost...pulsing.

Grampa nodded at it. Before I could ask, he explained, "It's an angel egg. I haven't seen one of those in a millennium." Looking up, he added, "May I hold it?"

"Uh...sure." I handed it to him, and he held it up to the security lights filtering through the windows. It subtlety changed colors, going from pink to blue to yellow, and other colors I couldn't even describe. I thought I spied some kind of tadpole-like movement from inside but maybe I was imagining that.

"So...that's an angel? An angel...unborn."

"Looks that way," he answered, his voice soft and almost reverent. He ran his hand gently over its surface and it seemed to sing. The melody felt haunting familiar to me. "I wonder how that fool got a hold of you, little one." He admired it for several seconds before giving it back to me to hold. I put it in my lap, where it continued to sing.

"Angel song," he added.

I did the thing he did, running my hands over it. It seemed to respond. "It seems so strange that something so beautiful can grow into such ugly monsters."

Grampa grunted. "Now, let's see to you, my brave boy."

He took my leg in his lap and ran his hands over my knee, cradling it.

"Fucking ow," I said.

"You dislocated it."

"Terrific. Are you going to do that thing like in the movies? The one—two—"

I didn't get the rest out before he twisted my knee, snapping the joint back into place.

I screamed like a little girl and almost dropped the angel egg on the floor.

Grampa waited until I was done, all screamed out and panting with the after-pain. Then he said, "Better?"

I swallowed against the nausea the pain had driven up my throat. "I...I think so."

He crawled up beside me and sat there, looking at me and, periodically, the angel egg in my lap. "You know what, grandson?"

"What?" I croaked.

He pinched my cheek and smiled. "I think you'll live."

"Heh."

***

When I was strong enough, I got up to check on Antonia. She was already up and about, pacing in circles in the vast living room. She had her cell phone out. "I'm going to call this in to the local PD, let them sort things out." Then she added, "The magus said there are some of us working there, so they should be able to tackle any unanswerable questions. At least...I hope."

I nodded, trusting Antonia to take care of everything. Then I asked, "Are you okay?"

She seemed jittery and her hair looked almost electrified. "Yeah," she said, stepping up to me. "I think I'll be okay." She patted her wild locks. "I just don't want to do that a lot."

I smiled. "Me too."

"What's that?" she asked, looking down at the angel egg I was still clutching against my chest.

A stroke of paranoia went through me, which was, again, ridiculous. It wasn't like Antonia was going to take the egg. I wouldn't let her. "Grampa says it contains an unborn angel."

Her eyes grew wide. "Like...a baby angel?"

"That's what he said."

She finally pulled her eyes away and looked back up at me. "Are you going to destroy it?"

"What? No!"

Flinching, Antonia stepped back. It took me a moment to realize my wings had come out. I didn't mean to do that. I forced them away and said apologetically, "Sorry. I'm just tired from…everything."

She looked me over with concern, and I thought perhaps she was on the verge of asking me if I was all right, so I told her I needed to talk to my grandfather right quick. As I turned away, I made a vow to make it up to her tonight. I hadn't meant to scare her. But, right now, I needed to find Grampa and ask him more about the angel egg.

But by the time I returned to the study, I saw he wasn't there. I went to the torn-up foyer, but he wasn't there either. Off to kill more human-angel hybrids, I reckoned, though he'd left a note pinned to the door with one of his special knives.

Dear Nicky,

Take care of the angel egg. It's meant for you—though I doubt I have to tell you that. You have good instincts. Listen to them. And don't let the bastards get you down. You're my grandson. Rise above it all. You're much more than the sum of your parts. Remember that, if nothing else.

I'll see you soon.

Love,

Grampa

P.S. I am and always will be proud of you, my beautiful boy.

***

Since Malach and Michael were no-shows, we decided to beat feet while our luck was holding. But before we left the mansion, I decided to explore the upstairs. The half-transformed Charles had acted like a guard dog needing to keep strangers away from a favorite bone. I wanted to know what kind of bone he was guarding.

Upstairs, I found the corridor went all the way around the foyer, with a plethora of bedrooms, all of which seemed to be empty. The doors were all closed but for the one at the end, which was open a crack. I took a deep breath, now on high alert as I tapped the door fully open.

It creaked open on absolute darkness…and one of the worst smells I had ever encountered.

The master bedroom was large and dim, the drapes drawn against the smoky orange security lights at the front of the house. I was sure I would find someone dead up here, especially with the flies buzzing about, but when I scanned the room, I saw some quivering movement on the bed.

A low moaning—barely audible.

"Hey," I said, not wanting to startle whoever was there. I didn't think I could take another assault so close on the heels of the last. "Are you okay?"

More moaning.

I reached around on the wall until I found a seesaw light switch, but when I pressed it, only a small, dim light went on atop the antique highboy in the corner. It was enough, though. I picked my slow way across the room—mostly due to my slowly healing leg rather than any real caution. Thankfully, whoever was lying there didn't look fit enough to jump up and attack me.

The smell increased. I had to cover my nose.

When I was finally standing over the bed, I saw who it was.

Papa Lacroix lay here in his own filth, looking pale and drawn. There were a few plates of uneaten food on the large bedside table, all of them covered in insect life. He watched me with huge, moist, red-rimmed eyes, his mouth set in a permanent open tunnel of horror. I wondered if he had looked upon the half-transformed Charles and lost it, or if something more sinister was at play. Had Michael done something to him before pulling up stakes?

I tried to check his pulse, but he screamed so shrilly, I jerked my hand back.

"P-p-p-pla...." he whimpered.

I backed away in case my presence was setting him off. "What?"

His eyes roamed a moment before fixing on me. He managed to spit out, "O...O..."

"O?"

"O...si...si..."

It took me a moment to catch on. "Osiris?"

He nodded frantically. He was sweating bullets, and his fists were clenching and unclenching beside him on the pillow

I got a very bad feeling suddenly. By the time he managed to string the words together that he was struggling with, I was already backing away toward the door, a stripe of tingling fear going up my back as if someone was touching it with a sharp feather.

Downstairs, I limped back to Antonia and told her to get an ambulance for Lacroix, as well as the police. She nodded and picked up her phone.

I wrapped the angel egg in my coat and decided to get out of that house of horrors, but I only made it to the driveway before I was forced to hunker down. Osiris. *The Angry Red Planet.* Somehow, Papa Lacroix knew about that godforsaken planet of hellish misery. I clutched the egg in my arms and worked on not having a panic attack.

| 14 |

The Greater Arcana

THE FIRST THING I did when I got back to the loft in Hell's Kitchen was sink onto the leather horseshoe sofa, a bag of ice on my knee, and text Malach. I'd called him three times already, and each time, it went to voicemail.

Where the fuck were you?

Nothing.

So I sent an even angrier text.

If you don't fucking answer me, I will come up to that cabin and beat the ever-loving feathers out of you.

That did it. A few seconds later, Malach texted back.

Don't come up here. Just walk away, Nick.

"Like hell!" I said aloud and then started to text that when a sudden, excruciating headache made me drop the phone to the floor and pinch the bridge of my nose. My ears were humming and the hairs on the back of my neck stood on end.

Something foreign was trying to come through, but the flat, like all the coven's holdings, was warded against such things. It was necessary to do craft correctly. You never wanted an unwanted passenger attaching itself to a spell and invading your space. Well, this thing had encountered the wards in the flat—and it felt distinctly familiar. *Malach.* Against my better judgment, I allowed him to bypass the wards and flicker into existence in the middle of the living room. He was still wearing that long leather coat, his face pinched and sour, speckled grey wings fully extended.

"You're done, Nick," he said in that familiar, growling baritone the moment he had a mouth and a voice to use. I supposed what he'd done was the angel equivalent of beaming down. "You're off the case and free to go back to Blackwater."

"What?" I demanded to know. "What in hell are you smoking?"

I started getting up, then thought better of the move. I was healing very quickly even without healer magick—I guess my angel genes were working overtime—but my knee still wasn't a hundred percent. And I didn't want Malach to know that. It wouldn't take much. One well-placed kick and I'd be laid up a whole day.

"You better explain yourself," I said from my sitting position, which wasn't nearly as dramatic as I wanted it to be. I pointed at him. "You were supposed to be at the mansion tonight to back me up with Michael."

Malach took a deep breath, his face cut with worry lines. It took him a moment to dissolve his wings. I'd never seen him so off his game. "The agenda's changed, Nick. We're not going after Michael any longer."

I looked at him, completely gobsmacked. "When were you going to tell me this?"

"It was…a sudden change of plans."

Maybe I hadn't heard right. Or maybe Malach had lost his nerve. I figured that was possible. Regardless, there was still Cassie to think of. "Michael is still out there."

"I realize that."

"Give me Cassie to look after," I told him. I had thought this through to some extent before contacting Malach. I'm not an idiot. "I'll take her someplace safe where no one will be able to find her—even you."

Malach scowled. "And then?"

"And then you can hunt Michael down. You and Cassiel. And you can air out your differences. Set up Celestial Fight Club. I don't give a fuck what you do. In the meantime, though, she'll be safe—"

But Malach shook his head. "You can't have her, Nick."

"Why?" I did get up then. I was surprised by how quickly I was healing. I didn't even limp as I took a step toward him, fists clenched and ready for action. "You still don't trust me with her?"

"It's not that." He took a step back, his expression stormy. "There is something I need to tell you. Something I should have told you before."

Oh hell! That did not sound good.

Malach looked around as if plotting an escape if I got too physical with him. "We are…well, we are in a bind. The Anointed One's coronation is set to take place in just three days' time."

I just gaped at him. "Explain that."

He glanced up, then quickly down at the floor in shame. "Michael isn't the only threat to Cassandra's ascension."

I watched him keenly. "Go on."

Sighing deeply, Malach went on. "Michael is working with a human man named Warren Szandor LaVey." He paused before continuing. "Yes, he is the grandson of Anton LaVey. No, you have never met him, he is not a Satanist like his grandfather, and, hopefully, you will never encounter him."

That name sounded familiar. I thought I might have heard his name in the news.

Reading me in a not-so-subtle way, Malach explained, "Yes, he owns a very large company that specializes in technology and social media. He is an American entrepreneur and a computer engineer. He is powerful and owns shell companies in America as well as all over the world."

"But he's not a Satanist?"

"No, Nick. He's Arcana."

I gaped. Then closed my mouth. The news made me sit down before I fell down. "You're telling me Michael is working with some shitty billionaire *angel-eater*? When were you going to tell me *this*?"

"I wasn't." He sounded defensive. Ashamed. "Cassiel and I discussed it and we decided we weren't going to involve you in that end of it. This is our business, not yours, Nick. The Lucifers have no part in this."

That pissed me off. I grabbed the cane that Antonia had left with me and pushed myself up again. I didn't even care that Malach knew my knee was jacked. "I beg to differ, Malach. This is *exactly* my business! Do you know what those fuckers have done to me over the years? Do you know what they did to Peter?"

He nodded once as if that wasn't a totally rhetorical question.

I pulled my shirt up and the edge of my jeans down to show him the bite scars on my lower abdomen. I saw him flinch. Good. "They tried to eat me. They ate parts of my fucking partner! How fucking dare you! The Arcana are involved and you didn't even think to warm me?"

"Nick," he begged, holding up his hands, "Nick..."

But I stomped forward, fuming. My wings extended across the goddamn room with my outrage. "How dare you try to cut me out of this? Putting Cassie on the throne is *literally* one of my family's jobs! We are the god-makers, or have you forgotten that?"

I might not be the best Lucifer who ever existed, but I knew my duties. And Cassie's coronation absolutely involved me on every level of her existence and mine. I was her guardian, her Merlin, her dark knight. Malach's job was to warn me about all possible dangers, including those of the Arcana.

Those goddamn bastards stood at every crossroad of my life! No matter what I did, no matter where I turned, I couldn't seem to shake them. God, they were like magickal herpes. I wanted to roar at the ceiling.

Suddenly, Malach looked highly uncomfortable. Which of course made him hostile. He grimaced and his hand moved to his holster. "Nick, your job was simply to find Michael for us...which, I might add, you did *not*."

"I was a little preoccupied with angel-human hybrids popping up all over the place, trying to kill me!" I pointed the cane at him. "Something else you did not bother to mention to me! Were you hoping they would kill me?"

Malach moved his hand away from his gun. "No, of course not!"

Still, my brain works in mysterious ways, and, quite suddenly, I got it. I understood everything.

"You son of a bitch," I told him. It was all I could do to keep from manifesting the Morning Star and driving it through Malach's stone-cold angel heart, as ill-advised as that would be. "You did, didn't you? You thought that the hybrids—or Michael, or this LaVey fellow, if no one else—would finish me off. Get me out of your way."

I threw the cane away and flew at him. To my surprise, I no longer felt the pain in my knee. I was too angry, too upset...too hurt. I slammed into Malach, hurdling him back against the fireplace mantel. There, I held him, my forearm pinning his throat as I stared into his icy cold blue angel eyes.

He didn't fight me; he just hung there.

I'd thought Malach was my friend. Well, maybe not a friend, exactly, but an ally at the least. We wanted the same things. We were on the same side. But he'd had no qualms about throwing me under the fucking bus!

"Nick..." he pleaded. He slowly raised his hands in surrender. "Nick, I'm sorry. It was all Cassiel. I should not have listened to him. I should have told you everything. I know that. But there were issues..."

"Issues my fucking ass!" I breathed in and out, in and out. I had to get myself under control before I did something stupid, something I'd regret. After a few more breaths, I let Malach go and stepped back. "You're not even worth it. You're nothing! God's Hitman, my ass!"

I started turning away, but Malach called after me.

So I swung around. "I'm done with you. And I am done with this. If you have a problem with the Arcana, then figure it out, Malach. If you've got a problem with Cassiel, throw him to the wolves the same way you threw me. Just don't call me to do your dirty work for you anymore."

"Nick..."

I threw my hands up, summoning the wards set around the apartment. Malach—indeed, no angel—was welcomed in this house any longer. I saw Malach's eyes when he realized this. They turned bleach white. I saw the pain build, and, with an open-mouthed shout, Malach was gone in a flash of light. Back to the cabin in the woods, the cowardly little shit.

A few seconds later, Antonia came down the stairs from the loft and stood there, just staring at me. In her hand was my grandfather's athame that I had given her for protection. I felt it was a better gift than even the Orisha Tarot. She was ready for a good fight.

Then I saw the question on her face.

"Everything is fine," I told her, sinking down on the sofa and running a hand through my hair. "Everything is good."

She nodded but didn't look convinced.

* * *

Near morning, my phone went off, waking me from a deep and disturbing dream about being chased by spiders through a house with endless rooms. I sat up in bed, dislodging Antonia's head on my shoulder.

She murmured something and shifted to the pillow.

"Sorry, darling," I told her as I grabbed my phone off the bedside table.

I saw it was Kiara. I wondered if she was calling about our family's genetic research, then saw the time on the phone. A quarter after five in the morning. No one in their right mind was going to call about some fun little fact they learned about the family at five in the morning.

It was going to be bad news. Then again, with me, it usually is. Holding the phone, I turned back to look at Antonia. She had dozed off again.

Giving Antonia my back, I cleared my voice and slid my phone to the green circle. "Hey, Kiara. Wassup?" I whispered.

A pause, and then her voice came, "Nick...sorry if I woke you. Are you okay?"

I cleared my throat. I sounded froggy and not myself—like I had a bad cold. "Y-yeah. I'm fine. It's good to hear from you." My eyes darted around the room until I recognized the shape of the small, ornately carved box sitting on the highboy across the room. The box had originally held a gazing ball that was in the magick loft, one of the many tools the coven used when it was here. I had moved the ball to a velvet drawstring bag and set the angel egg inside the box for safekeeping.

"Yeah," she said, sounding a little off. "I didn't wanna bug you, but..."

"No, it's okay." I got up and went to check on the egg, which was dark and quiet. It only seemed to come alive when I held it. The whole night had been fraught with a low-grade panic that had gotten me out of bed several times to check on it. I kept expecting it to be gone. This weird, sudden seahorse-dadding was driving me crazy.

I put my hand on the egg, feeling a slight pulse. "What can I help you with?"

"I'm not sure if you can." The edge to her voice worried me.

"What's happened? It's not Aunt Althea?"

"No...no, Mom's okay. It's...actually, it's T-Dawg."

"Troy?" I almost swore under my breath. "What kind of trouble is he in?"

A pause. "It's not like that, Nick. He's not in trouble—just really, really sick. I know he's been associating with some bad people...I don't know if that's the reason why he is like this now, but something is really wrong with him. And I'm afraid you're the only one who can help him."

| 15 |

Revelations

FUCK MALACH.

Fuck the angels.

Fuck their war.

Fuck the whole damned coronation.

I had finally had enough. When I got that call from Kiara, my priorities changed in that moment.

I had spent so much of my life fighting for others to the detriment of myself and my personal relationships. I'd all but ignored my family. Well, no more.

I was tired of being everyone's fool. Everyone's tool.

That call changed everything.

After I hung up, I called Antonia over and asked her to walk me through the tools and how they worked in the loft. Together, we went upstairs and she explained almost every single one to me, what it did, and what it couldn't do. I asked her to use layman's terms since I was still in training and knew I could really boff this up otherwise.

"Does your family know what's wrong with Troy?" she asked. "Maybe I can help."

I shook my head. "They don't know—not really. *I* really don't know, and I won't have a clue until I see him in the flesh."

She looked at me curiously. "Why are they asking you and not taking him to a hospital?"

I showed her the video on my phone that Kiara had sent me after her call.

"Oh," she said, growing very pale as she watched it. "And they think you can help?"

"I think they suspect I may be able to do something."

It took me a moment, but I decided to level with her. "They know my mom was a witch and that I inherited her abilities. It's been a point of contention in my family for decades. Y'know, why does the white-passing guy have powers when most of the family doesn't?"

She nodded.

"Plus, I think they know who my dad is on a subconscious level. Most people do when they meet him."

She absorbed that. "So, they think you can do something for him?"

"I think they're hoping I can, even though this stuff scares the hell out of them. Any port in a storm—you know."

Antonia nodded, then looked down. "I'm sorry they feel that way about you. My dad sort of feels the same way about me. The craft frightens a lot of people, and there isn't much you can do about it, especially if you aren't called to it."

Antonia—and, indeed, most of the Children of Endor—believed that for someone to wield the craft, they had to be called to it. They also believe people who play with it without being called or have little respect for it are the ones often responsible for spiritual disasters—spells that go wrong, hauntings, possessions, that type of thing. It's also a fairly popular belief among Indigenous people and the African-American communities. You only handled it if you had some natural talent with it. Otherwise, you left that work to an elder—a wise woman (or man).

Althea had never been called, and I think that was a point of conflict between her and my mom. Kiara, likewise, did not seem particularly inclined to the craft, though I had felt a brief spark from Troy while I was talking to him. A fat lot of good that did him, though. I wasn't about to question Kiara's motivations for calling me about Troy's worsening condition. I only wanted to help Troy.

I scooped some tools into my kit bag, debated taking the angel egg, then decided I didn't have a choice in the matter. If it left it behind, I knew I would worry about it endlessly, and that would interfere with my work. So I packed that as well into my magickal duffle bag.

After I was done, I turned to Antonia. "This is strictly a personal matter and has nothing to do with the Children of Endor, so I don't ex—"

"I'll come. You have me. You always have me," she said and gave me a little encouraging smile.

I set the bag down and moved toward her. I put my hands on her shoulders and rubbed them a moment. "I know I've been all over the place and not very attentive to your needs..."

Antonia stood up on tiptoes and put a finger to my lips, then leaned up farther to kiss me. "You've been preoccupied with protecting the future God, saving the world, dealing with asshole angels, and now family drama, so I'm not offended. It's a lot to handle. However..."

She gave me an arch look.

"Yeah?" I said.

That encouraging smile turned to something a little sassier. A little sexier. "I would like to spend some time alone with you after all of this is over, Nick. Like a little vacation. I don't mean a honeymoon. I'm not looking to be your number one. But I'd like to spend some intimate time with you without all the monsters." Her smile grew. "I mean, assuming we both survive this and the world remains in one piece."

I drew her close to me, lowered my head, and pressed my forehead against her. "Me too, Antonia."

* * *

I hadn't lied when I told Antonia that the craft frightened the hell out of this side of my family. My human bloodline was descended from witches. In fact, I wouldn't put it past the Puritans that they kept members of my family as much for their magical talents as for their ability to clean their fucking floors, and I suspected Kiara would learn that soon enough if she continued to dig through our lineage. But I also knew that Aunt Althea and Aunt Jo were devout Christians their whole life. They had rejected the craft—or perhaps, as Antonia believed, the craft simply had not chosen them. Aunt Jo had sung in a choir, and Aunt Althea had those crosses everywhere in her flat as if she knew there was something dangerous to keep out of her life. But desperate times call for desperate measures, and there are no atheists in foxholes or something like that...

When I got to the brownstone, Kiara was waiting for me outside, Lil' Nicky in her arms and a diaper bag over her shoulder like she was ready to run for the hills. Lil' Nicky was wailing like a siren.

"Nick!"

I got out of the car with Antonia but paused when I saw her face. "How bad is it?" I asked when I'd joined her.

At least Lil' Nicky stopped crying when he saw me and started doing grabby hands at me. I let him take my finger and hang onto it while I talked to my cousin.

Kiara shook her head, tears in her eyes. "It hasn't gotten any better. I'm afraid to go back inside, what with Lil' Nicky and all…" She stopped, sniffed, and looked over at Antonia. "Hiya."

"Hello, Kiara," Antonia said nicely, keeping her voice calm. She almost always had a calming demeanor and a pleasant demeanor when she spoke to anyone. She once told me she absolutely hated the stereotype of the Sassy Black Woman—even more so than being called "Toni." She'd never been like that, and she hadn't been raised that way. She gave Kiara one of her reassuring smiles. "Don't worry. Nick can handle this. He's very good at these types of things."

Kiara nodded and I saw her shoulders relax a little now that the cavalry had arrived.

"I'm Nick's friend, by the way," Antonia explained, holding out her hand. Kiara took it. "Would you and Lil' Nicky like to take a walk with me around the corner? I'm getting hungry and I saw a deli."

Again, Kiara nodded. "Y-yeah, I'd like that."

Antonia looked to me, and I nodded for her to continue. There was little she could do for me, given the current situation, but this would be particularly useful. And Antonia, in her way, knew that. After Antonia put her arm around Kiara and ushered my cousin and her son down the block, I went inside.

Aunt Althea stood by the rainbow-painted staircase, a silver cross in her hands. Her head was bowed and I could see she was praying over it. Her faith was so strong, it momentarily stopped me dead in my tracks. But then she looked up, her face full of tears, and the spell was broken. "Oh, Nicky."

I went to her and hugged her, careful not to let her cross touch my exposed skin.

"I dunno what happened, Nicky. It's just…it's like God left him…" She started to cry, which damned near broke my heart.

After another hug, I told her I would go look in on Troy. But she gently grabbed my wrist before I could climb the stairs.

"I know you ain't no Christian, boy," she told me. "I know you follow the left-handed path." She seemed distraught by that.

"No," I admitted. "I'm not a Christian." I wasn't about to lie, but I also wasn't about to go into further explanation, because, honestly, would you?

She nodded. "Normally, I'd get our local pastor...or maybe a priest. But I know you have power like Willa had power." She seemed to be consoling herself. "I can see inside you, boy, and I can see your soul is on fire."

Her words chilled me. "I'll do my best, Auntie."

Upstairs, the apartment door was unlocked. I went down the hallway to Troy's room.

Inside, the room was dark and the windows were boarded over, which surprised me. It was a lot of work to go through. Auntie and Kiara had also disassembled their beds and laid their queen-sized mattresses against the walls, one on either side where they shared a wall with the other apartments—to deaden noise, I assumed.

Troy lay on his bed, which was a shambles and smelled like urine. He was naked to the waist and wore only a pair of jeans that looked as if he had been shredding them with his fingernails before Auntie and Kiara tied his wrists to the bedposts with a pair of their scarves. The sight of him chilled me further. Troy was twisting and writhing in his dirty sheets, his teeth gritted and his eyes mere slits. His skin was waxy and pale, and he was sweating so horribly, he'd made a large wet spot around him. He looked considerably worse than when Kiara had taken the video she'd sent me.

The moment Troy spied me, his motions slowed and he watched me avidly for a few seconds. Then, suddenly, everything changed and he was clenching and clacking his jaws together in a way that was painful to listen to—trying to bite me even across the distance that separated us.

I closed the door behind me. I couldn't help but wonder if I'd looked like this when I was having my seizure a few days ago. But, of course, this wasn't epilepsy. This was so, so much worse.

Moving to the foot of the bed, I tried a few general exorcism spells. Of course they didn't work. Whatever was inside Troy wasn't a demon, which would have been easy for me to yank out. Demons were in my wheelhouse.

"Troy," I whispered. "Troy!"

Troy started writhing harder, faster, actually shaking the bed like he was going to tear the bedposts off—which he might have, had they not been made of wrought iron and presumably screwed to the frame. The bed jumped and rocked and rolled, and I took a reflexive step back.

"Troy, stop!" I said. Even though I sounded frightened, that didn't make me feel ashamed. I'd kept my cool in the mansion, but that had been Charles, and I'd had no emotional connection to the man. This was my fucking cousin…

"T-Dawg!" I roared so loudly that he actually stopped fighting against his restraints and just watched me hatefully from under his half-closed eyelids.

"Lord Lucifer," he said. Slowly, almost imperceptibly, Troy's whole body began to drift up and off the bed. There it hovered a couple of inches above the mattress. He started to speak in Divine. The voice of the angels. It sounded like a sick engine being turned over.

Had it been a demon in there, this would have been a piece of cake. I'd have been able to evict the bastard in seconds. But I had no dominion over the Holy Hosts, and it was pretty clear to me that, somehow, Troy had gotten some of Papa Lacroix's angel dust in him. I'm not even sure if it was intentional or not. Maybe he had messed with some of the Z-Quil. Maybe it was just the proximity to Charles.

Troy stopped talking and calling me names and began to moan and writhe again. I quickly realized why: His back was bleeding. Blood was dripping to the mattress while two pairs of feathered wings began to tear their slow, agonizing way through his flesh like swing switchblades. More purplish blood gushed, darkening the mattress under him. His eyes flashed with terror and pain as he looked at me, and for one second, his eyes cleared, and said, "N...Ni...ck...help...?"

"Troy?" I moved to the side of his bed and took his hand.

He began to scream, a shrill sound laced with anguish and outrage that tore through me like a scythe. The bony, black-feathered wings continued to push their way through his sweating flesh—a bloody, raw-meat birthing, with another pair on their way.

My heart began to triphammer and I gripped his hand tighter. God, I didn't know what to do. I couldn't manifest the bident and try to pin him with it. I couldn't take the chance I'd miss, stick Troy with the tines, and destroy him.

I let go of his hand long enough to find his office chair, turn it around, and try to press him down to the mattress with it, but with a roar, he flexed his body upward, destroying it and sending the shrapnel flying across the room.

I stepped back as Troy snapped those fearsome teeth at me, which looked longer and sharper now. Without holding him down, there was no way Antonia and I were going to be able to pull that damned angel out of him. I was so fucking useless!

His voice changed again, his eyes went black, and he started spewing holy profanities at me.

I made the mistake of trying to lean on him, but he flexed upward again, lashing out at me with his wings ripping a series of long tears in my pullover and scraping over the skin of my chest. I lurched back in response and hit the desk on the opposite side of the room. The Junkyard Dog action figure fell to the floor at my feet.

The angel in Troy started screaming at me in angel-speak, daring me to come closer, to allow him to kiss me, but Troy was in there somewhere. Amidst the sacrilegious bullshit, I heard my cousin begging me to come closer. He said he had something important to tell me.

I didn't think Troy was lying. He was quickly melding with the angel's mind. I imagined he had all kinds of arcane knowledge to share. Maybe even something that could help me.

But I was too afraid to approach. Not afraid that the Troy-angel would scratch me again, but terrified the angel would do something to Troy to get to me, hurt Troy, maybe tear right through my cousin's body to reach me.

Frantic, I looked around for something to use. There was a cross on the wall, but that was useless to me under the circumstances. Then I spied the Junkyard Dog doll. Picking it up, I held it out at Troy like a poor man's crucifix. Strangely, the sight of the doll seemed to calm him.

"Troy," I said, trying to keep the quaver out of my voice as I moved closer to him, the doll out in front of me. "What is it, Troy?"

The angel ranted. But Troy's eyes cleared and returned to their warm brown. They alone begged me to come closer.

I had no better ideas, so I did, trying to stay outside the reach of the angel's flickering wings.

Troy's eyes followed the doll. Bit by bit, I felt the angel lurch and recess just a little as Troy sought to retain control of his body. I held the doll up high and moved as close to the bed as I dared.

"N...Ni-i-i...ck," Troy managed, but then the angel made him hiss and spit as the battle for Troy's body continued.

I held the action figure up in front of Troy's face and slowly brought it down.

Troy watched it carefully until I had lowered it almost to the bridge of his nose.

"Troy," I tried again, "what are you trying to tell me? Is there something I can do?"

"H...im. Talk...to...him." His eyes moved sideways to find me. I saw the pain there and it brought tears to my eyes. "H...e...kn-n...o...w...s..."

"Who knows?"

Troy's eyes grew wide and my cousin began to convulse. I saw the foam forming in the corner of his lips. But he still managed to spit it out: "Th...Th...e...r...ion!"

I stepped back and just stared at Troy. I had a thousand questions, but there was no way Troy was going to be able to answer any of them.

Therion.

The Beast. The fucking Beast of Revelations.

Why in fuck would I want to speak to that bastard?

Then Troy turned his head, which was shaking like a palsied old man's, and nodded once as if to say, *Yeah. Him.*

I thought about it for one second, then nodded back. "If it means saving you, I'll even beg the bastard on my knees."

But Troy didn't answer that because his eyes had rolled up in his head and turned all black with his infection.

* * *

When I got downstairs, Antonia ran up to me. I explained the situation, and she insisted she could help me with another exorcism. I appreciated her desire to help, and her enthusiasm, but I told her the truth. "You didn't see him. There is no way we'll be able to restrain him with the bident. I really can't take a chance I'll stab Troy."

Auntie and Kiara looked on with low-grade horror at our conversation.

"You won't stab him," Antonia said in that always-calm tone. "I'll work fast. We can do this, Nick."

I considered it for one second before doubt began to creep in again. I couldn't see a way of holding Troy down with the Morning Star without hurting him—or even killing him accidentally—no matter how fast Antonia worked. But I was still willing to give it a try, under special circumstances.

I told my fam to stay downstairs. Then Antonia and I went up to Troy's room.

The moment she saw him, writhing and foaming at the mouth, his eyes all black now and two sets of wings sticking bloodily out of his sides, I saw the hesitancy in her eyes.

"There's no shame in tapping out," I told her. I looked Troy over. "I'm pretty sure whatever is inside him is an archangel. It's stronger than that Cherubim we pulled out, and it's not going to go without a fight."

Antonia took a deep breath to ground herself. "We'll at least try. If we don't try, then we're already defeated."

Troy—or the angel inside him, at any rate—began to scream even before Antonia moved to stand as close to him as she dared. Just like the last time, she put her hands over her eyes and started to recite her spell in angel-speak. He screamed so loudly, she had to stop and reclaim her place.

I manifested the bident and lifted it over Troy's bed—not touching him, but close enough I hoped the holy artifact would keep him down.

Antonia started the spell from the beginning. I stood at the foot of the bed and used both hands to steady the Morning Star.

The angel—if I'm being totally honest, Troy was more angel than himself at this point—glared up hatefully at the bident and began to snap his jaws again so violently, I was terrified he'd break his teeth. And the more Antonia chanted, the more violent the angel became, bending weirdly and at such angles, I started to hear the alarming crackle of bones that just couldn't move that way.

Antonia stumbled, then began again.

The angel writhed and its body snapped up and down on the bed like a tarp being stretched and snapped. I heard the metal of the headboard bending as the creature applied its supernatural force to it. It turned its coal-black eyes on me and spoke in English for the first time.

"I will be free, Lucifer. I will kill you! I will rip the hearts of everyone you love out and feast on their flesh!"

I brought the bident down, touching the angel's bare shoulder. The thing began to scream, a high-pitched, wheedling noise that put a crack in the panes of the windows. The hybrid began to writhe again, more violently than ever before. Then it began slamming its head against the headboard—a *thump, thump, thump* sound that made all the alarm bells go off inside of me.

"Stop...stop, stop, stop!" I yelled at Antonia, and she did.

Terrified Troy would break his own neck or smash his skull open on the iron headboard, I yanked the Morning Star away. That seemed to calm the hybrid somewhat.

Antonia dropped her hands and stepped back, her breathing labored and eyes wide at the dreadful sight of my cousin trying to kill himself.

"We can't keep going. This is going to kill Troy."

"Nick..."

"No, we're done," I decided. "Come on. We'll find another way."

| 16 |

A Discovery of Witches

NATURALLY, ANTONIA WANTED to accompany me back to Blackwater. She was my unofficial bodyguard. But I needed her to stick with my fam. I needed her to watch over them and to ensure that:

1. They did not call anyone for help. (No one would be able to help them with this, anyway.)
2. They stayed calm.
   And, most importantly—
3. Under no circumstances should anyone go into Troy's room, no matter how he begged or pleaded for their help.

That last one was going to be tricky. Aunt Althea, in her concern, wasn't going to be able to stay out of there for long. The angel had already begun to plead in Troy's voice to be let out, claiming that he was all right, that it was all over.

Before I left, I took Antonia aside. "They are going to bully you into letting them see Troy. You cannot let them see Troy."

She nodded, her eyes serious.

"I don't care if you have to use craft, but keep everyone away from that room."

After thinking about it for a long second, she asked, "There are coven members in the city, right?"

"Yeah?"

"What if I call them into a circle to help me keep Troy restrained and everyone away from him? I could even get some folks up from Blackwater to help."

I nodded. "That's a good idea. Make it happen."

An hour later, I had successfully warded the room against the hybrid trying to escape it. It was the same type of spell the coven used to prevent enemies from breaching sacred spaces, just inverted. It wasn't going to stop my fam from going in, though. And, if I'm being honest, it wasn't going to contain the angel for long, either. The stronger the angel got—or, more precisely, the more Troy became the archangel and less human—the weaker the wards would become and the bigger the chance of it breaking them. Right now, it was fine; Troy was technically *less* angel than I was, even being a hybrid myself, but that wouldn't stay that way for long. I couldn't calculate exactly how long it would take, but I estimated no more than a few days, at most.

I just hoped it was enough time for me to drive to Blackwater, complete my mission, and drive back.

After I slung my kit bag over my shoulder, Antonia joined me and put her hand on my shoulder. "You can trust me to take care of things, Nick. I know a lot of spells." Then she added, "But nothing that will hurt your fam."

I nodded. "Thanks."

Before I jumped into the Monaco, I took her into my arms and kissed her deeply. I even swiped a hand up her leg under her skirt, which made her smile. "That vacation," I told her, my forehead resting against hers. "Just think about that and make some plans while I'm gone."

"I will. I..." She stopped. I was afraid she was going to say *I love you*, so I got into the car quick fast. I didn't want her going down that road.

She waved me off and I hit the road. It was a little after three in the afternoon. I knew I would get back to town after dark, and that was if the traffic was good—but, this being a Friday, with tourists streaming up into the mountains for their weekend getaway, I knew it would not be. I would need to drive straight through to make good time, which I planned to.

I took my kit bag with me, the angel egg in its box inside. I dunno, maybe it would bring me luck or something. I stopped only once, and that was for an iced coffee from Dunkin Donuts. I didn't like it; I just needed some caffeine to keep me focused. It didn't help much, but the extra-large Snickers did, though I spent the next half an hour digging all the peanuts out of my molars.

It was after six by the time I reached the outskirts of Blackwater. Too late for Holy Name to be open, but I drove by the school grounds anyway on the off-chance it was open for some after-hours function like a game or sermon. As I had suspected, the parking lot was empty of vehicles. Thankfully, I had researched my old adversary Therion the Beast thoroughly. I knew he had a small raised ranch on the outskirts of town and about three miles from the school where he worked. It was one of several rectories that Holy Name provided their ordained teachers. They didn't believe in dormitories and liked the idea of affording their priests a minimal of privacy, which I imagined Therion (aka Dr. Theodore Lamb) enjoyed immensely, considering the nature of the creature.

I had encountered the "man" the year before. Like everyone else, I didn't think the Beast of Revelation was going to be a chubby, smiley, fatherly type of fellow with silver glasses and a warm handshake, but here we were.

It took driving slowly up a few roads and looking like a weird stalker before I found the right house and parked in the driveway that curved around behind the house. I settle d into a place just behind the man's station wagon.

Before I went up to the door, I glanced over the grounds. There was a cellar door peeking out of the ground, and I wondered what he had down there.

But even before I could begin speculating, a light flickered on and I heard a screen door screek open. I looked over at the stoop where Dr. Theodore Lamb stood, waving to me as if we were old friends. His porch light was on, and its light slanted across half his body. He was wearing his clerical shirt, tab collar, blue jeans, and a big, fluffy orange cardigan. He was holding a cup of tea and signaling I should approach.

With a sigh, I went up the cement stairs.

"Officer Nick! It's so good to see you," Lamb said pleasantly, a wide, cheeky smile on his face. "I spied you in Weis the other day, even waved, but I don't think you saw me."

I stopped almost toe to toe with him and said, "I saw you, Lamb. I was just ignoring you on purpose." I immediately regretted my bluntness, but damn, he got to me in a way very few could.

Lamb's expression never changed. You'd think I'd just rained down a compliment on him. He sipped from his teacup—I could smell the warm apple cider and cinnamon in it—and indicated I should follow him inside.

I didn't know what to expect from the Beast's abode. Torture devices and wolf traps hanging on the walls and maybe a series of childlike skulls on the mantel, but the house was all rustic brown paneled walls and gold carpeting, with one of those weird, ugly orange sofas with the big flowers on it that your great aunt probably had. An iron potbellied stove cooked in one corner to chase out the chill.

"I'm glad you dropped by. I've missed our little discussions," Lamb said as he led me into the little kitchen with its dark wood cupboards and yellow Formica countertops. "Can I warm you up some cider?"

"No," I told him, hanging by the counter with the dark wooden stools. He probably roofied it or something. "But I do need to talk to you about something important."

"Wonderful!" said Lamb, and he proceeded to warm up the cider in his saucepot even though I just told him I didn't want any. He looked at the plastic container of apple cider on the counter and said, "I love this stuff. Your farmer's markets here are truly a godsend!"

"Cut the shit, Lamb," I said as I sat down rather grumpily at the counter. Near my elbow was an Entenmann's box half full of coffee cake. It reminded me of how I'd had no real food today and was hangrier than I should have been.

Lamb indicated the cake. "I know you have a mighty sweet tooth. Help yourself." He sipped his cider and smiled, but I saw his eyes change, darken.

He was a daemon like me. And, more importantly, Dr. Theodore Lamb could not only glamour the almighty fuck out of people around him, but he was also something of a shapeshifter. A trickster, at the very least. Though whether he could physically change his shape, or only someone's perception of it—in other words, more glamour—I had yet to figure out.

When the cider was sufficiently warm, Lamb poured it into a second mug, added a cinnamon stick, and carried it to the counter to set it down in front of me. "Tell me what I can do for you, Officer Nick."

I decided to cut to the chase. "I'm not going to lie, Lamb. I don't like you. I don't trust you. And I know the feeling is mutual. But I need your help with something." I needed this too badly, so I added as an ego boost, "It's something only you can help me with."

Smiling as if we were best buds, he went to the other side of the counter and leaned over to stare me in the eyes. His glasses flashed at me in a disconcerting way. "I am, as always, your humble servant, my lord."

He wasn't lying. According to several annoying and unfortunate prophecies, the Beast was the divine servant of the Dragon. The Dragon being me, though I had to admit I didn't feel much like a Dragon at the moment. With everything I was dealing with, I felt like hardly a salamander. I was fatigued, my eyes bleary from driving too long, and I had a Charlie horse trying to start in one leg from stepping on the gas and the brake nonstop for the past three hours straight.

I sighed and rubbed my eyes. "It's a spell. I need to ask you—"

He interrupted me. "If you are weary, you are welcome to sleep in my room," Lamb offered.

I stumbled and looked up. "Oh, yeah? And where will you sleep?"

He never lost his smile. "In my room."

I snorted because that was actually funny. I'd forgotten about his weird devil fetish. Or maybe it was a fetish unique to me. A Nick fetish. "That's not much of a double entendre, you know."

"I don't do double entendres," Lamb answered bluntly. "I'm interested in having a night of intimacy with you, either tonight or one day. I suspect you'd find my more tender ministrations quite pleasurable…"

"You're a priest," I pointed out.

Reaching out, he put a hand on my arm, a fatherly touch. "We both know that isn't correct."

I quickly withdrew my arm, but he didn't even have the good grace to look offended. He simply went to fetch more warm apple cider.

"Tell me what's happened," he said.

With another sigh, I told him about needing information about how to remove an angel from a victim without harming the human side. I didn't tell him the victim was my cousin; he didn't need to know that. But I told Lamb I had good reason to believe he might have the answer I needed.

Lamb nodded once when I had finished my truncated story. "Your source is correct. I think I have what you need. However, you have to admit that the fact that you came to me for this means this is exceedingly important to you, Officer Nick."

"Your point being?"

He turned, stirring his cup. "You benefitting from my knowledge with me receiving nothing in return seems a tad...unfair."

I narrowed my eyes. "I thought you lived to serve Satan. Aka, me. It's your calling or some shit."

"This is true." He offered me a cheeky smile. "I receive great pleasure in being your servant, my lord. It gives me great purpose. But I can't see the harm in gaining a little extra...compensation, shall we say. Surely, it is worth your time?"

I watched the bastard, seething. If I could have gone to anyone else, I would have. If I could have done this without him, I would have done that too. And he knew it. He had me by the short hairs. Finally, I asked in a reasonable voice, "What do you want from me, Lamb?"

He seemed to think about that for an inordinate amount of time before narrowing his eyes as I had and saying, "Is saving your friend worth spending a night with me?"

I felt sick. It took me a moment to react. "So you want sex. You're not just fucking with me to make a point."

Juliette had long ago postulated that the Beast was unduly…attracted to me, despite his claims of being a hardcore (and self-professed) misanthrope.

Lamb tsked. "Officer Nick, you have such a dirty mind. It's always sex with you, isn't it? It's what everyone wants from you." He rolled his eyes comically.

I gave it to him straight. "It's usually about sex. Unless it's about power."

He smirked. "Well, let's leave it a surprise. When the time is right, you'll be mine. But only for one night. You will just need to trust in me. Shake on it?" He put out his hand.

I wanted badly to slap that hand away. I wanted to walk out of there and find another solution, but I didn't have one. Troy didn't have one. I thought about my cousin, suffering through his affliction in that dark room. If I let Troy die—rather, be absorbed by that archangel—I would never be at peace. And nothing Lamb did to me—"only for one night"—would compare to that pain. Still, it took me a moment or two to summon the nerve to reach out and take his hand. I felt an almost electrical spark. The Devil's Handshake, if you will. Our deal, or covenant, was sealed, never to be undone.

Relax, I told myself. *You've whored yourself out in the past.*

Lamb, not at all gloating and showing no reaction to the handshake, nodded to me. "Follow me."

He went to a door on the opposite side of the kitchen that I thought was a broom closet, opened it, and pulled a chain. A light bulb lit up a steep stairwell going straight down into darkness. Ah, the basement, then.

Down below, the space was full of extras from Holy Name, all the stuff they couldn't fit in storage there, I suppose, including a light-up plastic nativity display, old chairs and cafeteria tables, and some antique-looking desks from maybe the 1950s. A large bookcase full of old VHS tapes of Bible-themed cartoons that probably couldn't be played any longer because it was too expensive to try and find a VCR online dominated one whole wall. But beyond that was a small maze of more bookcases, these filled to the top with actual books. Lamb pulled another chain to light up the miniature library labyrinth.

"As you can see, no children in shackles," he explained as if he had read my fears from earlier, which maybe he had. He turned and gave me his angelic smile. "I keep them elsewhere."

I had no idea if he was telling the truth or was fucking me around.

Turning back to the library, he started running his fingers over the many collected tomes. I recognized a lot of Catholic seminary books, religious novels, and study guides—the usual suspects. But in between them, I spied a few books that the archdiocese probably would've frowned down upon—*Alchimia: l'oro della conoscenza*, *Fetichism in West Africa*, the *Vampyre Sanguinomicon*, *Sex, Drugs and Magick*, *The Diary of a Drug Fiend* by Aleister Crowley, and bunches of other questionable titles.

"Nice books," I said. I pulled loose a rather electric collection of *Penthouse* magazines.

"I litter them throughout the other titles to prevent my other brothers from noticing when they visit. The porn is the bishops," Lamb said without looking at me.

"How does the bishop tolerate you practicing witchcraft on church property?"

Lamb put on a pair of plastic gloves from a box on a shelf, picked up a book, and cradled it in his arms as if it were a baby. He turned to glance at me. "I keep his dirty secret. He keeps mine. It all works out. Here we are."

I suppressed a shudder as he approached and showed me a book that was mostly just fragile yellow manuscript pages bound together. It took me a few moments to realize it was a copy—or was it the original?—of *The Discoverie of Witchcraft* by Reginald Scot, the earliest known book in English explaining how to perform magic. The sight of it gave me a geekish little tingle, I admit. I'd read copies, of course, but it was rumored there were great swaths torn from later editions. The original was supposed to have spells that had not seen the light of day since the fourteenth century. Even the Children of Endor didn't have them in their vast, archaic online library.

"Your friend was right to recommend me. I have a spell here just for this situation, but you will need to memorize it. No pictures." Again that apple-cheeked, overly cherubic smile. "I can't allow such spells to get out into the public. They are simply too powerful."

I looked over the pages. In school, everyone used to think I was the cool, cute, but dumb blond. After a few years, I deliberately perpetuated the image because that's what kids do. And I never cared about quizzes, projects, or grades, which helped enforce the idea that I was as smart as a box of rocks. Truthfully, I was too preoccupied with trying to stay alive in foster care to care about something as mundane as schoolwork. But, unknown to my classmates, I did follow everything in class. And yet, even years later, while I toiled side by side with Morgana at our shop, the Idiot Blond image continued to dog me.

Then, a few months back, Juliette did a large number of tests on me to see where I fell in my magickal education and natural witchy talents. After the tests, she told me that I passed as an eidetic. She called what I had a "computer brain." I could remember things I saw and heard with almost one hundred percent clarity. She thought I may have a genius IQ, which I thought was just her trying to build my confidence. But then, I had always been good at remembering spells (when I wanted to), so remembering everything on the page of *The Discoverie of Witchcraft* was no trouble at all.

"Do you have it?" Lamb asked.

"Yeah," I told him.

"You'll still need an angel's feather for the ceremony. "A feather from one who is unfallen and living in the Grace of God, of course."

"I understand."

He closed the book. "Then you have everything you need to save your friend, my love."

Before I left, he took my wrist in his hand. "Remember our covenant," he reminded me. "If you don't, if you break it, we both die."

Just what I need, I thought as I shook off the Beast's surprisingly strong, cold touch. More complications in my life.

| 17 |

The Cabin in the Woods

THE FIRST THING I did when I got back to the Monaco was phone Antonia to see how she was fairing.

She sounded and looked tired when I Facetimed her. "It all went down like you said. Your fam was okay for the first hour, but then your aunt tried to bully me into letting her see Troy. I..." She paused as she turned to show me the living room. "...I put them both under a spell. Not a bad one, Nick. Just one so they were too tired or distracted by Lil' Nick's needs to fight me. That seems to be working."

My auntie and Tiara were sitting on the sofa, playing with Lil' Nicky, who was squealing from all the attention. *SpongeBob SquarePants* was on the large-screen TV hanging on the wall, the volume turned up—to muffle any sounds of distress from Troy's room, I presumed.

I felt so bad. "I'm sorry I put you through this, my darling," I told Antonia when she put herself back on.

She smiled—a tired smile. "Don't be. I knew what I was signing up for. Juliette prepared me for almost any eventuality."

I rolled my eyes. "I can imagine. 'He gets into levels of shit you can't even imagine. You'll find yourself in situations you never dreamed of.'"

She laughed. "Something like that, but not that cynical. Juliette likes you a lot, Nick. And she believes in you, which is the most important thing. When I talked to her last, she told me I was duty-bound to protect and aid you. Your bodyguard, so to speak. So, like I said, I knew what I was getting into."

I nodded. "And I appreciate it. All your help and sacrifices. I'm sorely running out of people I can depend on here."

She wanted to know what I'd found out, and I gave her a brief rundown of the last couple of hours, as well as an even briefer overview of my next move. "I know I won't be back till at least morning there," I explained. "That might not be early enough to save Troy. So, I'm going to messenger the feather to you as soon as I get it. I'll need you to confirm you received it."

She looked confused. "What do you mean 'messenger' it?"

"When I was looking at Lamb's *The Discoverie of Witchcraft* I noticed a spell on the opposite page for sending small items to someone in a hurry. It's sort of like corvine Uber. He doesn't know that I saw it or that I memorized it, but I did." I hesitated before going on. A lot of my plan was reliant on Antonia being able to handle advanced craft techniques. "If I can't get back there in time before the angel completely usurps Troy, I may need you to perform the ritual for me. Do you think you can do that?"

Her brow crinkled as she considered it. I knew that exorcisms weren't for everyone. "What's the ritual?"

"As part of my deal with Lamb, I can't write it down, but I can enunciate it and send you the spell as an audio file. You won't have to do anything but hold the feather over his face and play the recording. It's not more complicated than that. Do you think that's doable?"

She nodded. "I think that's reasonable. Send me the file."

I did. When I was done, I told her, "I need you to hold down the fort till I get back."

"Got it, boss."

"I appreciate you, Antonia."

A hesitation. Then, "Will you call me 'my darling' one more time? I liked that."

"My darling," I said in my best bedroom voice, "I appreciate you."

We said our goodbyes and I hung up. I was exhausted—mentally, physically, and spiritually tapped out—but I put the Monaco into gear and drove out to the cabin in New Hope.

* * *

Yeah, I know what you're going to say. I should have called Malach and asked him to meet me somewhere in town. He could have beamed down, and I could have gotten the feather from him there. But when I tried to call him, he wouldn't answer his phone. I just got the annoying voicemail gal over and over again.

I was pretty sure I had fubared whatever grace I might have had with him—not that he didn't deserve it because hell yeah he had it coming, the bastard. But, in retrospect, I probably could have handled our last confrontation better. I could have not controlled my emotions, not been a hothead about his betrayal. Hell, I should have half-expected it.

But I hadn't. I'd stupidly believed we were allies.

So here we were.

What all this meant was—you guessed it—more hiking through the damned cold, wet, miserable, foggy November woods with drops of freezing water from trees sliding down my back and me grumbling all the way. Thankfully, my hiking gear—boots and puffy jacket—had still been in the trunk of the Monaco from my first excursion a few days ago. They kept me warm, but they couldn't do a damned thing about my ongoing fatigue, my hunger, or the fact that I was worried my cousin was going to die.

Sometime after midnight, I reached the hill that sloped sharply down and led to the cabin, which was tucked securely behind some maples. The leaves were almost all off, so I could see it plainly—or as plainly as I could see it in the dark with my flashlight. Smoke was coming from the chimney—it was a frosty night—and there was at least one light on, probably a battery-operated lantern.

I would have made better time, but I'd gotten turned around at one point because my flashlight wasn't working well, I wasn't paying attention to where I was going, and I think I was briefly sleeping on my feet. Before I ventured down, I decided to rest on a dead and opened my kit bag.

I had added a few items before I set off from the car—a couple of bottles of water, some protein bars, a first aid kit, rudimentary camping stuff like a compass and fire starter kit, and two small, high-powered flashlights like the kinds you get at dollar stores. I checked to make sure I had everything, stuffed a protein bar down my maw because I was getting pretty cranky with every damned thing at that point, and switched flashlights because the one I'd been using was getting kind of wonky. I checked the wooden box to make certain the angel egg was all right, then started down the goat path that led to the cabin.

I kept flashing my light at the ground to avoid gopher holes and unexpected drop-offs. You'd think being part demon and part Frost Giant, I'd have fancy night vision or something, but nope. I kept having to stop, spin my flashlight around, and orient myself so I wasn't walking in a circle, which I promise you *will* do if you aren't careful in the woods. The temp had dropped to at least the twenties by now—but at least that didn't bother me too much. I suppose that was the Jotunn in me.

At a little after one in the morning, I reached the porch of the cabin. I kept my flashlight low to the ground so I didn't alert anyone to my approach. For some reason, I was on edge. There was nothing overtly obvious to set off my internal alarm bells. Maybe I was just dreading seeing Malach after our tiff. I even circled around the cabin before stopping at the back door. I peered in the windows, but they all had drapes drawn across them but one, and I couldn't see anything moving through that window.

The back door was open. For a safe house, that was odd. To be on the safe side, I manifested the bident, its weight comforting in my hand. Feeling more secure with my giant magical pitchfork at the ready, I kicked the door in but stayed on the porch just in case something flew out at me.

Nothing did but the heat from the oil lamp inside.

"Malach!" I said clearly, my voice echoing off the walls of the cabin. "Cassie!"

No answer. Not even an owl in the woods answered me.

I waited another minute before approaching the door and peering inside. I fully expected Malach to manifest in front of me and kick my teeth in, but the cabin appeared empty.

No, it wasn't *that* empty.

The inside was dim, and I recognized the lantern I'd seen from the hill hanging from a hook on one of the rafters, but the light was so weak, it took my eyes a few seconds to adjust, so I didn't immediately notice the figure sitting at a table at the far end of the main room.

The table, like the chairs and the rest of the furniture here, looked hand-made. Amish-made Shaker-style furniture carved from cedar for durability. There was a red gingham tablecloth covering the trestle table, and two simple benches were situated on either side of it.

Sitting at the table was none other than Cassiel. There was an assortment of items on the table, but another tablecloth covered them, so I couldn't make them out except as vague shapes.

"Lord Lucifer," Cassiel said. His voice was still that hitching, boyish timbre that would forever grate on my nerves. "Welcome back."

"Cassiel. Just the angel I didn't want to see." I stepped inside, but the moment I did, I felt a spark. It felt almost like someone had slammed a door behind me, though the door was still open. I turned, glanced around for signs of danger, then decided to exit, but I found a solid, invisible barrier blocking me from escaping. I put my hand out and touched the force field, which felt like touching an old-timey staticky TV screen.

"The fuck?" It was then I realized that someone—Cassiel, probably—had created a one-way ward. I could step inside, but now I was trapped until *he* let me go. And since this was not my dwelling and not my ward, I couldn't break it.

I turned around, clutched the Morning Star in an ever-tightening fist, and said, "Cassiel. What in the actual fuck?"

He lifted his face into the light, smiling despite the tears tracing down both cheeks—which was creepy on every conceivable level that you can imagine. "I like that human saying. It implies the existence of theoretical fucks."

"Cut the shit and tell me what's going on before I put this magic fork through your face."

Cassiel's smile grew even through his tears. "I knew you would come eventually. Malach hoped you would not—he even tried to dissuade you with that little betrayal stunt he pulled—but I told him you would not be sidetracked. Despite your otherwise usually chaotic nature, Lord Lucifer, you can be distressingly predictable at times."

He rolled his eyes and in a singsongy voice, he added, "'The little girl is in trouble. I must save the little girl! Because I'm Superman or some shit.'"

I felt the first twinges of rage. "What do you mean about Malach?"

But Cassiel ignored my question and just smiled on and on. Then he indicated the cabin with a wave of his hand. "If someone is in trouble, there you are. If someone needs help, there goes ol' Saint Nick again."

He folded those long—almost unnaturally long—hands in his lap. "Nicholas Englebrecht. Everyone's little guardian devil."

My fist shook, making the Morning Star vibrate in my hold.

With a sigh, he added, "My sweet lord, you must be so very tired, clawing at every corner of the universe as you struggle to keep it all tied together. Unfortunately, you've come too late to *this* rescue." He indicated the cabin, empty but for him and me. "As you can see, your buddy angel and your little girl are no longer here."

I was angry because I knew he was right about everything about me. He knew me too well, probably studied me, and I was mad as hell for his stupid fucking psychoanalysis. "What's it to you?" I demanded to know. "Why do you care what I do? And, more importantly, where are Malach and Cassie?"

"Malach served his purpose. He distracted you. He gave the meddlesome Lord Lucifer a mission to keep him occupied."

I growled at that. But, soon enough, it all started making sense in my head. The request to find Michael...was just a ruse, a way to give me busy work so I was out of town and not snooping around whatever it was Cassiel and Malach were up to. Hell, Malach had even succeeded in flipping the script and keeping me from coming back too early. He knew if he made me angry enough with his so-called betrayal, I'd drop the mission and tell him to go to hell. He'd played me. It was the only way he could keep me from pursuing my protection of Cassie…

I wouldn't even be here if I didn't need that goddamn feather!

I suddenly realized he knew me even better than I knew myself.

"Malach!" I roared, gripping the Morning Star so it burned in my hands. "Where is he?"

"I sent him away," Cassiel explained in a reasonable tone of voice as if I'd asked where Malach had gone off to and it was around the corner for milk and lottery tickets.

Taking a step toward the rogue angel sitting at the table, I said, "Sent him away *where*? And where is Cassie?"

"Malach took her, of course, but *she* is no concern of ours any longer. Truthfully, I'm pretty certain they are both dead. Osiris is a hostile place to both humans and angels and not easy for any creature to survive."

I glared at him. "Osiris? Where the hell is that?"

Then it hit me. Long ago, I'd seen a documentary on Osiris on the Discovery Channel, a hellish exoplanet millions of light-years from Earth that was in the long process of dying. See, I told you I remember everything—even if I misplace it from time to time.

I nodded. "The Angry Red Planet." I knew I was right. I took a threatening step toward him and my voice kicked up a notch. "You sent them *there*?"

Cassiel, suddenly looking very concerned, stood up and held up a hand to stop my approach. "No. I merely summoned the Simulacrum, who transported them there. You know how those fellows are…"

He never got a chance to finish his explanation because I'd moved fast. I grabbed him by the front of his robe and threw him to the floor. I was literally seeing red—as red as the sands of Osiris. I lifted the bident into the air and aimed the two silvery sharp forks at his smug, tear-smeary face. When he tried to move, I slammed my foot into his crotch to hold him down. He didn't react much because unfallen angels have no junk, heh.

"You've been working with Papa Lacroix," I deducted. "Not Michael. Or not only Michael. What's your endgame?"

No wonder Papa Lacroix had lost his shit back in that bedroom. Cassiel had probably been summoning those Simulacrum all over the place, and whenever someone on Earth got out of line or crossed him, bam, they were gone.

Cassiel sneered up at me.

"I don't know what kind of fucking game you're playing, you degenerate angelic shithead, but you better hope Malach and Cassie aren't harmed. And you better figure out a way to bring them back now!"

To prove my willingness to send him back to his God, I shoved the prongs so close to his throat that the tips scraped the floor to either side of his neck. "Do it!"

But Cassiel only laughed at me. "And how am I supposed to do that, Lucifer? I can call the Simulacrum back for you if you like, I know the spell, but I rather doubt it will take you, considering what you have done to its kin in the past. The Simulacrum regard you as a threat."

With a roar, I extended my wings, lifted the bident high, and drove the forks into the floorboards to either side of Cassiel's neck, kicking up sparks and pinning the angel. Outside, I heard a crash of thunder and a streak of lightning hit a tree on an otherwise still night. The smell of ozone filled the cabin. That was probably my fault.

"Nice display, and pretty wings, Black-winged Lucifer," Cassiel laugh-cried. "But I still can't help you. So, either kill me or get the hell off of me!" Raising his hand, he pantomimed a swipe at me.

I'd forgotten about the ward, and that he was king here. So his bitch slap really did hurt me and flung me backward so hard, I hit the trestle table behind me hard, upending it. I, and the table, both clattered sideways to the floor, and that's when the cloth tumbled away and I found myself with my back to the overturned table, an angel's head falling square into my lap.

I had to stare at it for several seconds to make sure it wasn't a wax prop or something. But no, it was real. I saw the sagging, surprised, half-mast eyes, the mouth open in a scream it would never utter, the blue angel blood (now turned to dust) covering it and still trickling from the severed neck. The hair was long, honey-brown, and the eyes staring at me witlessly a beautiful azure like two polished sapphires fallen from Heaven.

It was as beautiful as it was awful. So, I couldn't help myself. I screamed and threw my hands up, tossing Michael's severed head away from me. It bounced off the floor and rolled under the coffee table near the blue tartan sofa. It took me two tries to scramble up, and even then I realized I had forgotten to grab the Morning Star and didn't know where it had fallen.

But it didn't matter. Cassiel was already on his feet, and he had a big-ass sword in his seemingly boyish hands—the other item that had been under the cloth and which had slid across the floor and right into his hands when I upended it. He stood straight, holding Michael's sword—pure gold and full of glyphs in angel-speak—and smiled knowingly at me even as his tears continued to fall at his feet. The sword didn't ignite the way it usually did in Michael's hands, but it was plenty sharp. And it was plenty capable of ending me.

My Morning Star could destroy Cassiel or any angel, but the same was true of the sword he now wielded. I was just angel enough to die if he put that huge blade through my angel heart.

I glanced aside and spied the Morning Star ten feet away in a corner.

"Don't," Cassiel warned. "Just stand still and let me kill you, Lucifer. I assure you, the world will be a much better place with you out of it, meddling with everything."

I shook my head. "I can't let you do just whatever it is you are planning."

He took a step toward me, the sword extended and pointing at my chest like a finger, but then stopped. "And what exactly do you plan to do about it?"

I glanced around, hoping to spy a weapon, but there was nothing within reach that could kill Cassiel. "I'll figure something out. I always do."

Cassiel shook his head in wonder. "You're the biggest fool I've ever seen. I still live in a state of Grace. I understand what the world needs, and what it needs is a God that will rule hard and be unforgiving." His smile grew. "It's the only way the humans will ever learn to behave."

I hung my thumbs in my belt loops all casual-like. My fingers brushed the angel-eating knife still attached to my belt, the one Grampa gave me at Papa Lacroix's mansion. "And let me guess—you're just the angel for the job."

Cassiel snarled at me. "Well, it certainly is not you, Lu—"

While he was distracted with our mutual love-fest, I flicked the athame at Cassiel. I didn't even really have to aim; it was like it was drawn to him, and it nailed him in his belly, in his angel heart. Cassiel began to shriek and dropped the sword as his flesh began to smoke around the blade sticking out. He grabbed it with both hands and his shriek turned to a howl that bent him double.

"Consider that the middle finger from my grampa, the first Lucifer, by the way," I told Cassiel as I turned and dove for the Morning Star. Even though Michael's sword had fallen at my feet, I was fairly certain if I grabbed it, it would give me a great big ouchie the way the Morning Star did anyone not of my bloodline.

I grabbed the bident up and was back on my feet in seconds, and just in time.

Despite the angel-eating athame burning through his angel heart, Cassiel was staggering toward me, Michael's unnatural large sword in his hand. His eyes were pain-filled slits and his mouth was full of sharp, deeply clenched teeth. The tears on his face had turned blue like he was bleeding from the eyes.

"Trickster..." he managed as he swung at me, but not well. Pain was distracting him, and he was pretty obviously off his game. I was able to duck away from the blow and come up behind him.

He turned to face me, growling through the blood foaming up his throat and into his mouth.

I twirled the Morning Star in my hands. "The trickster thing is probably from my gramma," I informed him just because I could.

"God damn you, Lucifer. God damn you!"

I shrugged in a "whatevah" manner. And as he brought the sword up, I smashed the bident against the blade in a cross pattern to stop it. The two weapons screeked against one another, making weird music and even weirder light that filled the interior of the cabin.

"You can give up and walk out of here," I suggested. "All you have to do is let me go."

"No," Cassiel insisted. The light from our sparks made a colorful spectacle of his sweating, pain-riddled face. "Never. You die here, fallen one."

I gave him some serious stink-eye as I looked over his worsening condition. "You look like the one dying, chum, but okay, let's do it."

Secretly, I was glad that Cassiel was injured because 1. He was a full-blooded angel and I wasn't. I also wasn't so arrogant as to believe I was physically stronger than he was, and 2. I was fucking tired as shit and almost at the end of my rope here. So when he tilted the sword upward and pushed it down at me, I was pretty sure he was not at full strength, which was very good for me.

Taking in a sharp breath as if I was about to lift a great weight, I pushed up on the blade, keeping it blocked with the Morning Star. The bastard realized we were pretty evenly matched now and tried to kick me in the knee. He missed but got me in the thigh instead. Still, the impact knocked me back a few steps, causing me to slam into a nearby wall where someone had hung up handmade snowshoes, all of which fell to the floor. I stepped on them and almost skidded to my knees, catching myself against the side of the sofa.

But as I stood up, I saw a screaming Cassiel lunging at me, sword raised high and ready to cleave my head from my shoulders, and I wondered if, even with my small advantage, I would survive this…

| 18 |

Yahtzee

IT PAYS TO be limber.

As Cassiel sliced across the space where my neck was, I threw myself back against the sofa and leaned all the way back, my hair all over the cushions and the floor. Michael's sword sang, cutting through the air in an arc but missing me by inches.

Cassiel, frustrated, stood back and, with a roar, pulled the angel-eating athame out of his guts. Long, slimy blue internal organs that resembled a mass of umbilical cords came out with it, and when he dropped my grampa's blade, the entrails (or whatever they were) flopped around on the floor like dry-drowning eels.

"Shit," I said, sliding sideways and away from the sofa. I was supremely fucked, I figured.

Snarling through the blood and foam on his mouth, Cassiel brought the sword of Michael the Archangel down on my head again. It wasn't a focused strike, but the sword was so large, that didn't matter. The angel was taller than even I was, so he had the advantage of height, and even wounded and bleeding, his strength was freakishly enormous.

I only had time to raise the Morning Star and stop the blade from slicing into my skull. But the impact knocked me down to my knees, my arms up to hold the Morning Star in place.

The gold sword and silvery bident slid against one another again, the metal singing and causing sparks. I felt the electricity in the weapons as they moved over each other, the contact making them incredibly hot and hard to hold onto.

With a snarl, Cassiel raised the sword and slammed it down against my grandfather's weapon, making me tremble. At the same time, the action opened the hole in his body farther, making more of those blue eels escape, which made him cry out. I don't think he expected me to be as stubborn as I was. He tried twice more to stab at me with the blade, but I blocked it both times, the weapons sparking and sizzling each time they touched. The second time, I got mad, got leverage, and stood up, shoving the angel back.

Cassiel stumbled, almost tripped over the wrecked table, and let his big, heavy sword drop to his side. He was trembling with exhaustion and weakness, and I saw his hands steaming.

I looked down. Mine were smoking a little, too, and I was pretty sure the glyphs in the staff of the Morning Star were now permanently burned into my palms. But I was also hepped up on adrenals and rage and didn't have a ginormous hole punched through the center of my body.

Also, at this point, I was pretty much fucking sick of Cassiel's shit.

The angel, staggering on his feet, bared his teeth at me and extended his wings threateningly, two great golden wings that nearly touched the ceiling. "Why won't you fucking die already?"

I used the bident to drag myself back to my full height. "I live to annoy the shit out of you, you feathered freak."

He snarled. Not to be outdone, I snarled in response. I have angel teeth too.

We clashed in the middle of the living room. He tried to swing the sword around and get me low in the knees—cut my legs out from under me, literally—but I had the advantage of a much lighter weapon—one I knew how to use, incidentally. Juliette had insisted I practice with it, bless her.

I spun with Cassiel, blocking him. He swung the heavy-ass sword around the other way and tried to cleave my head off. I ducked and brought the Morning Star back around, smacking the bastard in the back of the knees. Using the bident like a bo staff, I upended him onto the coffee table with the wooden legs and glass top—some Wal-Mart piece of shit unlike the rest of the furniture—which exploded when he landed on top of it.

I stepped back gracefully while the angel thrashed amidst the glass and wood of the destroyed table. Unable to find leverage—that or his massive wound was getting to him at last—he started flapping his wings with distress.

Just to rub it in, I told him, "Michael tried to destroy my grandfather and failed. You chumps keep forgetting that the Lucifers may not be the strongest of the archangels, but we're durable and, more importantly, too stubborn to die. We always bounce back in a fight."

Enraged, Cassiel abandoned the heavy sword and flapped his wings, rocketing up to the ceiling and attaching himself to one of the beams by wrapping his wounded body around it. He crawled across the vaulted ceiling like a spider, his body shifting and moving in unnatural ways as he moved toward me, hissing like a goddamn snake.

Shit and double shit!

I didn't want him on top of me, so I turned tail and headed back out the back door, pounding against the back porch while I heard Cassiel racing across the beams, his fingernails clacking against the wood in a disconcerting way. By the time I'd sprung off the porch and hit the footpath that led into the labyrinth of midnight woods behind the cabin, the angel had fallen silent.

Keep running, I told myself as I pounded over the icy path, slip-sliding like crazy. I wondered if he was still following me. I took a chance and spun around, stumbling backward as I neared the tree line.

Some trees rustled. I tried to look everywhere, but I didn't have a flashlight, and the moon wasn't that bright, whatever you've seen in slasher movies. Everything was a black, amorphous blob. A few seconds passed, the branches rustled again, and then a screaming Cassiel burst through the trees and straight at me, eyes wide and mouth open in a howl of rage. All the hair stood up on my body. I tried to duck, but he was flying too fast and collided with me, knocking me through the tree line.

The two of us ripped through some bristly pines before we rolled over, him on top of me as we crash-landed in a huge patch of ice that immediately cracked under us. He started punching me in the face, his blows sharp, precise, and full of rage. I blocked most of them with my arms but a few got through. One mashed one of my eyes; another broke my lip. But it was obvious that Cassiel was quickly losing strength. His blows fell slower and slower until I was able to get a few jabs in, one hitting him square in the throat, which made him choke.

Not knowing what else to do, I drove my fist right through the hole in his belly—it felt horribly like the inside of a jack-o-lantern in there with the insides still intact, and I swear something alien crawled over my arm—and he cried out in pain. Sludgy angel innards exploded over both of us, some of it getting in my mouth. Ughk!

While he was shaking and screaming with pain, I rolled over and got on top. Then I let him have it. In school, I was a dirty fighter, always was. I pop-punched him twice before grabbing him around the neck and applying pressure. I didn't even want to kill him. I just wanted him fucking out so I could get the hell away.

But there was still fight in Cassiel and he broke my hold with frightening ease and slashed his nails across my face. I felt the fire of the wounds he'd caused across my left cheeks I snarled in response, grabbed his left wing, and ripped it half off before I'd even realized what I had done. Cassiel screamed and tried to buck me off, but I found my hair was doing all sorts of things now as well, including the fact that blond tendrils had coiled around his neck like I was Medusa and was trying to choke him, apparently.

He landed a punch in my family jewels—a weak one, but it was enough, the pain quickly expanding in my groin like a balloon—and with a cough, I rolled off and fell all scrunched up into some kind of thistle-y bush. After a few seconds, the pain subsided, but it took me a moment to kick the nettles off my legs as I struggled to get back up.

The damned angel was getting to his feet again, and I was getting too tired to fight him. I needed a plan. I needed to fight smarter, not harder. so I bent to retrieve the Morning Star, turned, and took off into the woods, shouldering against the trees and the darkness.

I could hear the rustling of Cassiel trying to fly after me with one wing half torn away. He was howling like a banshee, and the sound sent shivers razoring up and down my back.

I finally got a break when a full moon slid out from behind some clouds and I caught a glimpse of the glorified goat path I was stumbling down. Ahead, about a hundred feet, I spied a sharp drop off the mountain. But, just as quickly as the moon revealed it to me, everything went dark again when the clouds scuddled across the sky.

"Lucifer!" Cassiel howled in fury.

I took off at a jog down the path, trying to judge where the drop-off was from pure memory. I tried not to trip over any deadfalls or fall into any gopher holes. The path was icy and uneven and littered with rocks, but I kept up a steady pace until I'd judged I'd covered almost the whole length of the path to the drop. Then, I spun around.

The angel burst out of the trees, screeching as it reached for me with its long beclawed hands. The sound of its rage set my nerves on fire. I hiccupped with fright but held fast and tilted the Morning Star at it. Cassiel did most of the work for me, flying right onto the tines of the weapon. They sang into his chest, and I felt them catch between his rib bones, but that didn't stop him. He kept going right past me and off the edge of the cliff.

I held onto the bident with both hands, his momentum taking me over the cliff with him. For a few seconds, the two of us were airborne as we sailed off the rocks, Cassiel in front of me and my stupid ass attached to the bident sticking out of his chest.

A rush of wind...and then the ground left my feet.

The angel roared even as he began to disintegrate in mid-air. But by then, I was already off the cliff and in freefall. So I spread my wings. The fall was quick, but the updraft caught under my wings and jerked me upward brutally in a way that made me wonder if I had dislocated a few more joints. The moon slid loose of its cloud cover, and I got a nauseating eagle's-eye view of the whole valley—something I neither needed nor wanted—as I sailed over it and then, inevitably (and since I was not a creature made for flight) started plummeting toward the valley floor a hundred feet below.

I tried to coast, angel-fairy-dust falling magically all around me, but the landing was hard on me nonetheless. I rolled for about two hundred feet before my shoulder finally slammed into a tree, which hurt like hell but stopped me dead in my tracks. The bident, formerly in Cassiel but now in nothing but bluish dust, dropped, and the weapon went tines-first into the ground a few inches in front of my face.

Yeah, I kind of screamed at that. I repeatedly sucked in air and then let it out as I tried to catch my breath. My ears still ringing with Cassiel's dying cry, I tried to decide if I was actually alive or not. My heart was running like a clock in my chest, and I had to put both hands over it to check and see if I had all my parts intact.

Flipping over, I sat against the tree that had stopped me and looked up. I was exhausted and nauseated. I had to blink several times to keep from passing out. Blue angel dust was shimmering through the moonlit sky—the remnants of the rogue angel Cassiel. It looked like classroom glitter as it fell over the whole valley, making the trees sparkle and joining a light dusting of snow as it fell.

I watched it all in wonder. Blue snow. It was so very pretty.

***

After I decided I was in fact still alive and had survived this supreme bullshit, I started to laugh.

I laughed and laughed, and, still chuckling, I got up and limped back up the mountain, which wasn't easy—or fast. I had to pick my path to make the climb as easy as possible, and I used the bident as a crutch. The sun was partially up and the sky grey by the time I reached the cabin.

I looked around at the utterly destroyed cabin and let out my breath.

"Fuck."

Wood and glass littered the room, and every piece of furniture was damaged or destroyed, from the coffee table (reduced to kindling) to the ugly tartan sofa with the big holes in and the stuffing sticking out like entrails.

Speaking of which...

I looked around and saw some of those eel-like entrails lurking under the overturned kitchen table. I stabbed them with the bident and they died screaming.

"Thanks for the nightmare fodder, you fucking asshat," I told Cassiel, wherever he was, and then moved to the sofa to sit down and rest my weary bones.

On the cushion beside me lay Michael's head. I knocked that into a dark corner. If I never saw another fucking angel again, I'd be a happy man.

I pulled my kit bag over and dug out a water and a protein bar. I dreamed about waffles and my comfy bed at home, had breakfast on the wrecked sofa, then curled up on a cushion for a couple of hours of much-needed rest.

| 19 |

Cowboys in Hell

THE VIBRATING PHONE in my pocket woke me. I sat up on the slashed-up sofa and stared at the phone screen with gummy eyes. Antonia had left six voicemails and about a dozen texts over the course of the night. I had gotten none of them since I'd put my phone on silent while hiking toward the cabin the night before. I hadn't wanted the angry angels to hear my ringtone.

A headache beat sharp wings at the soft, burning place behind my eyes, but I still managed to answer the phone. "S-sorry. Rough night," I croaked into the phone.

A pause and then Antonia said, "Nick, are you okay?"

"Hmm…" I got up and went into the bathroom, found a mirror on the wall, and squinted into it. My hair was snarled all around me and full of twigs and leaves, my face was swollen and black and blue on one side, and my mouth looked like I'd French-kissed a Garden Weasel. Blue angel blood stippled my clothes up and down, and some had gotten on my face and in my hair. When I opened my mouth, I noticed two teeth were missing, with sharp little buds where new teeth were poking up.

"Y-yeah," I mumbled through my bruises and battle hangover. "I'm awesome."

"You don't sound awesome."

"I'm good," I assured her. As I stepped out of the bathroom, I almost stepped on the decapitated head of the dead angel, and, being both hungry and dehydrated, I gave it a quick, angry soccer kick across the room.

It hit the folding door of the closet, which crumpled inward, spilling the rest of Archangel Michael's remains across the floor where Cassiel had stashed them—mostly blue dust a few white angel feathers. "You should see the other guy."

The news wasn't great. Antonia said that Auntie and Kiara were slowly throwing off her spell and Troy was screaming and begging to be released. She was pretty sure my wards were wearing off, and she didn't know how much longer it would be until the noise in the flat alerted the police.

Lil' Nicky also wouldn't stop crying. "I found some formula in the cupboards...I changed him...I don't know what else to do, Nick," she said wearily. "I think he wants Kiara."

I could hear the baby wailing in the background. I had to think fast. I went to collect one of the dead Archangel Michael's feathers, but when I picked them up, they disintegrated in my hands and trickled through my fingers like sand. Swearing, I started tearing the remnants of the cabin apart, hoping to find something from Cassiel. Nothing. Had his feathers disintegrated when he had? Well, shit...

"Nick, what's wrong?" Antonia begged in my ear.

"Remember when I said I need a feather from an unfallen angel to do the spell to get the angel out of Troy? I can't find any, even after killing Cassiel."

"You killed Cassiel?" She sounded surprised.

"He had it coming," I explained. That led to: "Oh, and I found Michael. Well, I found what's left of Michael." I glanced over at the head, also falling to dust now in the light of morning. "Cassiel killed him."

"What about Malach? Did Cassiel kill Michael too?"

"Malach is on Osiris with Cassandra. Cassiel exiled him."

"Osiris?"

"The Angry Red Planet."

"Well, shit," she said, the first time I had ever heard Antonia swear. "I see a lot has been going on."

I kicked the sofa so hard, it flew against the wall, and a few pictures of the former occupants fell down. I wanted to scream. But that was useless, so I sat down on the debris-littered floor to get my temper back under control. I breathed in and out slowly while Antonia said, "You've been there, haven't you? To the Angry Red Planet? You can go there and get Malach and Cassandra back. You can get the feather from Malach."

I knew the spell to open a portal to the Angry Red Planet. That was the good thing. Unfortunately, an open portal usually summoned a Simulacrum. And that was very, very bad.

I ran a hand through my hair, pulled out a leaf, and moaned in defeat. "It's more complicated than that. The portals and the Simulacrum are linked somehow. Open the door and get a Spider from Mars. It's like the worst cereal box prize ever. And I'm in no shape to fight a monster right now."

Silence for several seconds. Then she said: "Open a portal, then kill the Simulacrum with the bident. You've done it before. After that, get Malach. I'll do what I can here to give you the time you need."

"But your spell won't last," I pointed out.

"That's true," Antonia acknowledged. "Which is why I've called in the other Children of Endor. They're on their way, and when they get here, I'm going to get them to help me form a circle. We'll be able to maintain the spell for at least a few more hours. I hope."

That gave me an idea. I recalled what Juliette said about drawing from the well of magic. I was only as powerful as my worshipers made me—but that was the key phrase. "Can you get them to help me, as well? And talk to the coven here in PA. See if they will mobilize?" I told her the truth. "I'm almost depleted and I'm going to need all the help I can get just to open that portal. And I don't have the time to explain everything to Juliette and the others. Malach and Cassie don't have much time."

"Yes! I'll call them right now. I'll tell them to form an emergency esbat."

Invigorated, I got up. The plan would need to change, but I was up for it.

And I had done this before, as Antonia had pointed out. The first time I opened a portal to the Angry Red Planet, I'd drawn on the deep magic of the coven. I would need to do that again. "When you talk to Juliette, tell her I plan to draw on her and the others like whoa. It won't be pretty. She should be prepared."

"Got it. Hanging up to call Juliette."

"And, darling? Thank you."

"You got it, boss," she said in a sultry tone just before she hung up.

Feeling better—at least I had a plan now—I turned and looked at the tattered remains of the cabin. I went to grab my kit bag. In a small compartment in the bag, I keep a few basic tools to make a magickal circle, just in case—black sand, candles, the usual. I checked to make sure everything was there, then I threw it over my shoulder and went out into the forest to form a circle and summon a Spider from Mars to take me to another world. Because this is my life.

* * *

I found what looked like a decent clearing in the woods and used a branch to draw a deep depression in the bare dirt in the form of the glyphs that I would need to open the door. I filled the depression with black sand, then added the candles. I even added a few pine cones I'd found. I didn't think the pine cones would help much, but I felt it showed I was making an effort.

After I had the rather complicated glyph drawn set, I sat in the center crisscross applesauce and tried to center myself. It took some doing. I was exhausted, mentally drained, and not exactly in the mood to do big magickal work. Plus, it was a cold morning, I could see my breath, and I kept thinking about having a big breakfast at the Perkins nearby. Hot tea, pancakes, and bacon. My stomach growled in agreement.

"Focus," I told myself (and my stomach). Perkins later.

Once I was certain I was in the zone, so to speak, I stood up, stripped off my puffy jacket, and pulled my sweater up so I could use Grampa's athame to cut a long, shallow line down my chest and belly. The wound burned from the blade of the angel-eating athame. I could only imagine what it had done to Cassiel.

My hybrid blood, more purplish than anything else, dripped to the ground at my feet in the center of the glyph. I summoned the Morning Star, said the words I had memorized, and spun the weapon around, plunging it into the ground. I did everything pretty much automatically, almost remotely, which is exactly the headspace I needed to do this kind of work.

With the tines of the Morning Star in the ground and my blood all around me, I felt the charge that meant I was tapping into the magickal well, as Juliette called it. I could even taste the individual magicks coming out of each member of the coven like different flavors in a great big magickal stew. For one moment, I felt I was surrounded by my followers and lovers—Juliette, Antonia, Sada, Amber, Henry, and the others. Even a bit of David flowed into me as if his residual energy was seeking its way back to me. That made me sad, and then angry, and that greatly increased my will, which made my power stronger.

When I opened my eyes, I thought I caught a glimpse of David standing amidst the trees, smiling and waving to me. Or maybe that was my imagination kicked into overdrive by all the crackling magicks around me.

The wind picked up and the trees went from absolutely still to thrashing around me in seconds. Leaves, twigs, and even small rocks flew past me as the funnel-like door began to take shape in the air in the center of the circle. I crouched low, my kit bag slung around my middle, the knife in my hand. This wasn't my first rodeo where these bastard Simulacrum were concerned, so I was fully prepared when the long, hairy black legs pierced the funnel and began to descend.

The skull-like head of the monster wasn't even fully birthed into our world when I spread my wings, let the wind take me, and jumped to its back. I felt like an ill-fated cowboy, but my aim was pretty spot-on. With a cry, I slammed the knife into the creature's gelatinous back, prayed it held, and heard it cry out in that screeching soprano voice from hell. I couldn't see a thing, of course. The wind, smelling of sand and ozone and hell—the stink of the Angry Red Planet—was too great, but it also meant that it couldn't see me as I dug my fingers and knees into its body and hung on. It was a little like trying to hang onto a waterbed amidst a hurricane—just a waterbed that was screaming at me.

Pops of ozone-laden electricity exploded around me. I smelled the hellish grit and heat of that other world. Osiris. It made me gag. But I used everything I had to hang on as the Simulacrum, suddenly panicked, withdrew into its own alt-world, dragging me along for the long, bumpy ride...

* * *

Another pop and we were through the portal.

My whole body felt like it was on fire and full of electricity all at the same time, though whether that was because of the scathing, arid winds of Osiris, or because we had broken the veil between two worlds never meant to touch, I had no idea. And no way of finding out.

The Simulacrum was bucking like a bronco under me when we emerged into the red-hot desert of this dying planet. It was hard to breathe, the oxygen extremely thin and laced with what always smelled like a sewer to me but which was probably methane. I tried to hang on, but when it gave a mighty kick, accompanied by a howl of indignation, I felt the athame come loose from its body and went ass over teakettle into the air.

Instinctively, I folded my wings about me, which helped with the impact when I fell some twenty feet to the sandy ground and rolled over a couple of times. But then the orangey-red sand shifted unstably under me, and I found myself sliding down a dune. I had to dig my fingers into the soft ground just to slow my descent. I still went down, but not as fast.

That gave the Simulacrum a chance to orient itself, shake off the pain, and turn to face me. I crouched low to the ground to make myself as small a target as possible as it topped the dune and looked down upon me angrily. This one was big, the size of a small bus, with twelve legs arched around it and that head that always reminded me of a demented baby doll's skull. Its eyes passed back and forth over me critically as if unsure about what had just happened. I thought maybe I had a chance to scamper away, but then, out of nowhere, it began to scream.

I thought it was screaming in fury or outrage, but after a second or two, I saw it trundle backward on those many legs as it put distance between it and me. "You!" it said. Its voice was reedy and weirdly female, not that it was necessarily so. They all sounded like that.

It was almost a porn movie voice, but it had the absolute opposite effect on me, I promise you.

"Lucifer, you monster!"

Its voice blasted over me, sending up puffs of sand everywhere, and that galvanized me. I scrambled up and stepped back, the athame at the ready in case it lunged at me. But the first step back caused me to sink into the sand up to my ankles, which put me at a disadvantage.

"Monster?" I said, then recalled Cassiel's words.

The Simulacrum regard you as a threat.

Surely not.

But when I decided to test the theory and ventured forward a step, my athame held out in front of me, the huge monster screamed like a little girl and even lifted several of its legs to cover its face as if I had smacked it. Again, sand and sound scoured over me from this gigantic creature that could probably crush me without even knowing what it had done.

Shrugging mentally but always willing to take advantage of a situation that meant I wouldn't need to fight and expend energy, I jabbed the athame at it and went, "Shoo...shoo!" like it was a noxious little fly.

With another horrid squeak, the thing backed up, its big black spider eyes full of fright, its arms scraping over its face like it couldn't believe what it was seeing. "No...nooooo!" it told me. It sounded like a 1950's television housewife standing on a chair, screaming about a mouse.

"That's right," I said, taking another bold, crunching step into the sand. "Get away, ugly. Run away!"

It danced back frantically. And then, when it seemed to think it was safe enough to turn around, I watched it scurry off over the sand dunes like I had set the hounds of hell on its heels. It screamed all the way into the hills.

Cupping my mouth, I said, "Don't come back! And tell your friends!"

It howled in absolute horror, waving its front legs as it trundled off into the horizon.

| 20 |

The Revenge of the Angry Red Planet

OSIRIS. A PLACE I had hoped to never visit again. But here I was.

No plant life existed here, and only the most twisted and bizarre lifeforms could eke out a living here. Just a flat, endless plane of burning red sand and small hills with outcroppings of rocks here and there.

I walked hunched against the brutal, relentless winds, pushing against the elements and leaving a long line of footprints in the red sand behind me. The last time I was here, I'd made slow progress. Knowing what to expect, I was more prepared this time. I had stuck a couple of snowshoes (the ones that had fallen off the wall of the cabin, incidentally) into my kit bag and included a long, light jacket I'd found in the closet. It was a woman's jacket in red, but I was Gumby thin, so it fit me well enough, though it was a bit short. Hood up, sunglasses on, and snowshoes on, I was able to make better time on this hostile alien planet. And the red of the jacket meant I also wasn't a blaring, walking target.

Still, it was hot, and the sand kept finding its way into my eyes. But at least I wasn't swimming through sand, lost and teetering on the edge of panic like last time.

After a few hours, one of Osiris's many storms blew up, blasting me with everything it had, but it was thankfully brief, and by the time the landscape cleared, I could see the next hill a quarter of a mile off. It took some doing, but I got to the top and sat down to take a break, drank some water, and took a gander at my direction with my camping compass. The poles on this planet seemed to be reversed, but that only meant I had to go in the opposite direction of where I wanted to go, not that I knew where the hell I was or even where Malach and Cassie had gone. But they were anomalies and likely to kick up a fuss; I figured if I kept my eyes peeled, I'd get a clue soon enough.

Another hour passed. I noticed the ground sloping sharply upward. It took some sweat to get to the top of the next ridge. There were more rocks and crumbly rocky outcroppings, and I began to suspect these were the remnants of a mountaintop before whatever disaster glassed the surface of this dead planet and rendered almost everything sand, stone, and storms.

The air was thinner here, harder to breathe. It forced me to gulp at the fiery air. But the heightened elevation paid off. From here, I could see for miles all around.

Off in the distance, I spotted a collection of caves poking up and, beyond that, something large, long, and squirmy moving threadlike through the sand. I thought about spreading my wings and taking flight to save time, but the wind was blowing against me and I was afraid of losing the precious ground I had covered. Instead, I took off my snowshoes, bound them together with the shoelaces off my boots, and sat on them, using them like a toboggan to coast down the sharp incline to the valley below. It wasn't as much fun as I had hoped, and I had a sore butt by the end of it, but at least I had cut the time I needed to reach the outcropping of caves. Slapping the snowshoes back on, I headed in that direction, moving as quickly as possible.

The land here was rockier, less sandy. Soon, the snowshoes became more of a hindrance than anything else. By the time I was within a few hundred feet of the cave system, I was doing a near-jog—well, more of a power walk, if I'm being honest. But then I had to slow down because I couldn't find the weird, snaky thing I'd spotted from a distance anywhere. Still, I had a good feeling about the caves. If I'd been dropped here and didn't know where to go for safety, that's the type of place I'd have looked for.

On a lark, I cupped my mouth and called out Malach's name.

He's not there. Cassiel was right. They are both dead—

"Nick!"

At first, I thought I was imagining the sound of my name coming out of one of the smaller caves, then I spotted movement and recognized Malach's long, dark leather coat fluttering in the gritty wind. His hood was pulled up and a scarf covered the bottom half of his face. He had muttered my name through the fabric.

"Malach!" I raised my hand in greeting but then lowered it when he started to gesture wildly to me. He was saying something, but the wind was tearing his voice away. When he realized I couldn't hear him, he gestured that I should back away.

I didn't even have a chance to react when the ground exploded in front of me in a geyser of red sand and rocks that rained down all around me. I had to cover my head to keep from being smashed to bits.

A living wall had thrust itself up in front of me, cutting me off from the cave system, and I saw a series of wide, overlapping scales that seemed to be *breathing* with their own morbid little lives and lots of small legs with black claws attached to them. A chirping noise brought my attention around, and I came face to face with the giant squirmy thing I'd witnessed from afar.

It looked like a cross between a segmented earthworm and a caterpillar. It was pale—anemic looking—and it had long, almost humanlike arms, with even longer pinchers at the end of them. Like the arms, the head was nightmarishly human-like, the face of a screaming old man with two large, red-rimmed eyes and a round portal of an open mouth full of sharp, glass-like teeth.

It glared at me hungrily before swiping one of its giant pinchers at me. Stupid me just stood there, gaping at it, because it was so bizarre and monstrous that my brain was having trouble processing it. Malach at least had the sense to raise his big golden gun at it and fire a few holy bullets into it.

The gelatinous white hide sucked up his shots. The alien creature screamed in response and shuddered, whipping around to face this new assault. The wind from its pincher swinging around knocked me straight to the rocky ground. I *oofed* on landing but my bag broke my fall.

Holy hell. And I meant that literally. I lay there stunned as I watched the Very Hungry Caterpillar turn on Malach, who quickly ducked back inside the cave.

I knew it wouldn't be more than a few seconds before it turned back to try its luck with me again—Malach had bought me seconds, if that—so I manifested the bident, and when it turned—moving with shocking agility for such a large creature—and lowered its grotesque face with its almost human expression, I jabbed at it, gouging it in one eye.

The tines of the Morning Star easily burst the huge bubble of the eye, and I was instantly awash in alien green-black ichor.

It didn't expect that. Shrieking, it reared back, its huge body thumping along the ground and making it tremble as it used a huge, paddle-like pincher to rub at its injury.

Quickly jumping to my feet, I made a wide path around it as it thrashed, shaking its head, its wounded eye raining down that thick greenish goop that slopped my shoulder as I made a beeline for the cave. I tripped over a rock as I reached the mouth of the cave, but, thankfully, Malach reached out, grabbed me by the front of the jacket, and dragged me inside.

Seconds later, the Very Hungry Caterpillar appeared at the mouth of the cave, peering in at us with its one eye, which was as large as a dinner platter. Its head was too big to fit inside, but that didn't stop it from trying to jam its misshapen head between the rock walls. Malach and I moved back a dozen steps. It screamed, its voice shaking the floor of the cave.

"What the hell?" I said. My voice sounded reedy and not super sane right then. "What is that thing?"

Malach shook his head. "I'm not sure, exactly." A pause wherein Malach looked sad. "But now we are all trapped in here." He indicated the back of the cave, where Cassie was sitting quietly on some rocks, playing with a handful of Malach's white and gold feathers. She was a fidgety child, I remembered, always needing something to hold and play with.

"Cassie!"

When she saw me, she put her hands out to me. I went to her and knelt, letting her play with my hair. "Are you guys all right?" I asked them both. "How long have you been here?"

Malach, hovering near the mouth of the cave, said, "I don't know. It feels like time is losing all meaning. Maybe a few days. Maybe a week. Maybe more than that." A darkness passed behind his eyes. I knew that looked. It meant he was supremely pissed and ready to do something about it.

"When we get back," he intoned, rubbing his big, golden gun, "I plan to hunt Cassiel down—"

I interrupted him. "Sorted."

His eyes slid over me suspiciously. "What did you do to him, Nick?"

I gave him my best smile and pointed to myself. "Angel-breaker, remember? I have mad skillz."

He seemed equal parts disappointed and relieved. Then, coming to terms with the fact that he was not going to have his revenge as he had hoped, he nodded and went back to peeking out of the cave. He was rewarded by a roar as the VHC lashed out at him, causing him to dance back a step. Grit rained down over the entrance of the cave.

I considered our predicament, including examining the ceiling of the cave. I couldn't see it holding up forever if the creature kept assaulting it. If it didn't eat us, it just might bury us alive. Things didn't look good either way.

Malach joined us and we hunkered down together and waited while the creature thrashed around outside the cave. After what felt like an eternity, it seemed to accept that it was not going to get noms right now and disappeared underground. That eerie apocalyptic calm fell over the whole area again. Just the wind howled distantly. It was as if the monster was never there.

I let out a breath I didn't realize I'd been holding it. "I think it's g—"

Malach hushed me. In a low whisper, he said, "It seems to be attracted to loud noises and vibrations, so keep your voice very low."

"Won't be a problem." I stood up and set my pack down gently on the sandy floor. "I'll be as quiet as I can getting a portal open."

He looked at me. "Open *where*? Earth?"

I felt a tinge of embarrassment at my limited inter-dimensional traveling skills. "Not Earth. It's going to have to be Dis. It's the only portal I can open at will, but at least the three of us will be safe down there." I shrugged. "I know it's not party city, but it's better than this place…"

Malach, though, was shaking his head. "You can't take me down to Dis, Nick. And you can't take Cassie."

His lack of faith in me made me grimace. I'd carried Antonia down to my homeland with no problem at all the other night. Shit, that seemed like a lifetime ago now. "I'm pretty sure I can. I mean, I may be a screw-up sometimes, but I do the whole go to Hell thing pretty well."

"Nick," Malach explained with a longsuffering sigh, "no unfallen angel may enter your realm."

"Now, that's not true!" He frowned and I remembered to lower my voice. "There were stone angel statues all over my dad's throne room." I knew because I'd had my au pair Baphomet remove all the creepy-ass-looking things from the little lighted alcoves in the walls. Dad seemed to think dead angels made great Pier One Imports decorations.

Malach's mouth pressed together. "And there is a reason all of the angels are stone."

I looked at him. Oh.

Oh…shit.

I felt my heart sink, and then I experienced a spike of anger. "Well, he never told me that! No one ever told me that!"

He hushed me and I lowered my voice. I expected him to gloat over my extremely limited angelic education, but Malach only looked sad. Instead of a reproach, he further explained, "No unfallen angel can enter Hell and live. Your dimension is completely off-limits to us. But, Nick, I appreciate you want to help."

A thought occurred to me. "But I can enter Heaven, right? The Lucifers do go up and down. I know that. Maybe I can manipulate the spell."

But Malach only shook his head. "That might have been a worthy plan long ago, but not now with everything...topsy-turvy. Not with the angels in revolt. They'll kill you—and they will most certainly kill the Anointed One—if you even try to go through."

I sighed and sat down on a rock. Goddamnit.

There was a disconcerting rumble in the floor, and we all stayed quiet for a long moment in case the monster was coming back. Once it had passed, I whispered, "I can at least take Cassie down to Dis. Then I can come back here for you and we can figure something out. Fight our way out of here."

But even before he said it, I figured it out. "Cassie is part angel, Nick. A Nephilim." He gave me sad eyes. "Do you think she'll survive it? Because I'm not sure."

I looked at Cassie, who was using a long strand of my hair like a blush brush on her cheek. Shit. Double shit.

Why were there so many complications? Why was everything being so damned difficult lately?

After our little sobering discussion, I tried hard to come up with a reasonable plan, but I had nothing that didn't involve putting us in an unacceptable level of danger, which just frustrated the hell out of me. I even tried my cell phone on the off-chance I'd catch a signal, not that I thought that would work. No Internet on the Angry Red Planet.

Triple shit.

Juliette said I had a computer brain, but she was obviously full of shit, or maybe my computer was broken. I couldn't see a way out for the three of us. Cassiel, in his final act, had thoroughly screwed us all over.

A short time later, Malach asked me if I had any writing utensils in my kit bag.

I dug through it until I found a small notebook for writing down spells or just directions should I ever get lost in the woods. I'd been lost in the woods in the past and I'd meant for it to never happen again. He also asked for a pen and went to work drawing something.

"There is a natural portal not far from here...maybe four or five miles. A weak spot in the veil between this world and ours. There are several that dot this land. It's how some humans, and even some angels, slip through to here by accident."

"How do you know that?"

He looked up. "I can feel its energy signature. You can probably feel it too if you try, Nick. I believe you are angel enough. Most importantly, though, you may be able to manipulate it to get the Anointed One across."

He gave me a keen look. "Do you understand what an anchor is?"

"Is that like a home base—an open circle?" That's what I had in the basement of the coven's house. The glyphs cut into the floor kept it open and available to be used even at a distance.

He nodded. "Yes, use your open circle." When he had finished his map, his head bobbed up. "There is a downside."

"What?"

"The weaknesses in the veils are always connected to the Simulacrum. That's why they come through when you open a portal. They..." He sought the right way of explaining. "...they create portals where they make their gardens. Understand?"

I shuddered. I'd seen those horrid "gardens" of theirs.

He knew what I was thinking. "As terrible as they may be, you need the Simulacrum to get you out of here." Turning the notebook around, he showed me the route, which was twisty and looked pretty long. "Do you think you can carry Cassandra there? You know she can't walk."

I gave him a sharp look. "Why are you asking me to do this?"

The big lug pulled his gold gun. "Because I think I can distract our friend out there and give you the time you need to escape."

His plan gave me a flash of panic. "Absolutely *not*. *You're* her guardian angel, Malach! Getting her out is your job." I really did not like where this plan was going.

But he was moving toward the entrance of the cave, so I untangled my hair from Cassie's grip and followed him. I had a sudden idea. "It doesn't like the Morning Star too much. I can use it to…"

But Malach wasn't listening to me. Without another word, and before I could even manifest the weapon, he darted out of the cave and into the open.

I stepped outside to try and stop him, but he turned, and I saw his eyes, which were crazed and holy with determination. "Mal—!" Reaching out, he grabbed me by the front of my shirt; I'd forgotten how damned strong he was.

"Nick, listen to me. This isn't my job," he insisted as he pushed me back toward the cave. "It was never my job. *You're* the god-maker. You're the only one who can put Cassandra on the throne."

"That's bullshit! I'm not even fully anything! I'm like one of those hybrids—!"

He clocked me across the jaw. The impact knocked me straight back into the cave as if I was a rag doll, where I fell hard on my side and shoulder. Not even feeling the pain, I scrambled up.

I did feel the nasally onslaught of tears starting. "Malach! Do not do this!"

But he smiled. I was pretty sure I had never seen God's Hitman smile before. "I'm sorry I betrayed you, Nick. I should not have listened to Cassiel." He spread his head. "Well, now, see where it has gotten me. I should have allied myself with you. You are a good man."

"Malach!" I got up, limping toward him. I wanted to tell him I wasn't that good, and that I had no idea what the hell I was doing most of the time...

But Malach didn't listen or wait. He threw Cassie a kiss, then ran out into the desert, shooting his gun off into the sky. I started going after him but stopped short at the entrance. Malach had stopped at a rocky outcropping to bang his gun against the rocks. I was too afraid to go after him and leave Cassie all alone.

"Malach!" I called, then shut up because I didn't want to alert that monster...

But it had already heard the ruckus that Malach had made. I felt the vibration under my feet before the creature burst out of the ground about two hundred feet away. It looked angrier than usual. My having put out its eye probably had not improved its temperament.

But Malach never flinched in the face of such horror. Turning, he faced the VHC trundling after him like a runaway locomotive head-on.

"Shit!" I roared, then realized I only had a short time to make our escape. It wouldn't take the monster long to make ribbons of Malach and turn its hungry attention back on us. So I ran back to Cassie, picked her up, and put her on my back piggy-back-style.

"Hang on, honeybee," I told her as I grabbed up my kit bag and some of Malach's feathers that had fallen to the floor. Those I stuffed in an inside pocket of my jacket. Once I was sure Cassie was secure, I raced back to the entrance of the cave to check to see if the literal coast was clear.

Malach was hundreds of feet away in the open by that time, a tiny dark blob on the horizon, with the huge creature writhing after him. It was using a creepy, inchworm-like locomotion to chase him across the desert deadpan, and it was covering great swaths with each movement. Malach had to run like hell just to stay a little ways ahead of it.

"Malach!" I screamed at him.

He turned and, still running backward, met my eyes. He waved me on.

Scanning the horizon, I realized they were both heading for a sharp drop-off. The cliff of some long-buried mountaintop. The creature screamed as it closed in on him, its entire body pulsating with hunger and rage.

I knew I should run but I stood there like an idiot, rooted to the spot as Malach and the VHC closed in on the cliff. At the last possible moment, Malach spread his winds and an updraft of air carried him up and up, almost to the level of the creature's head. He was beautiful to behold in full angel form. That's when he twisted in mid-air, raised his gun, and pounded a half-dozen bullets into its face like some action hero in a movie.

The VHC opened its huge maw to scream. Malach put some of his bullets in there, too, creating spasms in its body, and more green blood flew everywhere like ugly paint. But by then, the creature was too close. It was right on top of him.

In one last, dying effort, it sprang forward and swallowed Malach whole as it went right off the cliff, which was a longer drop than I first thought. It roared as it soared off the cliff and disappeared into teh blackness of a void down below.

I never heard it hit bottom.

| 21 |

Beyond Escape

IT WAS THE longest five miles of my life.

I kept having to stop to check my direction on my compass or to look at Malach's map. Then we moved on. If there was a formation of rocks that created a windbreak, we'd stop to rest. If there wasn't, we would just sit down in the middle of the sandy ground and I would create a protective shield around Cassie with my wings and lower my head into it until I had the strength to go on.

I was tired. Soul-weary.

Sometimes, it was hard to see the map through the veil of my tears. Which was stupid. I hadn't even liked Malach. He's made a habit of punching me in the face and ruining my life.

When it was time to go, I bundled Cassie on my back, wrapped a scarf over her head to keep the sand off her face, and trudged on. I didn't tell her about Malach, but I think, given her silence, she knew. While we trekked across this hellish landscape, she held onto the collar of my jacket with one hand while the other stroked the side of my face where my tears were dripping down.

I didn't want her getting upset, so when we rested, I tried telling her the story of *The Velveteen Rabbit*, the story I'd entertained her with when I first rescued her all those years ago. But I was brain-tired and beaten down, and I could only remember snippets of it. I think I mixed up the events pretty badly, too, not that Cassie complained.

At one point, I stumbled over what may have been the broken remnants of a statue and fell, scraping my knees up pretty badly. I set Cassie under an outcropping of rock and went off a few feet so I could crouch down and scream into my hands for a few moments. I hoped it would help me get myself back under control, but I didn't feel any better. There was just this huge, empty, hopelessness inside me.

After a second or two, the sand shifted about ten feet away, and a small animal that looked like it had an upside-down skull head and little crab feet emerged and skittered a few feet toward me, making me jump up. Why did everything on this goddamn planet have to be nightmare fodder?

We're never getting out of here. We're going to get eaten out here and no one will ever know what happened to us...

Suddenly frightened, I raced back to Cassie and got her back on my back. I didn't have time for self-pity. If I didn't do something, we were both finished and so were a bunch of other people in our world.

We moved on.

Time passed. And it didn't. It started to feel like time was losing all meaning.

Cassie began coughing, probably from sand and dehydration. I wasn't used to caring for someone so fragile. We stopped once more for water and to share an energy bar. I was perilously low on food and water. If we didn't find the portal soon, we were both going to fucking die out here, but I kept my fears to myself.

A couple of hours later, I finally found the high ridge that overlooked the valley where the portal was located. I knew this was it even without consulting Malach's map because the whole place was crawling with Simulacrum.

* * *

We sat behind a large boulder and finished the last Snickers bar in my kit bag. I let Cassie have most of it even though she kept trying to feed me pieces.

"You finish it, honeybee. I have to figure out a way down there."

While she nibbled the chocolate, I lay down on my belly and scooched out from behind the boulder in a military crawl. I needed to stay low and observe what was pretty obviously a hive. I mean, I have no idea what Simulacrum called their colony. But it reminded me of a hive of busy bees.

The desert formed a small bowl-like valley that was maybe the size of a football field from end to end, though irregular in shape. It was surrounded by an outcropping of small and large rocks. Small Simulacrum—juveniles, I thought—were digging random holes at the bottom of the hive, while a much larger one just stood in the dead center like a black tank, doing nothing but enduring the red sand blowing over it. The big one had its ugly Halloween head cocked upward but its eyes mercifully closed. Its front legs lay crossed in front of it as though it were sleeping. I thought it might be the queen—or what passed for one among these monsters.

After observing the activity down in the valley for the better part of an hour, I scooted back behind the rock and rested. Cassie opened her hand to reveal a small bit of the candy.

"Thank you, honeybee." I popped the bite into my mouth and chewed slowly to savor it. I was so damned tired, and I desperately hoped the bite of chocolate would jump-start my brain.

Cassie's eyes suddenly went wide and her lips formed words she couldn't quite speak. I turned to look.

The queen was shuddering and making weird clicking noises. I recognized those sounds. It was the same noises the creatures made while they were coming through one of those portals and into my own world. As if on cue, one of the little ones stopped what it was doing and joined the big one in making those noises. After a few seconds of this back-and-forth discussion, the little one raised its long black arms skyward, the wind suddenly picked up, and I saw a dark funnel form directly over its hard.

I swallowed hard at the sight. I realized I was seeing what happened when one of the Simulacrum was summoned into my world, but I was seeing it cross over from their point of view.

As soon as the funnel was fully open, the little one pierced the center with its arms and then easily crawled into the hole hanging in the air. The other little ones didn't seem to notice; they were too busy tending to their holes.

The Simulacrum that had passed over didn't stay gone for long. A few minutes later, the creature slipped out of the funnel with a sleek wiggle of its grotesque, shiny black body. This time, though, it wasn't alone; it was dragging an unconscious young man by one leg.

The funnel unraveled and disappeared. The little one had a lively, chirping conversation with the big one before racing off to dig a fresh hole for the new occupant.

I ducked back behind the rock. I didn't want to watch the rest because I knew what the Simulacrum did with their victims. I knew they buried them deep in the dead red sands, and that, over time, the roots and tangles of deep-earth intestines sewed themselves through the living body of the unfortunate victim until that person became one with the earth—feeding it much-needed nutrients. Because that was apparently the only way anything survived in this place. The only way this dying world got by.

Sitting there, a hand scrubbing at my eyes to get the grit from them, I thought about how I could get the Simulacrum out of the nest long enough to perform a rite reversal to open the portal. I had that anchor in the open circle in the basement of the coven's house, so that wasn't going to be an issue. But doing a complicated rite amidst all those creatures wasn't going to work.

I thought about just going over there and waving my hands. Maybe my reputation was terrifying enough that I would scare them all off. But then again—I eyed the big one—maybe not. Maybe the queen didn't care. Maybe she even had it out for me. After all, I'd killed her offspring in the past.

Slowly, an idea took form. It was a really stupid, dangerous idea, by the way. Too bad I didn't have any better ones.

After resting a few minutes and getting my bearings (and hyping up my courage), I told Cassie to be quiet and stay where she was. My honey bee nodded her understanding. I then started moving around the edge of the valley from rock formation to rock formation, picking up any loose stones I could find and putting them in my kit bag. By the time I had a whole bag of them, I had made a full circuit of the nest and was back with Cassie.

"Things are going to get very loud and scary. But you have to remain absolutely silent." I put my finger to my lips. She mimicked my motion.

Leaning against one of the boulders, I took a rock from my pack and threw it up and down in my hand to get the heft of it. Then I heaved it at the hind end of the juvenile Simulacrum that was digging the hole for the new victim. Because I had the advantage of the high ground, the rock picked up some serious momentum before it pinked off the hard shell covering the creature's back.

As I'd hoped, the creature made a chirp of surprise and stopped digging to glare at the others. But all of them were busy with their own holes. After a second or two, it went back to work.

I took up a new position behind one of the other boulders, made sure I was close enough to hit another of the little ones, and repeated the motion. I hit that one even harder than the first. Even though it could not possibly hurt that much, it squealed and turned to chitter its indignation at the first one, who ignored it. But I got lucky in that it was a grudgey sort of fellow because it picked up a rock of its own and threw it at its fellow. The rock pinged off its brethren's head in a way that looked like it hurt, and the first one turned to chirp angrily at the second, then went back to its work.

I moved back to my original position and tossed two rocks this time in quick succession at two different targets. I hit one in the thorax and the other in the head. The two immediately stopped what they were doing and turned to face each other, screaming and posturing with their front legs in the air.

The first two, who had apparently not gotten over what I'd done to them, also screamed in rage.

With chaos ensuing amid the hive and everyone getting cross with one another, I returned to sitting beside Cassie to watch the fireworks. Quick to anger and highly competitive, the Simulacrum started lashing out at each other for the perceived slights. Rocks were thrown back and forth, and what sounded like insults.

"I used this technique once on a bunch of bullies at school," I told Cassie. "Sat up in a tree and threw chestnuts at them until they started beating each other up." I had no idea if Cassie understood what I was telling her, but she did nod appropriately. "You'd be surprised by how fast stupid things get ugly."

And, boy, did things get ugly. Two of the Simulacrum locked their arms together and started to scream and push, while another jumped on the back of its perfectly innocent neighbor and began thumping on its head. The remaining three postured and jabbed at each other's eyes. I was afraid the queen might break the row up, but she seemed perfectly all right with the battles taking place all around her.

Eventually, one of the more wounded creatures tapped out, scuttled up the slight slope of the bowl, and off into the desert. Two more started after it—to finish it off, I suppose. That left four little ones down in the valley. One was savagely cutting into its fellow with the razors on its arms, and the other two had sort of balled themselves up and were kicking and eviscerating each other. After a few more minutes of this, another battered-looking fellow took off with a second in close pursuit. The other two lay dead at the bottom of the bowl, their alien guts strewn all over the place.

I was wondering what to do about the queen when she suddenly came awake. Lowering her arms, she moved to the corpses of her children and quickly ripped them to pieces, consuming each part as if she were starving. The second one she'd attacked quivered slightly, and I decided it wasn't quite dead when she started to swallow down its pieces, which was kind of gross to watch. But I guess in this harsh landscape, you did what you needed to do to survive.

When all was said and done, the queen, looking disappointed by her destroyed hive, started climbing up the side of the bowl. I crouched low and covered Cassie with my body, pulling my coat up over us as I attempted to make us as small and innocuous as possible while she passed overhead. She made sharp clicking noises as she headed into the desert.

I waited until I was certain she was far off. Sighing with relief, I sagged and threw my coat back. But I had no time to celebrate. I was only half done.

Because now I had to perform a spell I had never practiced before and that probably didn't even exist.

* * *

Malach said he could feel the portal, but that was probably an angel thing. Being only part angel, I had more trouble. It took me walking around the bottom of the bowl for about ten minutes before I located it. And even then, I wasn't sure.

"What do you think? This look right?" I asked Cassie, looking up at where I thought it might be.

Cassie raised her hands, but I didn't know if she mimicking me or if she had actually found it.

"Okay, sounds good," I told her and opened my gig bag to get my magickal things out. I used Grampa's athame to draw a circle, then I started on the glyphs in the sand. I stopped halfway. I wanted a reversed rite, so maybe a circle with backward-drawn glyphs was the way to go? I felt that was correct and redrew them as best I could. I had no more black sand, so I would need to skip that part of it.

I was getting a little nervous by then. I had no idea if the Simulacrum would return at some point or if something equally horrifying would show up, so decided to get a move on. Standing up, I set the little nubs of candles that I had left in their proper place, then manifested the Morning Star. I started saying the words of the rite—

But, suddenly, out of nowhere, a hand grabbed my ankle...and I damned near jumped straight in the air.

After swearing and jumping around a bit, I realized a human hand was sticking out of the center of my circle—the man the little one had buried only an hour ago.

I couldn't possibly leave him, so I got down on my knees and started the process of digging him up. He was young, cute, maybe late teens or early twenties, black leather jacket, Black Number One hair, guyliner, and two lip rings. He was pale, gritty, and almost catatonic with terror. After I pulled him from the sand, I wound up holding him like some unholy Pieta as he trembled in my arms, his hands spastically grasping at the air and his eyes ping-ponging all over the place.

"Hey...hey, what's your name?" I asked him. I bypassed asking if he was all right. After his ordeal, he was most assuredly not all right.

He coughed up some sand, then cringed at the sight of me. "A-A-A...Angel," he finally managed.

I thought about the probability of finding a goth guy named Angel on this godforsaken planet, planted by the intergalactic Spiders from Mars, then laughed because why the hell not? These were the types of things that happened to me on the regular. So, instead of commenting on his situation, I took Angel gently by the shoulder and looked into his terrified eyes.

"I know you're scared and confused, Angel. But I may need your help. My name is Nick and I need you to watch this baby while I try to get us out of here." I pointed to Cassie. "Can you do that?"

He looked at her, then turned back to eye me. He cringed at the sight of the big, scary forked weapon in my hand. "I...I...what is that?"

I was beyond tired, beyond making up excuses, so I just told Angel the truth. "This is the Morning Star bident. I'm the Devil. Cassie is the future God. And we're all stuck on a hostile alien planet millions of light-years from Earth. So, I need to fix that. I need to get us home."

I hesitated and watched his eyes. He looked a little left of sane. "I need you to hang onto Cassie. Can you do that for me?"

"Uh...y-yeah?"

"Good man." I had Angel hold Cassie in his lap while I returned to working on the spell to open the portal. I drew the blood. I said the words. Angel looked horrified by it all, though Cassie seemed fascinated. When the portal finally swirled open above us, I felt a wave of relief, though nothing about Angel's expression changed.

My assumptions about the spell and knowledge of the craft had paid off.

I got Cassie up on Angel's back. Then I turned to the frightened young man. "Up you go," I said, making a saddle with my hands to help boot Angel and Cassie up to the level of the portal. I had to bump them both up to reach the funnel, but as soon as they were close enough, the winds took them.

I experienced one moment of euphoria that something had at last gone right, but that didn't last long. A chittering noise drew my attention. When I turned around, I realized the queen Simulacrum had returned from the desert and was lunging right at me.

Well, hell.

* * *

I instinctively swung the Morning Star around to bring it to bear in front of me, but the queen caught me by surprise and lashed out too quickly. Her blow packed some power, let me tell you, and it knocked the weapon clear out of my hands. The bident slid away in the sand, leaving me open and defenseless.

The queen loomed over me, her eyes crazy with rage, legs curled over my head. She opened her almost humanlike mouth and cried, "You! You monster!"

That was pretty funny. So I laughed.

"Me?" I struggled up into a kneeling position, my hands up as if I were the victim of a stick-up. I didn't dare stand up with her legs curled over my head. "You know who I am?"

"You destroyed my nest!" Her voice rumbled out over the desert in a near-screech that left my ears ringing. "You destroyed my children!"

This was bad, I decided. She didn't seem as impressed with me as the little ones—or as afraid. But I guess she had good reason to be pissed with me. I had a bad reputation for compulsively reducing the Simulacrum population.

"S-sorry," I said and lowered one of my hands to the sandy ground. I clenched a handful of sand. "I seem to always be in the wrong place at the wrong time."

She eyed my hand. Clearly, she anticipated my next move. Lowering her head, she spoke directly into my face. "And for your infractions, you will be punished, Lucifer."

"Now, now, lady," I told her, "don't threaten me with a good time." We were nearly eye to eye. And while she was looking at the sand in my fist that she thought I was going to throw in her face, I moved my other hand, which already had Grampa's athame from my belt in it. I drove it upward and under her skull-like chin with great force and determination in the swing.

With a sharp popping noise, the blade went all the way in. I immediately removed it, and out of the hole came a gush of thick, black, almost tar-like substance. She screamed as I knew she would —so loudly, it rendered me temporarily deaf—and hit me across the head. I felt the ground leave me before everything went black.

I must have been out for a little while because when I came to, I found myself face down in the sand. I was half breathing it in, which made me cough and gag. Sitting up, I clutched my head. Either the slap to my head or the queen's screams had left a ringing in my ears because it took me a few seconds to reorient myself.

The queen was lying motionless in the center of my circle, the funnel hovering above her. A huge wet black spot had spread out under her, but the sands of the Angry Red Planet were already absorbing all of her moisture. I looked for motion, signs of life, but saw none. Her eyes looked as empty as paint pools.

Grampa's athame lay under her huge body, lost forever. I realized this was the second knife of his I had lost.

After I was sure I could stand and walk straight, I spread my wings, took a running leap, and sprang to the top of the dead queen's glassy black body. The lift helped, as did my wings. I felt myself being sucked up into the vortex above my head.

But as soon as I came out the other end—I recognized the basement study immediately and felt a wash of comforting familiarity—I realized something was wrong. The top half of my body slid out, and my wings helped, but I found myself hanging there upside down. I couldn't get my bottom half to emerge. I started to panic and scrape at the open air.

"Nick!" Down below, I spotted Angel standing in the center of the circle of runes cut into the floorboards of the study. He seemed to have recovered somewhat, and when he saw me struggling, he jumped up and grabbed my hands, pulling down.

Kicking hard as if I was underwater, I slid out another inch—but that was all. I was fucking stuck! And that's when I saw two slender black, spider-like legs tangled in my jeans, I heard the not-so-dead queen laugh, and I felt her trying to yank me back through the portal.

| 22 |

Sweet Home Pennsylvania

I TOLD ANGEL to pull. Angel pulled.

My jeans ripped. So did my skin.

"Aaaaahhhh!" I said, and then I said it a lot louder and longer when he pulled harder on my arms and more of my skin started to tear. Angel immediately let go.

"No...pull!" I told him, reaching for this stranger while I prayed that he would save me. Hanging upside down, my long hair flying all over my face, the blood was rushing to my head and I couldn't see shit. I also thought it was possible I might pass out. I needed Angel to midwife me out of this fucking hole in time and space or I was going to die!

He jumped up and grabbed my arms. Pulled. He also pulled some of my hair in the process, which made me scream, but that was all right. He didn't mean to.

"Oh god, oh god, oh god..." he kept saying over and over again as he tried to drag me out of the portal. The large silver cross around his neck bounced around as he pulled. Sometimes it slapped me in the face, which hurt.

He pulled. The queen Simulacrum pulled back. I went in and out in a very double-entendre way that was not at all sexy to my way of thinking and hurt rather a lot. I didn't know what else to do, so I told Angel to unbuckle my jeans.

Angel looked at me oddly, then seemed to catch on. He let go of one of my wrists to work on my jeans while trying to hold onto my other hand. The queen yanked me pretty far back while he was working my belt open. I tried to help, but that bumbled things and only slowed him down. I manifested the bident and told him to stop, which he did. I sort of curled myself up and jabbed at the queen's face with the tines of the weapon. She screamed and let me go a few inches. I slid back out, but not by much. I then dropped the bident and told Angel to hurry the fuck up.

He was breathing harshly as he got my jeans open. "I don't...I don't usually do this on the first date," he said.

"Ha, that was a good joke," I said as I started wriggling my jeans over my ass and down my legs. Thankfully, I was not a fan of skinny jeans and they went off pretty fast. I told Angel to grab my wrists and pull again—hard!

Between the two of us, we got my hips loose and I slid the rest of the way out of my jeans, out of the portal, and down to the floor. I was wearing only the jack-o-lantern boxer briefs that Amber and Henry got me for my birthday as a joke. I lay there stunned a moment, then twisted around to watch the queen drag my Levis 501s into another world.

Angel, suddenly and rightfully nervous she might come through the portal and into our world, raised his hands and said, "Nick!"

"Got it." I raised my hand and said the words to undo the portal.

The queen made one last effort to push through, eyes wild and full of hate for me, teeth gnashing, but the portal was closing quickly and cut right through the space between her head and thorax. The skull-like white head dropped to the floor like an alien watermelon.

It screamed a remarkably long time before the light went out of its black eyes and it lay still and slowly turned to black dust in the center of the rune circle.

Angel plopped down and Cassie crawled into his lap to play with the crucifix around his neck. He put his hand on her head and let out his breath in a pained sigh. "Jesus fucking Christ, I should have stayed home tonight."

* * *

Angel, Cassie, and I walked up the stairs from the basement. Well, Angel limped. I sort of slouched along, Cassie in my arms, my long jacket hiding the whole no-pants situation.

Angel, whose name was Angel Hernandez, said he had car in the parking lot of this popular nightclub in east L.A. So, I had the unsavory task of explaining he was currently in Eastern Pennsylvania.

He had to swallow a few times as we emerged into the darkened kitchen. "P-Pennsylvania? Like in the east?" He thought about that for a long second. "I was having a bad breakup, so my friends said I should come out and dance. I don't like to dance, by the way, but I figured why not? It was better than eating junk food on the couch and watching the new *Charmed* show. So here I am." He swallowed again, a hard click in his throat, as he glanced around the old Victorian. "I went to the can to piss out all the cheap beer I'd drunk and there was this…thing…waiting for me. It grabbed me. I don't remember much after that till you pulled me out of the ground."

Angel shuddered, wrapped his arms around himself, and turned to me. "Was I in the ground, Nick?"

I stopped too. "Do you want me to tell you the truth or do you want me to tell you a nice, pretty lie?"

He thought about that a moment. "I can't handle the truth right now."

I looked around the darkened kitchen. The shades were drawn, but it was clearly daytime from the little light peeking around the blinds. I even checked the clock. It was eleven in the morning. And yet the house, usually bustling this time of day, was as silent as the grave. That gave me a very bad feeling.

Cassie was fussing and chewing on her fingers. I knew that meant she was hungry. I looked over at Angel. "I need to feed her and get us some water."

Angel nodded as he fell into a chair at the trestle table.

I was exhausted and running on fumes, but I got some bottled waters out of the fridge, and even some eggs to make scrambled eggs for Cassie because there didn't seem to be much food in the huge industrial-sized fridge, which was also strange. With so many people to feed in the house, it was usually stocked.

"I wonder where everyone is," I said, more in fear than wonderment.

Angel took the water I gave him. "Thanks, man," he said and poured some into a plastic cup so Cassie could drink.

While I was making Cassie some breakfast, I glanced at myself in the window glass over the sink and almost lurched at the sight. My face was sunburned to the color of a red delicious apple, and my hair, which had been formerly braided back, was sticking out in every direction and looked like I had stuck a fork in an electrical outlet. It and my eyes—always a pale grey—looked almost white as if I'd been bleached under the horrors of the Angry Red Planet's three suns.

"Are you okay?" Angel asked. "You look sick."

"Y-yeah," I told him, set my rubber spatula down, and wandered out into the hallway. I suddenly had this very bad feeling that something wasn't quite right.

I picked up my phone to call Antonia but the device was acting oddly. Maybe there was sand in it or something. "Something is wrong with my phone," I said to no one.

Then the phone jumped to life and I saw a bunch of emergency alerts. They'd been delayed because I was stuck on an alien planet with no Internet. It was mostly COVID alerts—whatever that meant. Something about a lockdown and a curfew in the city. But the most curious thing of all was a sound clip of a presidential address from the night before. Problem was, it wasn't President Obama. It was Warren LaVey behind the Presidential seal.

I had a thousand questions, but before I could even start wondering about what was going on, I heard the low sounds of a TV coming from the common room down the hallway. I lowered the phone and walked down to the doorway at the end.

Glancing around, I noted the room was different, all the furniture replaced. And none of the Children of Endor were present—though a strange man was sitting in an elaborate wing chair near the hearth. His head was bowed and he was watching the presidential address on his phone, the same one I'd seen.

I looked him over, but he was no one I knew. "Who the hell are you?"

The man's head bobbed up. It took me a moment, but I suddenly recognized Warren LaVey. The man in the smart, tailored suit who had given the speech in the Oval Office was sitting in the common room. He looked me up and down before smiling. "Nicholas Englebrecht? Yes?"

"Maybe."

"Oh, come now. I'd recognize you anywhere, your lordship."

LaVey stood up. That weird third-eye business that happened whenever I was in the presence of Arcana hit me. If I didn't look directly at the man, I could see he had wings. Four sets as I did. Warren LaVey the Arcana had ascended to archangel status and was eyeing me steadily in my own house. "Lord Lucifer," he said in a sibilant hiss, "Welcome home. You've been gone a long time." His seedy smile grew.

My slow, damaged mind finally caught up to what was happening, and I thought to look at the time stamp and date on my phone again. I choked at the sight. "Fuck!"

Angel, looking worried, stepped out into the hallway. "What's the matter?"

I looked again at the screen—and at a mystery that, at present, I could not fully wrap my tired brain around. But while that was happening, other men—other Arcana—began appearing in the room with LaVey. Some came from other rooms. Some seemed to materialize in place like the hybrids they undoubtedly were until I was completely surrounded.

"It was my birthday a few days ago. November 1, 2018," I explained to everyone and no one. "But according to my phone, it's June of 2020."

To be continued in
The Devil's Heart

ABOUT THE AUTHOR

K.H. Koehler is the bestselling author of various novels and novellas in the genres of horror, SF, dark fantasy, steampunk, and young and new adult. She is the owner of KH Koehler Books and KH Koehler Design, which specializes in graphic design and professional copyediting. Her books are widely available at all major online distributors and her covers have appeared on numerous books in many different genres. Her short work has appeared in various anthologies, and her novel series include *The Kaiju Hunter, A Clockwork Vampire, Planet of Dinosaurs, The Nick Englebrecht Mysteries*, and *The Archaeologists*. She is the author of multiple Amazon bestsellers and was one of the founders and chief editors of KHP Publishers, which published genre fiction from 2001 to 2015. She has over fifteen years of experience in the publishing industry as a writer, ghostwriter, copyeditor, commercial book cover designer, formatter, and marketer. Visit her website at https://khkoehler.net.

www.ingramcontent.com/pod-product-compliance
Lightning Source LLC
LaVergne TN
LVHW031610060526
838201LV00065B/4801